"Leslie Gould's *The Shop Down the Lane* is a touching Amish romance of second chances. Lois Yoder, pressured to marry for convenience, finds her life upended by Moses Lantz—her new landlord and the man who once broke her heart. An anonymous connection through bird-watching letters leads to a tender, unexpected journey of healing and true love."

Suzanne Woods Fisher, bestselling author of *A Season on the Wind* and an avid birder

"*The Shop Down the Lane* is a sweet, tender story about two people nursing their own 'broken wings' who find renewed love through grace, friendship, and faith. A must read for fans of Amish fiction and bird lovers alike."

Kathleen Fuller, *USA Today* bestselling author

"She's quirky and accident prone, and he's broken her heart once already. A delightfully entertaining Amish twist on *You've Got Mail*. This book has a sweet cast of characters who leave your heart overflowing and keep you turning the pages. Leslie Gould never disappoints!"

Patricia Johns, *Publishers Weekly* bestselling author of *Green Pastures*

The Shop
Down the Lane

Books by Leslie Gould

THE COURTSHIPS OF LANCASTER COUNTY

Courting Cate

Adoring Addie

Minding Molly

Becoming Bea

NEIGHBORS OF LANCASTER COUNTY

Amish Promises

Amish Sweethearts

Amish Weddings

THE SISTERS OF LANCASTER COUNTY

A Plain Leaving

A Simple Singing

A Faithful Gathering

PLAIN PATTERNS

Piecing It All Together

A Patchwork Past

Threads of Hope

AMISH MEMORIES

A Brighter Dawn

This Passing Hour

By Evening's Light

LETTERS FROM LANCASTER COUNTY

The Shop Down the Lane

An Amish Family Christmas:
An AMISH CHRISTMAS KITCHEN Novella

LETTERS *from*
LANCASTER COUNTY

The Shop Down the Lane

LESLIE GOULD

BETHANYHOUSE

a division of Baker Publishing Group
Minneapolis, Minnesota

© 2025 by Leslie Gould

Published by Bethany House Publishers
Minneapolis, Minnesota
BethanyHouse.com

Bethany House Publishers is a division of
Baker Publishing Group, Grand Rapids, Michigan

Printed in the United States of America

Library of Congress Cataloging-in-Publication Data
Names: Gould, Leslie, author.
Title: The shop down the lane / Leslie Gould.
Description: Minneapolis, Minnesota: Bethany House, a division of Baker
    Publishing Group, 2025. | Series: Letters from Lancaster County
Identifiers: LCCN 2024041943 | ISBN 9780764244223 (paperback) | ISBN
    9780764245015 (casebound) | ISBN 9781493450787 (ebook)
Subjects: LCGFT: Christian fiction. | Romance fiction. | Novels.
Classification: LCC PS3607.O89 S55 2025 | DDC 813/.6—dc23/eng/20240909
LC record available at https://lccn.loc.gov/2024041943

Scripture quotations are from the King James Version of the Bible.

Cover image of Amish woman by Laura Klynstra / BPG
Cover design by Peter Gloege, LOOK Design Studio

The author is represented by the literary agency of Browne & Miller Literary Associates.

Baker Publishing Group publications use paper produced from sustainable forestry practices and postconsumer waste whenever possible.

25 26 27 28 29 30 31   7 6 5 4 3 2 1

In memory of my parents,
Bruce and Leora Egger,
who deeply loved each other,
the beauty of the earth,
and their four children.

A deep voice at the back of the shop startled Lois. She stumbled off the step stool under the birch tree display, the birdhouse still in her hand. A deep and familiar voice, although she couldn't place it.

She climbed back up and hung the birdhouse next to a crocheted bluebird as the door buzzed. She grabbed the stool, stashed it under the counter, adjusted her *Kapp*, and moved toward the front of the store. It was the third Friday in April. Tourist season never stopped in Lancaster County, but it was beginning to take off for the summer peak.

"*Willkumm* to Paradise Found." Lois smiled at the middle-aged *Englisch* couple.

"What a darling shop." The woman glanced around as she spoke. "I love the play on words. Paradise Found—in Paradise, Pennsylvania." She smiled, showing her laugh lines. "Cute." She turned from the antique iron rack's display of kitchen towels adorned with birds to the birdhouses.

"These are adorable."

"Aren't they?" Lois pointed to the hummingbird feeders

made of copper and stained glass. "These are big sellers too." She foresaw a sale or two in her near future.

Lois called it right, although it took a half hour for the woman to browse through the shop and make her selections. Five other customers came in during that time. As Lois waited on them, she kept listening for the familiar voice. She guessed Scotty Harris, the owner of the shop, had a visitor, and they had stepped into the back room. Perhaps the voice simply sounded familiar.

When the last customer left, she pulled her father's watch from her apron pocket. An hour until closing. The door buzzed again.

On cue, Lois stepped out from behind the counter to greet the customer. Except it wasn't a customer. "John. What are you doing here?"

"*Guder Nummidag.*" John Miller swept his hat off his head and grinned. "I came to see you."

She returned the smile, although a little dubiously. John was twenty-one, four years younger than she. He came by the store quite often. He was the last of six sons, and his *Dat* planned to turn over the family farm to him in a few years. He was cute with his wide smile, thick eyebrows, and gray eyes. Plus, he had broad shoulders and a muscular build. And, more importantly, he was caring. And kind of . . . simple. But not in a bad way. In an uncomplicated way.

"How's the birding going?"

"*Gut.*" She clasped her hands together. "How did you know I bird?"

"I saw you at the park last week with your bins."

That was birding slang for binoculars. She tilted her head. "Do you bird?"

He laughed. "Oh no."

"Oh." She hadn't taken John for a birder, although it was common among the Amish. Personally, she tried not to be obvious about her bird obsession. In fact, she did her best to hide it, not taking her binoculars from her backpack until she was at her birding destination. Her brother didn't think it an appealing look for someone who needed to find a husband. Thankfully, the bird-themed items in the shop were top sellers. She ordered them not because she liked them but because they brought in money, which ensured she had a job. "I don't bird much," Lois said. At least not as much as she wished she could.

"That's good to hear."

Her heart fell. Not only did he not bird, but he wasn't positive about it either.

John cleared his throat, wiped his palms on his pants, and asked, "Would you go to the singing on Sunday at our place with me? Mark and a girl he's dating plan to go too." He spoke quickly. "We can double date. We'll pick you up at five after we pick up Evelyn."

Lois tilted her head again. Was John Miller actually asking her out? She stepped to the counter and repositioned a stack of gift bags. *Jah*, she was stalling. Just for a moment.

Lois raised her head and met John's gaze. "*Denki*," she said. "May I tell you Sunday at church?"

He frowned. "I guess so." Perhaps she should tell him *no* now, so he could invite someone else. But what if he intended to court her? Could she be interested in John? She wasn't sure. She needed more time to decide before she went on a date with him.

He took a step backward, raised his hat a little, and waved with his free hand. "See you at church."

She nodded. "See you then."

As Lois stood on the step stool again, this time to dust the hummingbird feeders to the left of the register, she heard the voices of Scotty and the other man, this time in the office. They must have slipped in while Lois chatted with John. Again, the other voice sounded familiar. Perhaps one of the vendors who regularly came into the store had stopped by.

The front door buzzed, redirecting her attention again. She forced herself to smile to keep from groaning as she climbed down from the stool. Bishop Stephen Mast. She hoped he wouldn't bring up her marital status, one of his favorite topics of conversation since he'd found out she was living above the shop—as she'd been doing for the last two years—instead of with her best friend, Amy, and her family, as the bishop had been assuming.

"Lois!" Why did he sound surprised? "How are you doing today?"

"Fine," she answered. "How are you?"

"*Gut.* I'm looking for a birthday gift for Dorcas. Do you have any ideas?"

"What does she need? Personal items?"

He gave her a blank stare.

"Lotions? Soaps?"

He shook his head. "*Nee.* She makes her own. What are some other options?"

"Household items." She pointed to the hand towels.

He shook his head again.

Lois pointed to the blocks of wood that read *Peace*, *Hope*, *Faith*, and *Family*.

He wrinkled his nose.

"We also have tablecloths and cloth napkins." She turned toward the birdhouses. "And we have items for the yard. Birdhouses. Garden art." She pointed at the blown-glass balls and metal sculptures. "Packets of wildflower seeds."

"So many choices." He stepped toward the birch tree and stared at a crocheted male cardinal. He spoke as he shifted his gaze to a birdhouse. "I saw John Miller heading away from here. Did he stop by today?"

"Jah." Lois's face grew warm.

"*Gut, gut.*" Stephen stepped over to the tablecloths and touched a gingham-checkered one. "We've had a couple of long conversations." He picked up a cloth napkin. "John is a good man. Very mature for his age. And ready to marry."

Lois stayed quiet.

Stephen turned toward her. "Any more thought to going back to Big Valley?"

She nodded. "I'm putting quite a bit of prayer into it." Prayer about how to keep from ever having to return to where her brother lived, over a hundred miles from Paradise.

"*Gut, gut,*" he said again and gave her an awkward nod. "I'll put more thought into a gift for Dorcas. Perhaps I'll be back. See you Sunday."

"Jah." Lois forced a smile. She feared it appeared half-hearted. "See you then."

After Stephen left the shop, Lois walked to the front door and peeked out the window. The bishop climbed into his buggy. Why was he so determined to have her go back to Big Valley and live with her brother and his family? Why, when she belonged to a community of believers, did he want her to be under the authority of a man? Specifically, her brother.

Lois's church district had recently grown so large that

it split in two. She stayed in the original, but Amy and her husband, Bennie, were assigned to the new one because of the location of their farm. That was when Bishop Stephen realized Lois lived in the apartment above the shop.

Bishop Stephen waved at someone. Were Scotty and whoever he was with outside again?

Stephen pulled his buggy around, and Lois stepped back from the window. Clearly, Stephen thought John Miller would be a catch for her. And he was right. He would be. She would be well taken care of. But would he love her the way her father had loved her mother? Her parents never had much money, but they always had a lot of love.

Perhaps they *had* spoiled Lois for marrying, as her brother claimed.

She turned her attention to tidying the shelves. She guessed John Miller wanted to marry soon. And Lois *needed* to marry. The bishop was intent on her not living alone.

The door buzzed again. This time Scotty entered the shop with a serious expression on his face. He cleared his throat as he approached Lois. "I need to talk to you about something."

Alarmed, she stumbled backward. Had the books been off the day before? Had she ordered too many birdhouses? Not enough greeting cards?

He ran his hand through his gray hair. "I've had a couple of offers on the store."

Lois gasped. "What?"

"Barb wants me to retire. This time for good."

Lois felt ill. "What are you talking about?"

"We hope to be in Florida by October."

Lois put her hand to her chest. "You're kidding, right?"

14

He shook his head.

She placed her free hand on the shelf to steady herself. "What about the farm?"

"We'll be selling it too." His expression turned sympathetic for a moment and then, with a bit of a quiver in his voice, he said, "I've been talking with a prospective buyer. I've told this person I'll only sell the shop if he promises to keep you on and let you continue to live in the apartment."

Lois opened her mouth to speak, but nothing came out.

"I wanted to tell you, so you wouldn't be surprised." He stepped behind the counter and opened the cash register. He held up a key. "I need to show Moses the shed."

She sputtered, "Moses?"

"Yes. Moses Lantz." Scotty gave her a questioning look. "Do you know him?"

Lois put her hand over her mouth. She *had*—she didn't anymore. But she did know he was the last person in the world she wanted to buy Paradise Found.

After Scotty strode out the door, Lois moved to the back window and craned her neck to get a view of the shed. A giant of a man, dressed Mennonite, stood at the open door. He held his straw hat in his hand. He was clean shaven—but not all married Mennonite men wore beards like married Amishmen did. She squinted.

She had last been in the same vicinity as Moses Lantz nearly five years ago at a party along the Susquehanna River, one of her favorite birding spots, the week before Amy married. Moses, at twenty years old, was tall then, at least six foot four—and he appeared even taller now. Had he grown another inch? Then again, at only five foot two, everyone appeared tall to her.

Moses had always been tall. On Lois's first day at the Paradise one-room school, they'd both been in the third grade. She'd taken him to be in the sixth grade, while he'd assumed she was in the first.

Now he tipped his head back, making his thick golden hair flop against his neck, and watched the tree towering over the shed. There'd been a red-tailed hawk nest in the crotch of the loblolly pine at the edge of the woods. Had the birds returned? She had hoped they would.

Amy had been baptized a year before she married. Lois was baptized after she moved to Big Valley to live with her brother and his family. But she'd been miserable there and moved back to Paradise two years ago.

Scotty and Barbara had welcomed her back from Big Valley, given her a promotion and a raise, and allowed her to live in the apartment again, where she'd once lived with her mother. There was no way a new buyer would keep a commitment to Scotty to retain her as an employee. Especially not Moses Lantz.

Since Lois had returned from Big Valley, she hadn't seen Moses once. Nor had she asked anyone—Amy specifically—where he'd gone. In fact, she'd told Amy five years ago she didn't wany any updates on Moses at all.

She knew, obviously, he didn't attend church in the nearby Amish districts. She'd guessed he attended somewhere else, but now it appeared he'd joined the Mennonites.

Lois returned to the counter and stared at the collage of painted buntings. She'd almost let Moses Lantz ruin her love of buntings, the birds that had sparked her interest in birding, when he had called her Baby Bunting in the fourth grade. But her father talked her out of it. Dat had asked, *"Why would you let Moses take something you love from you?"*

Why, indeed? Now she needed to prevent him from taking Paradise Found and her apartment. She was stronger than she used to be. But was she stronger than Moses Lantz?

―――――――

Fifteen minutes later, Lois walked up the lane to the mailbox on the highway. Old ornamental cherry trees with gnarly trunks lined the lane. A chipping sparrow sat on the low branch of the third tree, singing. Other birds, hidden in the trees, added to the song. Lois smiled at the sparrow, shading her eyes. The bird hopped to the next branch and flew farther up the tree. Lois peered up into the fluffy white blooms of the tree but couldn't find a nest. However, in the winter, abandoned nests filled the bare branches of the trees.

She focused on the highway ahead. The clouds from earlier had disappeared, and the day had grown warm, the warmest of the year so far. She retrieved the mail and turned back toward the shop and scanned the property. The pink and orange tulips bloomed in the flower beds in the front of the shop. And the grassy area around the back and side of the shop had grown in and was an emerald green, the perfect shade of spring.

The shed door was open. She headed back to the shop, leafing through the mail as she walked. Three bills for Scotty and a letter for her from Amy. Even though Amy lived only a few miles from the shop, she sometimes mailed a letter. She had four *kinner*, four and under. A letter could often travel faster than Amy.

Lois!

   I found a circle letter perfect for you—one
about birding. I've enclosed the info. Just write the
facilitator and tell her you're interested. Maybe you'll
meet someone—besides more birds, haha. ☺

Lois laughed—she adored Amy—and glanced at the second page. The woman's name was Teresa Schrock, and she lived in West Hempfield Township, across the county. At the top of the information letter, Teresa had written with exceptional neatness:

   Birding connects us to the Creator, educates us
about nature, and builds community. I invite you to
join the Flight of Doves Plain Circle Letter, facilitated
by me.

Lois found Teresa likable, along with the name of her birding community. A flock of doves was called a *flight*, and doves were birds of peace, fitting for a Plain group striving to follow Christ's teachings.

As interesting as the circle letter sounded, she forced Amy's letter and Teresa's sheet of information back into the envelope and slipped it into her apron pocket. She had no desire to join a circle letter. After she'd moved back to Big Valley, Amy, three other friends from their days as scholars, and Lois started one. By the time the letter traveled from one member, who wrote a page, to the next, who wrote another, to the next, the whole process became painfully slow. How would it work with birding? By the time a letter came around, it would be the next season—or worse, the next year.

18

When she stepped back into the shop, Scotty and Moses were standing by the birch tree, looking at the birdhouses and birds.

Moses, due to his arrogance and lack of self-awareness, most likely didn't realize he was an *accidental*—a bird who showed up where he shouldn't have. Like a mangrove cuckoo in Pennsylvania.

Scotty turned. "Lois." He stepped toward her, and she handed him the envelopes. Scotty took them and motioned toward Moses. "Moses, this is Lois Yoder. Lois, Moses Lantz."

"Hallo," Lois said, keeping her voice as neutral as possible. She extended her hand.

He stepped forward as if he'd never seen her before in his life. Either he was an excellent actor or a complete jerk. He was definitely a strange bird. His grip was firm and professional, as if they really were meeting for the first time.

In his deep voice, Moses said, "I'm pleased to meet you." She forced herself not to roll her eyes.

He shifted his gaze past her to the wall and dropped her hand and stepped around her. She turned. He headed toward the bunting collage, perhaps relieved to have a distraction. "I have to have this." Lois suppressed a groan. Not the painted bunting collage.

Moses took his wallet from the pocket of his jacket. "I'll buy it now."

2

Moses climbed into his SUV and placed the collage on the passenger seat. Lois had tucked it into a cardboard sleeve, wrapped it in brown paper, and meticulously tied string around the packet. He started the engine and backed out of the space, swinging in front of the shop toward the lane. Lois stood in the window, her arms crossed over her chest. Staring at him. In her yellow-green dress, the color of a painted bunting, white apron tied around her waist, and white Kapp positioned over her brown hair, she hadn't changed a bit in five years. Except perhaps to grow even prettier. Definitely feistier, which showed in her fiery blue eyes.

He shifted into drive and sped up the lane, between the cherry trees. A sparrow flew up from the ground into a tree. A white blossom floated down. He slowed for the stop sign and waited for a buggy traveling toward him before he could turn left onto the highway.

Then a car appeared over the knoll from the south. Moses's face grew warm as he imagined Lois still staring. She had acted as if she'd never seen him before in her life. He knew she hadn't forgotten him, though. He certainly hadn't forgotten her.

They'd been friends when they were scholars, teasing each other and competing in their schoolwork. Then, when they were twenty, he'd realized Lois Yoder was the girl for him. For a month they—courted. But not officially. They met up at *Youngie* events and parties. They were on their *Rumspringa*, but he intended to formally court her in the months to come. He planned to join the church as soon as possible, and she did too.

But the last time they were together hadn't gone well. It had at first—they'd ended up at the same party along the Susquehanna River the week before Amy's wedding. Lois spilled her soda. He replaced it and sat down beside her on a log near the fire. He put his arm around her. All was going well until Sara Fisher arrived. Lois shrank back and then disappeared. Moses panicked when Sara took her place, and he didn't go after Lois. Tall, confident Sara had been pursuing Moses for over a year. He wasn't interested. At the time, he had eyes for only Lois.

Why, when Scotty Harris had said his one requirement was that whoever bought Paradise Found keep the manager, hadn't Moses at least asked the manager's name? He would have made up an excuse not to be interested in buying Paradise Found after all, even though he was already deep into the process.

But he really wanted the shop and the entire property. He planned to develop an Amish farmers market like the one he operated in Delaware. He would need to build a structure for inside booths and a large concrete pad for outside booths, plus a place for food carts and for restrooms. He had already looked into the zoning laws.

When he'd first toured the property a couple of months ago, Scotty's wife was working—not Lois. It must have been her day off. Soon after, Moses's lawyer had drafted a letter of intent, and Scotty came up with a purchase agreement. Another buyer had been interested, but Scotty said he preferred Moses.

Moses eased forward to turn onto the highway, but a semi appeared over the knoll. He braked as his phone rang. He glanced at his navigation screen. *Scotty Harris.* He pressed Accept, and the call came over his speakers.

"Moses!" Scotty spoke in a loud and friendly voice. "I crunched some numbers. One option for you might be a loan for half of the cost, and then I could finance the rest through payments. If you can circle back, we can talk through it more."

Moses hesitated. Why would Scotty Harris offer to finance half the cost of the shop? Didn't he need the money for whatever he planned to do next?

"Moses?" Scotty's voice was kind and patient.

And could Moses return to the shop today and face Lois again? Maybe he should wait until tomorrow.

"Or you could stop by tomorrow," Scotty said.

"No. I'll swing back now. See you in a few minutes." Moses ended the call. His father always said not to put off a business meeting if possible.

A buggy crested the knoll. Moses glanced in his rearview mirror. Was Lois still standing at the door? The buggy passed and Moses swung onto the highway and accelerated to the next farm, where he pulled into the driveway to turn around. He would visit his mother later.

As he pulled back into the parking lot, he scanned the front of the shop. Lois no longer stood at the door.

She certainly wasn't reason enough to *not* buy Paradise Found, not when it came with ten acres of land, counting the woods. Where else in Lancaster County would he find a spot he could develop into a market? Besides, he had worked on the idea for the last couple of months, since he gave Scotty a letter of intent.

The fact that Lois worked at Paradise Found and lived in the apartment above it certainly complicated his plan but didn't negate it. He would keep Lois on. But based on the way she'd treated him five years ago and today too, she would most likely quit soon regardless. Then he wouldn't be on the hook to keep renting her the apartment, which would make the perfect home for him. And he liked Scotty's office. It was much better than his current space in back of his grocery warehouse, in the studio apartment that came with the property. The previous owner had gone through a variance process to get the commercial building zoned for a residential unit. But it was a small, dark, depressing space. All he needed to do was bide his time. There was no reason to let Lois Yoder keep him from doing business with Scotty.

When he stepped inside the shop, Lois wasn't at the counter. She didn't seem to be in the shop at all, despite the Open sign still sitting in the window. Moses sauntered back to Scotty's office, knocking even though the door stood slightly ajar.

"Come in," Scotty called out.

Moses stepped inside. Scotty was sitting at his desk. A window behind him showed the grassy acreage where Moses hoped to build the Amish market.

"Thank you for coming back." Scotty stood, shook Moses's hand, and motioned to the chair in front of the desk. As they both sat, Scotty said, "I really hope you'll buy the shop. I want someone Amish to have it."

"I grew up Amish." Moses brushed his jacket. "But I'm Mennonite now."

Scotty smiled. "I know. But you have an Amish background, and I like your idea of an Amish market. It will be good for the local community and for Lois too. She could be a help to you. She knows everyone around here, both Amish and non-Amish. Plus, she has good working relationships with our vendors."

Moses clasped his hands. "I hope to open the market by June."

"Two months." Scotty rubbed his bare chin. "Might be a little optimistic. Maybe by mid-summer."

Moses pulled his phone from his jacket pocket. "I've already talked with—" he pulled up his notes app—"Jeremy Reynolds from J&R Contractors about the building permits. I'll apply as soon as the sale goes through. I think June is realistic."

"Maybe so." Scotty shrugged. "Maybe not. But I like how you work." Scotty placed one stack of papers on top of another. "What about financing? How is that coming along? Like I said, I can help if needed."

Moses shook his head. "I have that figured out, thank you."

"Have you run your numbers? Taking into account unexpected expenses?"

"Yes," Moses said.

"And what does your bank say?"

Moses's face grew warm. "My finances are in order."

"All right, all right," Scotty said. "I knew your father—I'm not surprised."

Others often told Moses what a good businessman his Dat had been. "I still need to look at your books before we continue negotiating."

"Of course. I'll get those ready."

"Perfect." Moses stood. "I'll talk with my lawyer on Monday and let you know if I'm overlooking anything."

Scotty stood too and extended his hand. "The community will be lucky to have such a fine young man operating this business."

Moses stood outside Scotty's office for a moment after he stepped into the hall. He hadn't seen the apartment where Lois lived, and he wanted to. But he feared if he asked to see it, he would make it obvious he hoped she wouldn't stay for long. And it seemed a little creepy. But it was only fair he be allowed to inspect the entire property before he negotiated a price.

For a moment, he was tempted to sneak out the back door just in case Lois was at the front counter. But what if she was outside? The staircase up the side of the building most likely led to the entrance of her apartment.

He squared his shoulders and headed toward the front of the shop. Then someone—Lois—cleared her throat and said, "You're back." She was standing by the bird feeders, under the tree that looked like a liability. It would have to go.

Without turning toward her, he said, "Scotty called me back."

She cleared her throat again. "Why did you pretend not to remember me?"

He slowed but kept walking. "I didn't."

In a commanding voice, she said, "Moses."

He stopped. "You pretended not to remember *me*. And, I must say, you were convincing."

She shook her head. "Same old, same old."

His face grew warm. "If you're saying I haven't changed in the last five years, I agree." He puffed out his chest.

She rolled her eyes. "No, you haven't."

His voice dropped. "I could say the same about you."

She crossed her arms, holding the duster to the side, and stepped toward the counter. Moses moved to the side to let her pass, just as she did the same. The two collided, sending Lois flying. Moses reached out and grabbed her, lifting her off the ground.

"Let me go," she hissed.

He hadn't meant to jerk her off her feet—just to stop her from falling. But he'd overestimated her weight. He let go of her. She stumbled. He grabbed her again.

"I'm fine." She glared at him.

He let go of her slowly, and she grabbed the counter.

"Sorry," he muttered. "See you next week."

"What's happening next week?"

"I'll be back." If not sooner. His face grew warmer as he strode toward the door. He couldn't get out of the shop fast enough. As he closed the door behind him, Lois stood in the window turning the sign from Open to Closed. Then she locked the door—he heard the click.

Surely she wouldn't want to keep working at Paradise Found once he bought the shop. After a week or two, she would give her notice. It would be best for both of them. He didn't want to be reminded of his failures when it came to Lois—and she obviously didn't want anything to do with him.

3

After Moses drove off, Lois jogged up the lane to the highway, grabbed the sandwich board that read Paradise Found: Gift and Tourist Shop, and lugged it back. She snatched up the board from beside the entrance and dragged it inside too. Next she retrieved the vacuum from the back closet and began doing the final cleaning of the shop, working as fast as she could. Back and forth. Back and forth. She rushed past Scotty's office door. When she finished, she put the vacuum away and called out to Scotty from the hallway. "I'm done for the day. See you on Monday."

"I'll be in tomorrow." His voice grew closer, and the door opened. Scotty stood in front of her with a grin on his face. "Moses is very interested in buying the store. He has all sorts of plans—good ones."

A wave of nausea swept through her.

"I think you'll really like him," Scotty said. "Both of you are smart, with a keen sense of business. He grew up Amish, although he's Mennonite now, which is perfect for the Paradise community. And he's ambitious."

Lois tried to smile, but she feared it came across as a grimace.

Scotty frowned. "You're not happy about Moses being your employer?"

She sighed. "I'm sad you and Barb are selling. It's a shock, honestly."

His face softened. "That's part of the reason I'm selling to Moses—he's local. You'll be able to relate to him, and tourists will be thrilled with his suspenders and straw hat."

She knew she should say something positive. Instead she said, "See you tomorrow."

Scotty smiled. "See you then."

Lois had known Scotty and Barb Harris since she was eight, when she moved to Lancaster County from Big Valley with her parents, who leased the Harrises' farm and farmhouse on Meadow Lane. At the time, Scotty and Barb lived in another house they owned in Gordonville. Right after Lois turned fifteen, Scotty hired her to decorate for holidays at the shop. When she turned seventeen, he hired her to clerk, Tuesdays through Saturdays.

After her father died, Scotty and Barb moved Lois and her mother into the apartment over the shop, and they moved into the farmhouse, leasing the land to another farmer.

Lois double-checked the front door, exited through the back door, and then took the steps up the outside staircase two at a time. When she reached the top, she ducked under the maple branch that hung over the landing to her apartment. She unlocked the door and stepped inside, breathing in the scent of the fresh air from the open windows, the sprigs of daphne in the vase on the tabletop, and the fresh bread on the counter from her morning baking, trying to distract herself from the emptiness. It had been five years since her mother passed—but the pain of losing her hadn't eased one bit.

A male blue jay ate at the bird feeder, which she'd purchased in the shop and attached to her window with suction cups. She gave him a wave, but he ignored her.

She stepped into her tiny kitchen to check her hummingbird feeder. The nectar appeared to be at the same level as when she filled it two days before.

She glanced at her father's pocket watch. *6:12.* She sliced a piece of bread, buttered it, and ate it, along with a few slices of cheese and an apple, for her supper.

After she ate, she shuffled into her bedroom and sank onto the bed, which was more of a nest with its extra pillows on top of the quilt her mother made the year Lois turned fifteen. The border was the yellow-green of Lois's childhood dresses, the same color as the dress she wore now.

Her binoculars from her father sat on her nightstand next to her journal. She picked them up and stepped to the window, directing them toward the loblolly pine, looking for a red-tailed hawk nest. But she couldn't find one. She sank back down onto her bed, the binoculars still in her hand.

Her father used to tell her that everything she needed to know about life in their Amish community she could learn from birds. Rise early. Sing to *Gott.* Flock together. Work hard. Take care of yourself and others. She didn't remember a time when her family didn't observe birds. They had a bird feeder in their yard, out the living room window. A hummingbird feeder hung from the eaves of the back porch. Their only outings, except to visit members of their church, were to go birding.

She'd never stop learning about birds.

She had two hours of daylight left. Why not go to Paradise Park?

She grabbed her sweatshirt and her reflective vest and put her binoculars and journal in her backpack. Once down the staircase, she retrieved her red kick scooter from where she kept it at the back of the shop. It was the only mode of transportation she possessed. Although it had a basket on the front, which she used when she did any shopping, she always kept anything valuable in her backpack. She didn't want to risk taking a spill and having her birding notebook and binoculars fly into a ditch.

~~~

As Lois picked up speed along the highway, one foot planted on the scooter and the other pushing alongside and propelling her forward, she tipped her face upward toward the blue sky and the lingering warmth of the sun. A flock of Canada geese flew north. One honked. Then another. They'd be stopping soon for the night. She increased her speed. Scootering was the closest she would ever come to flying.

She held on to the handle with one hand and stretched out her other arm as if it were a wing, leaning into a curve. A pickup sped by, honking as it did. Lois pulled closer to the ditch and raised her hand in a wave. Sometimes drivers yelled as they drove by, but she still tried to expect the best of people. Behind her, horse hooves clopped along. She inched over as far as she could.

A bird, one she couldn't identify, flew up into the brush on the other side of the ditch. She laughed as it flapped its wings and the horse and buggy sped by.

She slowed as she reached the village of Paradise. The

park was in the middle of town, but she decided to stop at Denlinger Pond, just before the train station, and follow the waterway to the park, which meant leaving her scooter. She walked the scooter off the highway and down to the pond, hiding it behind a row of bushes. Then she slipped off her vest, rolled it, and stuffed it into her pack as the Strasburg train rolled into the Paradise station, whistle blowing.

She walked to the pond, where several goldeneyes were floating on the water. She took out her journal and a pencil and recorded what she saw and then kept going along the bank of the run. High on a branch of a hemlock tree was a platform nest. She took out her binoculars and focused in on it. A hawk swooped down and landed in the nest. She squinted, making out a rusty breast. Dark red eyes.

A Cooper's hawk. The hawks lived in the area year-round. They were monomorphic—the female and male looked the same. But she guessed this one was female because of its size. Most likely there were eggs—two to four—in the nest.

She jotted down the sighting in her notebook and continued on her way until the run reached the park to her right. To her left were the baseball diamonds. The Harris farm, which her Dat had leased, sat a little to the northwest. She could make out the barn, silo, and farmhouse through the trees.

Who would Scotty sell her childhood home to?

A wave of sadness swept over her. Long shadows fell. The daylight dimmed. Sometimes being close to the farm made her feel better—but sometimes worse. Today was the latter. Probably because, with Moses taking over, she would need to find a new job and a new place to live soon. Neither would be easy. She missed having a permanent home.

She turned back toward the pond. As she neared it, a heron

swooped down. Lois took several quick steps to the water, lost her footing, and slipped on a rock.

She gasped as her right foot fell into the water, and then she scampered back up the bank, sloshing a muddy mess up the grassy slope.

Feeling defeated, she took her vest from her backpack, slipped it on, and wrestled her scooter out from behind the bushes.

She should have stayed home.

When she reached the pavement, she stamped her feet, trying to force the water out of her right shoe. Then she put her left foot on the scooter and started east on the highway. Ahead was Paradise Café, a new restaurant that had opened a few weeks before.

As she approached, a black SUV turned into the parking lot. Moses's SUV. Her pulse quickened. He hadn't seen Lois. Or perhaps he didn't realize it was her. Or, most likely, he'd chosen to ignore her.

Moses jumped down from the driver's side and stepped around to open the passenger door. He held his hand up. Someone took it, and then Sara Fisher climbed down.

Immediately she locked eyes on Lois, who quickly glanced away. "Lois! Is that you?"

Lois grimaced and then directed her attention toward Sara. "Hello!" She held on to the scooter with one hand and waved with the other. "Hi, Moses." Hopefully they didn't expect her to stop.

Moses mouthed "Hallo" as Lois hit a patch of gravel. Her free hand flew to the handle and she braked too hard, and the scooter slid out from under her. She stumbled but caught herself, for a second. But the scooter kept sliding toward the parking lot, and before she could let go it pulled her down too, on top of the gravel. As she slid, her dress pushed up on her thigh.

She came to a stop, her skin covered with road rash, her dress twisted around her left leg, and her wet shoe a foot away. She tried to stand but fell back down. Sara, who towered over her, said, "Let me help."

Lois took her hand and let Sara pull her to her feet, hopping on her one shoe and tugging at her dress as she stood.

Sara, who had to be almost six feet tall, wore a Mennonite Kapp over her blond hair. She had hazel, doe-like eyes and wore a pink print dress and a pair of sandals with a little bit of a heel. Sara had always been gorgeous—something Lois was aware of from the first day she met her at the Paradise school. And tall. Those were the two things that impressed Lois the most.

Obviously, Sara had become Mennonite too. She and Moses made a perfect couple.

Moses grabbed Lois's shoe and handed it to her, interrupting her hopping and her staring at Sara.

Lois managed to get it back on her foot.

"Moses." Sara's voice dripped with sweetness. "We need to give Lois a ride home."

"No." Lois's gaze fell. Blood was trickling down her leg.

Moses reached for the scooter. "I'll put this in the back."

"No," Lois pleaded. "I'm fine. It's not very far." She shifted her backpack into place and reached for the scooter. "Thank you, though. I appreciate your thoughtfulness."

Moses glanced at Sara, who shrugged. Then he asked, "Are you sure you're all right?"

Through gritted teeth, Lois repeated, "I'm fine."

A half hour later, her leg cleaned and bandaged, Lois sat on the top step of the staircase to her apartment and watched the sunset. Had she been ungracious in refusing a ride home from Moses and Sara?

She was used to being lonely, but she felt extra so tonight. Was it from seeing Moses and Sara together? The sun disappeared below the horizon, taking the light and warmth of the day with it. Amy was home with her husband of five years and their four children, the youngest just four months old. Lois's only blood relatives were her brother, who was nineteen years older than she was, and his family.

Was John Miller her only hope of having any kind of stable life in Lancaster County?

Moving to Paradise with her parents from the Yoder farm in Big Valley had changed Lois's family, and looking back Lois realized moving had to have been hard on *Mamm* and Dat. They'd left the only home they'd known and their first-born, their only son. That must have been hard no matter how many disagreements stood between them. And it wasn't as if, like in most Amish families, there were other children to depend on.

For years, her parents believed Randy would be their only child. But when he was nineteen, Lois came along. Eight years later, she and their parents moved to Lancaster County. The next ten years had been a blissful time—her parents deeply loved each other and Lois, as well as Randy even though he was far away. They delighted in the natural world, and not just birds. Flowers, trees, stars, the sun and moon, the weather, wild animals, domesticated animals. Everything.

Until her father died in a farming accident. Two years later, her mother, who never recovered her strength after Dat died, suffered a stroke and passed away too.

Randy swept in and moved Lois back to the family farm in Big Valley. After three years, Lois managed to escape and return to Paradise.

But now that was coming to an end too.

Dusk faded into darkness, and Lois stepped into the apartment and took Amy's letter from her apron pocket. What would it hurt? She needed a distraction, especially while she was looking for a job and a new place to live.

Perhaps John Miller *would* love her—and perhaps she could come to love him too, Gott willing. He seemed to be her best plan. But a relationship wouldn't happen overnight. She'd still need a new job. And a new place to live. A distraction, which the circle letter would be, might help pass the time.

Although she wouldn't want anyone—except Amy—to know she'd joined a birding circle letter. She could envision someone showing up at the store, perhaps when John had stopped to see her, and bringing up the circle letter.

Her brother thought Mamm and Dat wasted too much time on birding and flower identification and looking at the clouds and nature in general. He'd cautioned Lois against showing that side of herself to a man who might want to court her. She thought Randy was ridiculous with his concerns, but John's comment about birding made Lois wonder now if perhaps her brother had a point.

Lois sat down at her small kitchen table. She'd write Teresa Schrock and ask to join the circle letter. Then she'd go to the post office the next day and pay for a mailbox. She didn't want

Moses snooping through her mail—not about a future job or a new home. And not even about a circle letter.

What pseudonym should she use for the letter? After putting some thought into it, she decided on her middle name, Jane, along with her mother's maiden name, Weaver.

As she started the letter, an owl hooted in the distance. She took it as a good sign.

4

oses drove around the back of the Amish market
he owned in Byler's Corner, Delaware, located at
a crossroads with a couple of shops a few miles
from the nearest town. But enough local and tourist traffic
stopped to make it worth opening the market on Fridays
and Saturdays. It consisted of a building with booths and
an outdoor concrete space for carts and picnic tables during
the warmer weather. Like today.

Amish from the Dover area, to the south, brought their
wares to the market to sell, as did Amish from Pennsylvania.
Several Mennonite families also had booths at the market,
along with local farmers and craftspeople.

A text popped up on the dashboard screen.

I need you at the café. Having a few unforeseen
troubles this morning.

He sighed. He'd been looking forward to spending the
day at the market, but it wouldn't do any good to ignore
Sara. He pulled into his parking space and dictated a reply.

I'll head your way as soon as I can.

He climbed out of his vehicle, entered the building, and then walked through the rows of stalls. First he checked in with Joey Williams, who managed the market. His wife operated a coffee and pastries booth.

"Hallo, Boss!" Joey called out. "Things are looking good today. Yesterday too."

"Great," Moses replied. "I'll only be here for a little bit. I need to head back soon. Text me if anything comes up."

Moses had inherited the market when his father died. When or how his father acquired it wasn't clear, because Moses hadn't known about the market until after his father's death. Joey had seen to its operation, while Dat collected payments from the vendors and paid the bills. When Moses asked Joey when Dat bought the market, Joey shrugged and said, "I'm actually not sure how it all came about." Joey never clarified his answer, even though Moses rephrased the question a few times.

He continued on toward Casey Smucker's wooden toy stall. After saying hello, he asked if Casey wanted to ride to Paradise with him. "I need to check on the café and see to some other stuff."

Casey glanced at his younger brother, Walter, and back at Moses. "Then you're coming back here?"

"For sure. I'll be back by midafternoon, before closing."

Walter said, "Go ahead. I can handle things." The market was busy but not swamped.

Casey grabbed his cane and limped out of the stall and then turned to his brother. "Denki."

Walter gave him a wave.

As they walked, Moses slowed his pace to try to match Casey's. Moses slowed even more. Casey stumbled over the uneven ground.

Moses hesitated, but once Casey began to fall he reached out and steadied him, saying, "I'm sorry," as he did.

Casey planted his cane and straightened. "You don't have anything to apologize for."

Moses hated when Casey said that. Casey's bad leg was Moses's fault.

A few minutes later, Moses backed out of his parking place and pulled onto the highway, heading north. He'd told Casey a few years ago about the Amish market and suggested he hire a driver and sell his products. But he asked him not to tell others in Lancaster County Moses owned the market. Perhaps he felt compelled to keep his ownership private because his father had. But he also felt uncomfortable with people knowing all the businesses he owned. He knew people criticized him behind his back. He didn't want to give them another reason to do so.

"What's going on at the café?" Casey asked.

"Sara's managing it now. We stopped by for supper last night, and things were a mess. The manager quit on the spot. Sara's there this morning trying to sort things out and needs me to stop by."

"Does she know how to manage a restaurant?"

"Jah," Moses answered. "From working at her Mennonite uncle's restaurant."

"That's right."

"She lived with his family and worked for him for a couple of years, after the accident."

When Casey didn't respond, Moses shot him a glance. His

friend stared straight ahead. Maybe Moses shouldn't have mentioned the accident. It was something the two of them didn't talk about. Moses pressed the brake to slow for the tractor hugging the right side of the lane.

"You don't think Sara is the right choice to manage the café?" Moses asked.

Casey's voice was a little raw. "I didn't say that."

"But?"

"It takes a lot to manage a restaurant. Dealing with deliveries and supplies. Managing people. Being flexible when deliveries are late and people don't show up for work. You know how it goes."

Moses did. He had the same problem at his grocery store, the first business he'd bought after his father passed away.

Casey asked, "Do you regret buying the café?"

"No. It's just taking a while to work out the kinks. I expected a few problems."

"Are you and Sara courting?" Casey asked.

Moses hesitated. Why was it difficult for him to answer Casey's question? "Jah, we are." He needed to marry sometime soon, within the next year or two. He'd waited long enough.

Casey didn't reply. Instead, he pulled an envelope out of his jacket pocket. "Walter gave me this, but I don't have time for it."

Moses paused a moment and then said, "I have no idea what's in the envelope, but do you think I have more time than you do?"

Casey didn't respond again, which made Moses feel uncomfortable. He'd just valued his own time over his best friend's.

"It's a birding circle letter," Casey finally said. "Walter knows I've gone birding with you a few times—but you're the one with the passion for it. A woman named Teresa Schrock is starting it. It's for Mennonite and Amish people."

"Sounds like it could be a lot of older people," Moses said.

"I don't know about that." Casey pressed the envelope between his palms. "But even if it is, you need to do something besides work."

"I've got Mamm—" He visited her several times a week, although he hadn't visited her yet this week.

"Jah, you're a good son."

Moses winced. There were plenty of people who thought otherwise, including himself. He'd put her in the Green Hills Care Center instead of caring for her himself. If he'd been a good son, he would have married someone by now and moved Mamm into his home. As it was, all he had was the studio apartment in the back of his grocery store warehouse.

"You need more of a normal life." Casey tucked the envelope into the console. "Read it and see what you think. Maybe there will be younger members in the circle letter. Young women. You might meet someone new."

"You don't like Sara, do you?"

"No. I do. I just think if she was right for you, you'd know by now."

"Yeah, well, I've been a little busy." He'd done it again, commenting about his time. He sighed. "I'm going to slow down in a month or two when it comes to work. I need to launch one more project. It will be my last."

Casey placed his palms on his thighs. "Care to share?"

Moses grinned. "I'll show you before we head back to the market."

When they reached the café, the parking lot was full. "Are you hungry?" Moses pulled around the side of the building.

"Starving." Casey opened the passenger door and climbed down.

"Let's go through the back." Moses led the way into the storage room, followed by Casey.

Moses heard the voices before he saw anything as his eyes adjusted to the dim light.

"Put your apron on and get out there."

"Sorry. My babysitter was late," a woman said. "She had to take her mother—"

"Go!"

Sara was yelling at an employee. Moses waited for his eyes to adjust. Casey closed the door. Sara turned toward them. She was wearing a yellow print cape dress, brown shoes with a bit of a heel, and her rounded Kapp. Like most days, she wore makeup—but not much. Her blond hair showed at the front and under the sheer Kapp. She was attractive, even when she was angry.

"Moses." She squinted. "And Casey. What a surprise."

Moses asked, "Do you need help?"

"I do." A strand of hair had escaped her Kapp, and she tucked it behind her ear. "We're swamped."

"What do you need us to do?" Moses asked. "I can wait tables."

Casey stepped forward. "I can do dishes."

"All right." Sara reached for aprons on the hook in the hallway. "Take these and wash up. An hour of help should get us through brunch. You can hang your jackets here." She pointed to the row of pegs behind them, by the door. The ones Moses had installed.

Moses and Casey each took an apron.

Sara pointed toward the dining room. "I'm hosting today. Moses, would you show Casey the dishwasher?"

"Yes, ma'am." Moses hoped he had a hint of playfulness in his voice.

Sara didn't respond but kept walking toward the doorway to the dining room. She walked with her head held high and her shoulders squared. Moses had always liked that about her.

Turning toward Casey, Moses pointed through the door to the kitchen. Casey grinned as he limped forward. "Hello, dishwasher, my old friend." Moses and Casey both had worked as dishwashers at a restaurant in Gordonville as teenagers.

"Have fun." Moses turned toward the restroom to wash his hands. After he finished, he stepped into the makeshift office and grabbed a notepad and pen. Then he strode out to the floor. The woman who had just arrived, who Moses hadn't met, worked the far-right side of the dining room.

Sara led a couple to the middle area, where a family of six sat at a nearby table. She nodded to both tables and mouthed to Moses, "This is your section."

Sara had always been brave and ambitious. Perhaps her beauty, height, or both had given her a confidence unlike most of the Amish girls he knew. She'd always been a little abrupt, even harsh at times, but since the accident she'd been even more so. He thought perhaps, with time, she would completely heal from her injury. But she continued to seem more irritable and more easily triggered than before the accident, which he still felt guilty about.

44

An hour and a half later, at one, Moses told Sara he and Casey needed to grab some food and leave.

"Already?"

He nodded.

She exhaled. "We didn't have enough staff this morning, but they slowly trickled in."

"What do you mean? Were more people late than the waitress who came in right before us?"

"I thought the others were late but then checked the schedule."

"Oh." Moses had made the schedule. He'd staggered the starting times because they were never busy at seven in the morning, not even on a Saturday. "Well," he said, "I need to see to a few things and get Casey back to the market. We'll take sandwiches to go. I already put the order in."

Her mouth turned down. "Will I see you this evening?"

"I'm going to stop by Mamm's," he said. "See you at church tomorrow."

"See you tomorrow." She turned back toward the dining room.

A few minutes later, Moses grabbed the to-go order and coaxed Casey out of the kitchen.

As they reached the back door, Moses turned toward the hallway. Sara stepped into the kitchen, carrying a sandwich on a plate. She raised her voice again. This time to the cook. "The order was without mayo. Read it again."

Moses winced. He expected Casey to say something, but he didn't. Sara had a lot of positive qualities, and Moses needed to remember that. He'd certainly used the wrong tone and said the wrong things to employees on occasion over the last four years. She'd learn.

Casey pulled a sandwich from the bag and handed it to Moses. "What are you going to show me?"

Moses took the sandwich and slowed his SUV. Scotty's car was in the parking lot. "Paradise Found."

"I tried to sell birdhouses there. Lois said no."

"You knew Lois worked here?" Moses took a bite of the sandwich as he parked next to Scotty's Buick. "Why didn't you tell me?"

Casey muttered something incoherent.

"Why didn't Lois carry your birdhouses?"

"She said they were too rustic." Casey took another bite and added, "She was right."

"Well, I'll change that. Rustic or not."

"You'll change what?"

Moses pointed toward the shop. "This is my next acquisition."

"Really?"

Moses nodded and took the last bite of his sandwich.

Casey sounded surprised as he said, "How many more businesses do you plan to buy?"

"This will be it." Moses crumpled up the sandwich paper. "Grocery store, Amish market, café, and a tourist shop. Plus, I'm going to add a market here too."

"That's good news," Casey said. "Walter and I won't have to hire a driver to take us to Delaware."

"Or one of you could run a booth there and the other one here."

"True," Casey said. "Although we'd need to up our production."

"Hire someone to help." Casey should learn to think ahead. Moses opened the door. "I need to talk to Scotty Harris for a few minutes about the sale." He'd thought of a few more questions to ask. "Want to come in?"

"To say hello to Lois?" Casey grinned and wrapped his remaining sandwich back in the paper. "Sure."

Casey and Lois had always been close, even when they were kids. But Casey had assured Moses five years ago he wasn't interested in Lois romantically—nor was Lois interested in him. He'd said he and Lois were friends and he planned to keep it that way. But Moses didn't entirely believe him. When they entered the shop, Lois stepped out from the counter with a smile on her face. It disappeared when she saw Moses.

Then she grinned at the sight of Casey. "Hallo! How are you, Casey?"

Joy filled Casey's voice. "I'm doing well. How are you?"

"*Gut!*"

Moses cleared his throat. "Is Scotty in?"

Lois tilted her head to the side. "Jah. He's in his office. Go on back."

Moses took a few steps forward. "How's your leg?"

Lois's smile faded. "Just fine."

Moses kept going as Casey asked, "What happened to your leg?"

He couldn't hear Lois's response, but he felt like a jerk for asking about it. Obviously, she was fine.

He knocked on Scotty's door, saying, "It's Moses."

"Come on in!"

As Moses pushed the door open, Scotty stood and walked around his desk, his hand extended. The two shook hands and Moses said, "I was hoping I could look at your books before I speak with my lawyer Monday afternoon."

"Definitely," Scotty said. "I'm getting everything in order. Mine will draw up the papers by Tuesday."

"Nice! So we have an understanding?"

Scotty nodded.

"Could I go through your books this evening?"

"That won't work." Scotty glanced toward the computer. "But I'll text you tomorrow and let you know when you can. Perhaps Monday morning."

"All right." Moses had hoped to look at them sooner.

Scotty put down the pen he'd been holding. "This has all gone faster than I expected. I'll have them ready soon." He stood. "Do you have any other concerns?"

"Just one."

"Oh?"

"Lois Yoder."

"Lois." Scotty laughed. "What about Lois concerns you?"

"She doesn't have the best customer service."

"What are you talking about? We have customers who come in solely because of her, and I'm not just talking locals. We have tourists who come back to the shop year after year asking for Lois. Heck, I think some of them come to Lancaster County specifically because of Lois."

Moses's face grew warm. "That's reassuring." It seemed Lois was only rude to him. He stepped backward. "See you soon."

As he stepped back into the shop, Lois spoke with a customer. "We have hand-painted cards of Lancaster County scenes—farms, covered bridges, horses and buggies, and farms, as well as paintings of both birds and flowers." She pointed toward the far wall. "Along with the photographs there and—" she pointed to behind the counter—"the collages here."

"Thank you." The customer, a woman in her fifties, had her arms full of kitchen towels and aprons.

Lois extended her hands. "Let me take those while you continue to browse."

The woman slipped her load into Lois's open arms.

Moses stepped to Casey's side.

"This is cool." Casey stared up into the birch tree. "It has more birdhouses on it than the last time I was here."

Moses whispered, "It's a liability."

"It seems sturdy. . . ." Casey reached in and grasped the trunk.

"I think I have everything I need," the customer said.

"*Wunderbar.*" Lois sounded genuinely warm. "I'll ring you up." As she worked, she asked the woman where she was from—Virginia. And if she'd been to Lancaster County before—this was her second trip. And where she was staying—the bed and breakfast on the edge of Paradise.

"Moses?"

He turned toward Casey, who stepped closer and spoke quietly. "We should leave after Lois finishes. I need to help Walter pack up the booth, but I want to tell her goodbye first."

Lois said to the customer, "That'll be two hundred forty-eight dollars and fifty cents."

"Yeah," Moses said to Casey. "We need to go." He'd hoped to have time to stop by and see his mother, but he couldn't be late getting Casey back. Besides, Moses needed to check in with Joey again. He wouldn't go back to Delaware until next Saturday.

As Casey told Lois goodbye, Moses tried to ignore a pang of envy.

A half hour later, while Moses sped back along Highway 41 toward Delaware, Casey leaned his head back against the headrest and closed his eyes. Casey had been happy to see Lois—but not so happy to see Sara.

Moses glanced down at the envelope with the information about the circle letter. His life *had* been all about business lately. He did like to go birding—but he didn't do it.

Maybe he would write Teresa Schrock and ask about joining the circle letter. It might not help, but it couldn't hurt either.

5

Sunday morning as Lois cooked her oatmeal, a male ruby-throated hummingbird flew near the kitchen window, flitted about, and then found the nectar in the feeder. Lois froze. Her heart fluttered as fast as the bird's beating wings. It was her first sighting of a hummingbird for the year.

After it flew away, Lois grabbed her notebook from her backpack and recorded the sighting. She and Dat and Mamm used to celebrate the sighting of the first hummingbird each spring after the birds' long journey home from wintering as far south as Costa Rica and Panama. One time Dat said he wished they could follow the hummingbirds to Central America, although they all knew it would never happen. They had no one to take care of the animals on the farm nor the money to travel. Lois couldn't imagine such a trip.

She put her notebook away, ate her oatmeal, and washed the pan and her bowl. As she scootered to church services at the Millers' farm, her bandage pulled against the road rash on her leg. She did her best to ignore it.

The weather had turned cool overnight and clouds scudded across the gray sky. The wind picked up and raindrops began to fall. By the time she arrived, the rain had soaked her fluorescent vest and her Kapp, even though she'd worn her hood. Her raincoat protected most of her dress but not the bottom of it.

As she zipped past the row of buggies, a few people called out greetings to her. She waved and kept on going. People gathered outside the shed, huddled under umbrellas. She parked her scooter under the eaves of the building and hurried toward the entrance. She was too cold to wait outside.

As she stepped through the door, someone called her name. She turned. *John.* She shed her backpack and vest and waved.

He approached with a smile. Before he spoke, she said, "I would like to go to the singing with you tonight."

His smile spread into a grin. "I'll pick you up at five."

She smiled and wiggled out of her raincoat. Thankfully she had a fleece on underneath to ward off the chill in the cold shed.

"I need to go help my Dat," John said. "I'll see you after the service."

Lois gave him a wave and then stashed her backpack in the corner. She spread her vest and raincoat over the top to dry. She waited until everyone started filing in and joined the unmarried young women.

After the singing ended and the sermon began, her mind wandered. Where should she look for a job? She didn't want to work as a mother's helper or in a restaurant. Perhaps another shop. She should find a job first and then figure out where to live, a temporary place, if, in fact, things worked out with John.

The Miller farm was immaculate with its white barn, shed, and other outbuildings and the enormous two-story farmhouse. Could she marry John Miller if he asked? That would certainly offer her an appealing place to live and a job—being an Amish farmwife. It was more than full-time work. She hadn't been *glicklick* in her first two tries at love, but perhaps a third would be the proverbial charm.

She had the feeling someone was watching her. But who? John was sitting across the aisle a couple of rows ahead of her. He wasn't watching her. She turned her head slightly.

Moses was sitting a row back. Lois jerked her head forward. What was he doing in the Amish service? Sure, it was his old district, but he didn't live here anymore. And he was Mennonite. Why would he come back?

After the service ended, Lois stood and did her best to sneak a glance at Moses—without letting him see she was looking for him. But he was gone.

She sat down to eat the simple meal of bean soup and bread with the other members of her district. She'd known many of the people since she'd arrived in Lancaster County with her parents.

Until then, Lois's father had worked with his father and his son on the family farm in Big Valley. But when Lois's grandfather passed away when Lois was six, they all discovered he'd willed the family farm and house to Lois's brother—not to Dat—skipping a generation.

Randy had always been their grandfather's favorite, but it was still a shock he'd leave the farm to a grandchild instead of his own son.

Nevertheless, at first it seemed nothing would change, allowing her father and brother to continue working in the same way they had for the last several years. But soon Randy started to disagree with Dat about the crops and the finances and where to reinvest the profits from the farm. After Randy and Deanna's third child was born, Randy insisted Dat, Mamm, and Lois move into the *Dawdi Haus* so his family could have the bigger house to themselves.

It made sense, but once they settled in the Dawdi Haus, Randy became cold to his parents. He stopped asking Dat's advice and made several mistakes when it came to farming. Instead of admitting his mistakes, he became defensive. Their grandfather had been a harsh and demanding man, and Randy had taken after him, not their kind and loving father. Around then, Randy's wife started refusing Mamm's help and instead Deanna's mother, a widow, moved into the farmhouse. A month later Dat found the farm in Lancaster County, and in the following years Lois and her parents never returned to Big Valley, nor did Randy and his family travel to Paradise to visit.

"Lois."

She turned.

John stood behind her. "Are you finished?"

"Jah." She stood and picked up her half-full bowl.

"Not hungry?"

"I guess not." She took a step toward the kitchen. "I should start home. I'll see you soon."

He grinned again. "At five, on the dot."

She smiled back at him. "I have a question for you," she said before he could leave.

"Oh?"

"Do you know why Moses was here?"

54

John shook his head. "I didn't have a chance to ask him. He left during the last prayer." He smiled again. "Maybe he plans to rejoin us."

Lois doubted that. In fact, she hoped not. She didn't want to have to deal with him at church too.

John leaned toward her. "More likely, he left early to get over to the Mennonite church before it started at eleven."

Lois guessed that was the case. Although she still thought it odd he would worship with the Amish at all.

She retrieved her backpack and her damp vest and raincoat. After she put both on, she made her way out of the shed. As she scootered back down the highway, a buggy approached from behind. Again, she moved to the right. Until someone called out her name.

"Lois!"

She spun to a stop. It was the voice she wanted to hear most in the entire world, besides Mamm's or Dat's.

"Get in!" Amy leaned out her window. She grinned and her rosy cheeks pushed up toward her sparkling eyes. Her dimples flashed.

Lois broke out laughing as she stepped off the scooter. "Amy!" The two had been friends since Lois's first day of school in Lancaster County. "Where are you going?"

"To pick up the kids at my parents'."

"Where's Bennie?"

"Home with a laboring cow." She waved her hand toward the rear of the buggy. "Put that thing in the back."

Lois rolled the scooter alongside the buggy, barely managed to lift it in, and ran around to the passenger side. As she climbed in, she said, "Denki for the letter about the circle letter. I'm going to join."

"Oh good! I hope there's an eligible Amish bachelor in the group."

Lois let out an exaggerated sigh. "So do I."

As they reached the lane, Scotty's car was ahead of them, making its way under the white canopy of cherry blossoms. He parked close to the shop and walked around back. He never worked on Sundays—of course the shop was always closed on the Lord's Day.

"What's Scotty doing?" Amy asked.

Lois shifted on the bench and turned toward her friend. "I'm not sure, but you won't believe what's happened." She told Amy about Scotty wanting to sell the shop and Moses wanting to buy it.

"Moses Lantz?"

"Jah," Lois said.

A smile crept across Amy's face as she turned into the parking lot.

"What?" Lois demanded.

Amy placed her hand over her mouth. "Sorry."

Lois grumbled, "That's even worse than smiling."

"I never guessed Moses Lantz would come back into your life."

Lois slumped down on the bench. "Neither did I."

~

At five on the dot, John knocked on her apartment door. Lois grabbed her cloak and followed him down the staircase. The sun had come out and warmed the world some. The grass was still damp as they walked to the buggy, which was one of the newest and nicest around.

John opened the passenger door. Lois climbed up to the

seat. In the back sat John's brother Mark and a young woman Lois didn't recognize.

Lois turned her head and said, "Hello, Mark." Then she turned toward the woman. "I'm Lois."

"I'm Evelyn." She had dark eyebrows and dark-blond hair. "It's so cool that you live above Paradise Found."

Lois smiled. "I agree." She had been more thankful than ever the last three days for her job and her apartment, knowing two of the biggest blessings in her life would soon come to an end.

"I've wondered who lived there for the longest time."

"Are you from around here?" Lois asked.

"No." Evelyn shot Mark a smile. Her voice grew sweeter. "We met at a Youngie gathering over by Elizabethtown. But my grandmother lives near here, which is where I'm currently staying."

"Have you ever been in Paradise Found?"

"Only once. Just to look. You were helping a customer." Lois was surprised Evelyn remembered her.

As John flicked the reins and then turned the buggy onto the lane, Evelyn asked, "Do you live by yourself?"

"Jah," Lois answered. She wasn't going to say, especially in front of John, that the bishop wanted her to move—and now she did too with Moses taking over the shop.

Mark said, "Didn't your mother used to live there with you?"

"Jah," Lois said again. Until Mamm passed away.

Evelyn sat back against the seat. "I'd hate to live by myself."

"It's not so bad." Lois faced forward. At times—more than she liked to admit—she was lonely, but that was far better than living with someone she didn't love. Once Bishop Stephen began pushing her to give up her independence, she realized how much she preferred living alone.

As they passed the park, a hawk swooped down and then up toward the trees along the run.

John ducked. "What kind of bird was that?"

"A kestrel," Lois answered.

John laughed. "I think I've been attacked by one of those even after offering him all the mice in the field."

"That one was female." Lois smiled. "Perhaps it was a *she* who attacked you."

"Oh." John glanced at her. Lois frowned. Perhaps she'd said too much about the bird.

John asked, "So is Moses Lantz buying Paradise Found?"

"What?" Evelyn's voice grew closer. "Is that a real thing?"

John turned his head toward Lois again. "Do you know anything? Everyone's talking about it."

"I don't know anything for sure."

John snapped the reins. "I hope Moses will let you have a wiener roast in the field this summer, like Scotty did the last couple of years."

Lois had hosted wiener roasts in the grassy area behind the shop the last two summers for the Youngie. Perhaps that was when John first noticed her. The event had been a hit and surprisingly fun for her too, but she doubted she'd be working in the shop by summer.

"Moses owns the new café," Evelyn said. "I'm thinking about applying for a job there. I'd have to keep living with my grandmother. . . ."

Lois stifled a yawn. The road rash on her leg had woken her up whenever she'd rolled over during the night.

Evelyn kept talking. ". . . Moses also owns Creekside Market."

John shifted in his seat. "I still can't believe he'd sell his father's farms, three to Englischers, and blow his profits on businesses. He can never get that land back."

Lois felt oddly defensive of Moses. Why? She agreed with John. There was nothing like a family farm.

Lois tried, she really did. She attempted to be attentive toward John before the singing when the couples all gathered outside the Miller family shed, but her mind kept wandering. Finally, she headed to the house to see if she could help John's Mamm with the snacks.

"Denki, Lois," Wanda said. "I could use an extra set of hands. How have you been?"

"*Gut.*" Lois grimaced. Why couldn't she be chatty like Evelyn? She asked Wanda, "How have *you* been? How many grandchildren do you have now?" That was always a safe question to ask older Amish women.

"Twenty-three," she said. "My five oldest children have been quite prolific. As you know, we only have two more to marry off." She gave Lois a smile.

Lois forced herself to return it. "So I've heard."

Wanda yawned, quickly covering her mouth.

"You've had a long day with the service and meal. And now the singing," Lois said. "Go sit down and put your feet up. I'll take the snacks out."

Wanda's shoulders sagged a little. "Denki. I will." She glanced down at her sturdy shoes. "No one told me how much my feet would hurt with age." She reached between the counter and the stove and pulled out a tray. "You should be able to get everything out in two trips with this."

Lois took the tray.

Wanda gave her a wave. "You always have been a dear. I'll never forget how well you took care of your Mamm—working all the while. You'll make some fortunate man a good wife."

Tears pushed against Lois's eyes at the mention of her Mamm, and she turned back to the counter and loaded the gigantic bowl of popcorn and the plate of crackers. She had taken good care of her mother until that last night in the apartment. She hadn't been there when her mother needed her the most. Lois headed out the door with the tray. She'd return for the peanut butter cookies and the bowls of apple and orange slices after she'd set up the snack table.

By the time everything was ready, Mark had started the singing. John and Mark sat on the boys' side and Lois sat next to Evelyn on the girls' side in the back row. There were twelve girls in attendance and, she counted, nine boys. Girls and boys. How about men and women? Although perhaps she was the only one considered a woman. Everyone else appeared to still be a girl.

The singing started with "*Lebt Friedsam*," which translated "live peaceably," and then a praise song. Mark led them in "Amazing Grace" next and then "Rock of Ages." Lois shifted on the hard bench. Birds courted each other with songs too. And dancing—something the Amish Youngie would never do, not at a church-approved event, anyway.

⁓

After "How Great Thou Art," the Youngie gathered around the snack table and filled their plates again. Lois scanned the shed and saw a cup on the floor. She went to retrieve it and when she stood, John was beside her.

"You served the food and now you're cleaning up. You don't need to do that."

"Sure I do," she said.

"Mark and I told Mamm we'd clean up."

"I'll help."

He took the cup from her. "Come visit with everyone first." She'd much rather clean.

On the way home, Lois asked John to drop her off first. She didn't want to ride to Evelyn's grandmother's house and then back to her apartment.

"Are you sure?" He sounded disappointed.

"I'm tired. I work tomorrow." She knew he did too—and earlier. Still, she didn't think she could stand another minute of this particular courting ritual.

When John pulled into the parking lot, she made herself wait until the buggy came to a complete stop before she opened the door. "Denki," she said. "I had a wonderful time." She turned toward the back of the buggy. "It was so nice to meet you, Evelyn. Come by the shop soon."

"I will," she answered.

"Wait," John said. "How about the volleyball tournament next week?" He perked up a little. "Can you go to that? I'll find a ride for us. Mark and Evelyn are going—" he turned toward the back seat—"right?"

"Jah," Evelyn and Mark said in unison.

Lois swallowed. "Sure," she said. She started to say *I'd like to*—but would she really? She stopped herself. She needed to ask Amy for pointers on how to navigate the mating game of Amish Youngie. If only she were still young.

John climbed down from the buggy and hurried over to help her down. She thanked him again and said, "*Guti Nacht.*"

"*Guti Nacht.*" He jogged back around to the driver's side of the buggy. Lois waved as John drove the buggy to the lane, which was protected by the two rows of cherry trees with their white blossomy tops looking like *Kappa* in the night. She watched as they turned onto the highway.

Once the buggy was out of sight, Lois pulled her keys from her apron pocket and unlocked the door to the shop. She flicked on the light. Scotty's wife, Barb, usually worked on Mondays to give Lois two days off each week. But Scotty had said they needed Lois to work the next day. Perhaps Barb wouldn't be coming in any longer. She hoped she'd have a chance to tell her goodbye.

She wondered if Moses would expect Lois to work on Mondays. If so, he would need to pay her overtime. Of course, it wouldn't be for long.

Lois stopped at the counter and tidied it up, stacking flyers and business cards. She had been so ready to be done on Saturday, she'd simply locked the door and left without doing her usual cleaning.

She headed to the utility closet to grab the broom. There was a light on under the door of Scotty's office—but his car wasn't out front. He never walked to the shop and certainly wouldn't at night.

There was a rustling behind the door and then the sound of the office chair against the floor.

She continued on to the closet, grabbed the broom, and stepped to the office door. She raised the broom like a baseball bat and barked, "Who's there?"

No one responded.

She raised the broom higher.

Footsteps fell across the office floor. The door swung open.

A giant of a man dressed in black sweatpants, a sweatshirt, and a backward baseball cap stood in front of her. He was handsome—but that didn't mean he wasn't a thief.

Lois whacked him, aiming for his head, but she hit him across the chest. She pulled the broom back and swung again, but he grabbed it and twisted it away from her. "Lois! Stop!"

She took a step backward.

Moses crossed his arms over the broom.

She sputtered, "What are you doing here?"

"I could ask the same."

"Getting ready for work tomorrow. And you?"

"Going over Scotty's books. He let me in. He said to go out the back door and lock up when I left."

"Where's your car?"

"I ran over."

"You ran?"

He nodded. "Which is why I'm wearing running clothes."

"How are you getting home?"

"I'll run. Or get a rideshare if it's late."

Lois put her hand out for the broom. "I'll leave you be."

He didn't uncross his arms. "I'm not sure I can trust you."

"Trust me? You're the one lurking in the office, scaring me half to death."

He chuckled. "Did you think someone was robbing the store?"

"For sure."

"And attacking said robber with a broom would force him to leave? Did you think about calling 9-1-1?" He smiled.

"For certain on attacking said robber." She extended her hand and scowled. She'd forgotten how attractive Moses could be. She found the fact disconcerting. "And no, as far as calling 9-1-1. Give me the broom."

He stopped smiling, handed her the broom, and closed the door.

6

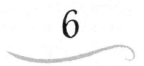

Moses left the office door all the way open as Lois swept the hallway, vacuumed the shop carpet, took out the trash, and then stomped around, banging who knew what. Neither one of them should be working on Sunday, and yet both of them were.

He tried to concentrate on Scotty's accounting program but kept thinking about Lois. Fearless Lois. Feisty Lois. Fiery-eyed Lois.

Beautiful Lois.

He squinted and forced himself to focus on the monitor again. Sales began picking up in April, peaked in August, and then fell flat by November. Perhaps Moses could come up with a Christmas festival or something connected to the market to increase sales in November and December. January would be slow no matter what. Maybe a Valentine's Day event would bring more people in during February.

"Will I see you tomorrow?" Lois stood in the doorway. Her white Kapp with the heart-shaped back was a little askew. He'd always liked the heart-shaped Kappa. His mother still wore them, but he knew the staff at the care home tired of bleaching and pressing them.

"Moses?"

He cleared his throat. "I'm not sure. I'll call Scotty and see where we're at."

"All right." She tightened her apron and then flipped her cape over her dress, which was the same color as an indigo bunting. "I'll see you when I see you."

"I guess so."

"Make sure and lock up."

His gaze drifted back to the computer. She harrumphed and must have left. He didn't hear her again.

Two hours later he noticed the time. *11:05*. He yawned, stretched, and stood. He put his notebook in his satchel and slung it across his chest. He'd run home. He turned off the office light, closed the door, and made his way down the pitch-black hallway. And then he tripped. As he sprawled out on the floor he felt the bristles of the broom. He tried to stand, but his foot landed on top of the handle and he slid again. Not sure where the broom ended up, he stayed on all fours and crawled to the back door. When he reached it, he pulled himself up.

His knees hurt but he wasn't sure whether it was from falling or crawling.

He opened the door and stepped out into the night. A near-full moon shone. An owl hooted. A light turned off from above. Had Lois been waiting until she heard the clatter of him falling before she went to bed?

Suddenly exhausted, he fished his phone out of his satchel and ordered a rideshare. But as tired as Moses was, once he crawled beneath his old quilt, sleep eluded him. He wasn't sure why he'd gone to the Amish church service. Probably just to torment himself. Seeing Lois again had impaired his judgment and transported him back in time five years. He needed to get a grip and put that behind him—again.

He climbed out of bed, unlocked the door to the warehouse, shuffled through it, and then unlocked the door to the dimly lit grocery store. A car slowed on the highway, and Moses waited. He didn't want someone calling the police on him for "breaking" into his own store. After the car passed, he took a chocolate milk from the cooler and a bag of popcorn from the snack aisle, noted the items on a pad by the register, and then retraced his steps back to his studio apartment. After sitting down at his desk, he turned on the lamp and stared at the collage of the painted buntings for a minute. For a second he felt a sense of peace, even a hint of harmony. Then he opened the envelope Casey had given him. He might as well write Teresa Schrock and ask to join the circle letter. He decided to use a nickname—*Menno*, the name Casey sometimes called him after he joined the Mennonites, in memory of Menno Simons, the Catholic priest who became an Anabaptist in the 1500s. Followers of his beliefs became known as Mennonites.

He needed a good solid Amish surname to go with Menno. The last thing he wanted was for someone to figure out who he really was and share their opinions about his business ventures. *Stoltzfus.*

Menno Stoltzfus.

He'd mail his letters from Delaware to further protect his identity.

After he finished the letter and addressed and stamped the envelope, he crawled back into bed, going over his to-do list for the next day. Stop by to see his mother, finally. He'd failed at that again today. Check on Sara at the café. Spend some time in the grocery store, besides raiding it for a late-night snack. Call Scotty. See to payroll. And figure out what to do about Lois Yoder.

⁓

Moses stared out the window as the aide helped his mother to the bathroom. A robin hopped across the grass. A crow swooped down alongside it. Then another crow. Soon there were five crows on the lawn, and the robin flew up into a dogwood tree.

"Denki," Mamm said to the caregiver as they returned. Moses turned away from the window. Mamm's face lit up. "*Sohn.*" She reached out to him. "You're such a good son." He wasn't sure she remembered his name—but at least she remembered he was her son, although she hadn't remembered he'd arrived fifteen minutes ago. A double bonus was she thought he was good. If she only knew.

She wore a nightgown and robe. Her gray hair hung down her back in a braid. He would let the aide get her dressed when she had time, but in the meantime he could do her hair and cover it.

He motioned to the chair at the end of her bed. "Mamm, sit down. I'll do your hair."

"Denki." She sat a little awkwardly.

The aide said she'd be back in a half hour.

Moses began undoing Mamm's braid. She had been diagnosed with early-onset dementia six years ago, at the age of fifty-seven. A year and a half later, Moses's father had a massive heart attack and died in his sleep. Mamm was found the next morning wandering the lane in her nightgown. Thankfully the neighbor called Moses, who was living at another of his father's farms near Strasburg, instead of the police. The neighbor had already found his father and called for an ambulance when Moses arrived.

In the next week, Moses made all the arrangements to bury his Dat and found a woman to come in during the day to care for his Mamm, after a quick lesson from their family doctor on her diagnosis. Something his father had kept from him.

His family had always been different from others in their Amish community. He was an only child. His parents were older than his friends' parents. And they didn't have any relatives in the area. His Dat had grown up in Ohio and sold a hundred-acre family farm he'd inherited there when he was in his thirties, and moved to Lancaster County, where he married Mamm and invested his money into two properties before prices in the area skyrocketed. Over the years, he purchased and sold farms in the area.

When Moses started to notice Mamm's memory problems, without knowing the diagnosis, he thought he'd have another decade or two with Dat, at the least, to learn more about the businesses and their family history.

Instead he was thrust into caring for his mother and sorting out his father's finances and figuring out how to pay for Mamm's care without any insurance. He feared the ongoing expense would break their district's mutual aid fund and determined to pay for it on his own, or at least as much as possible. That meant he needed at least a couple of businesses to turn an ongoing profit. He had never enjoyed farming, so he decided to sell the properties, buy the grocery store, and hold on to the rest of the money to invest over the next few years. That was how his business journey began.

Moses picked up the silver-plated brush on Mamm's dresser top. As he brushed her hair he said, "I went to church yesterday." He'd told her several times he'd left the Amish and joined the Mennonites, but she never remembered. Nor did she remember he was spending time with Sara Fisher.

"How's Lois?" Mamm asked.

He didn't answer, hoping she'd forget what she'd asked.

Mamm waited a moment and then said, "Lois Yoder. How is she? Have you proposed to her yet?"

Moses took a deep breath. Mamm remembered Lois's name but not his. "Why do you ask?"

"You were such good friends in school."

They weren't. They'd hated each other in school. No, that wasn't true. He'd actually adored Lois—he just liked to tease her. She hated him. But then there was a time she'd liked him, really liked him, almost as much as he liked her. But he didn't want to think about that.

Mamm sat up a little straighter. "Lois is full of life. And cute as a . . . bird."

Moses suppressed a smile at Mamm's play—or fumble—on words as he grabbed the bunch of bobby pins off the dresser. "She moved up to Big Valley."

Mamm leaned back in the chair. "She's back."

As Moses brushed all of Mamm's hair into his hand, he asked, "How do you know?"

"Amy Kauffman told me, a couple of years ago."

Either Mamm was unusually lucid today or she had a special file in her brain for Lois Yoder that included Amy

Kauffman. Although now her last name was Dienner. Moses had sold one of his father's farms to Amy and her husband, Bennie.

"You and Lois cared about each other." Mamm's voice grew louder. "I don't know why you aren't married by now."

Moses slipped her hair into a fastener, ignoring what she'd said. He'd kept Mamm at home for a year with the help of several caregivers, including one who took the night shift, before he moved Mamm into a care center. Moses had reached a point of exhaustion after Mamm woke him three or four times a night for an entire year. He feared his father's heart attack was brought on by exhaustion—and stress.

Mamm had been in two previous care centers before this latest one. She received better care here, plus therapy. He hoped he wouldn't have to move her again. Her memory kept deteriorating but her body remained strong. The doctor said she could easily live another decade. When she was gone, he'd be all alone. Except for Sara.

He put the brush back on the dresser and twisted Mamm's hair into a bun at the nape of her neck. It would make sense to cut her hair short, but she still cared about it and her Kappa too. In another year—maybe in just a few months— she wouldn't. But he wouldn't approve a haircut for her then either. It wasn't what she would want.

"Paul, I'm tired," Mamm said.

Here it came. She'd been confusing Moses more and more with her little brother Paul. Moses had no memory of him.

"Didn't we have fun down by the creek when you were little? We were bookends, the oldest and the youngest."

Moses patted her shoulder. "You were a good big sister. And a good mother."

"I'm tired," she said.

"You can nap as soon as I'm done."

A bird flew by the window and her head jerked to the side. "Oh, Moses. A cardinal."

Tears sprang into his eyes. She remembered his name. And she'd identified a bird. "Jah, you're right, on both counts." He began pinning her bun.

"I need a feeder in that window."

"What a great idea." He pinned her white Kapp on her head. "I know just the place to get one."

He'd skip going to the café and head straight to Paradise Found. He could have the bird feeder in place before she awoke from her morning nap.

He'd stop by the post office and mail the letter to Teresa Schrock on the way.

7

As Lois flipped the Closed sign to Open, a black SUV came up the lane. What was Moses doing back so soon? Scotty hadn't even arrived yet.

She stepped back to the counter, pulled out the feather duster, and turned her attention to the birdhouses. Dust in the shop was a big no-no. Any dust implied the inventory was old—and neglected. Lois kept an immaculate shop.

The buzzer rang.

She stepped toward the center of the floor and forced a surprised smile and greeted him.

"Moses."

He wore black trousers and black suspenders over a white shirt. He held his straw hat in his hands. After attempting to deny that he appeared as handsome as he had the night before, she asked, "What are you doing here so early?"

"I'm curious. I know you liked birds when we were young. Are you a birder now?"

Her face grew warm. "I don't have time for that."

"Why all the bird feeders and houses?"

"Supply and demand."

That got a little bit of a smile out of him. "I'm here early to do some shopping. I need a bird feeder."

"Oh?" Why in the world would Moses Lantz need a bird feeder? "Are you a birder?"

His face reddened a little. "It's for my Mamm." He closed his mouth, but it seemed perhaps he wanted to say more.

Lois stepped back toward the feeders. "Is it for a tree? Or window?"

"Window," he said. "I'll need to hang it from the eaves."

She pointed toward a feeder made out of cedar with an open log-cabin look. "This design works well in a window. Or this one." She pointed to an acrylic feeder. "It attaches easily but very securely with suction cups. I have one on my window upstairs."

He glanced toward the back door.

"Go take a look," she said. "It's the window right above the back exit."

"I will." He stepped around her. "I'll be right back."

She continued dusting. She wouldn't tell him how much joy the feeder had brought *her* mother.

He returned a couple of minutes later. "The feeder looks good from the outside. Any chance I could see it from the inside?"

Her face fell into a scowl, which seemed to have become her resting expression. Then she forced a smile. Of course she wouldn't let him in her apartment. She hadn't even made her bed, and no doubt the door to her room was open. She said, "No. Absolutely not. I can assure you the feeder looks as nice from the inside as the outside."

His face reddened again. "All right. Are you sure the suction cups work well?"

"Yes. I bring it inside for the winter and then put it back outside in March. I've never had it even slip, let alone fall, even when crows try to perch inside. I bought it several years ago." It had been in storage from the time of her mother's death until Lois moved back to Lancaster County from Big Valley, but she wouldn't mention that.

Moses hesitated a moment and then said, "The suction cups will make it easier to install."

Lois nodded in agreement. "Do you have birdseed?"

He shook his head.

"I have some in the back." Lois put the duster on the counter and headed toward the storeroom. When she returned with the feeder in a cardboard box and the birdseed, Moses was standing at the front window. He turned toward her. "A red-tailed hawk just swooped by."

"*Wunderbar*," Lois said. "I've been waiting for them to return. They've had a nest in the loblolly pine for the last two years."

"In the loblolly pine?"

"Jah," Lois said. "It's the pine tree by the shed." She rang up the feeder and then put it in a large paper bag. Then she placed the seed on top.

Moses took out his wallet from his jacket and pulled out a card. "You forgot to add the birdseed."

"We include the bag with the purchase of a feeder—it's a small bag."

"Oh." Moses handed her his card. "Does that bring people back into the store?"

"I think so." Did he think it was a bad idea? "It adds to

the experience. Several people have started collecting bird-houses after buying their first one here." She lowered her voice as she ran his card. "I believe it becomes a sort of addiction."

He said, "I see." And then frowned.

Lois returned his card, along with the receipt. "Thank you for shopping at Paradise Found today." She gave him her shopgirl smile. But then she added, "I hope your Mamm enjoys the bird feeder. Please tell her hello from me."

Were those tears that sprang into Moses Lantz's eyes? He blinked several times in a row. "I will," he replied. "She'll be happy to hear from you."

That surprised Lois. Why would Moses say that? She doubted Anna Lantz remembered her.

~

Lois pulled her father's watch from her apron pocket. Three o'clock. She turned the sign. Barbara usually closed early on Mondays from the first of November through the end of April. Lois wanted to send her letter to Teresa Schrock in the afternoon mail—and rent a mailbox.

She scootered down the highway, past the café, past the park, and past the stone church, her bandage pulling on her leg as she rolled along. Then she veered right at the fork and arrived at the small brick building with the Paradise, PA Post Office sign over the door. She parked her scooter in the bike rack and hurried up the steps and through the entrance. She approached the counter and told the clerk she needed a post office box.

"We have one available," the woman said. "We just had a cancellation on Friday."

After Lois filled out the form and paid the fee by writing a check, the woman gave her the key. "It's on the bottom row near the middle."

Lois found her box and tried the key. It worked. She added it to her key ring, alongside the shop key and her apartment key. Then she wrote her new return address on the envelope and slipped the letter to Teresa Schrock in the outgoing mail slot.

Once outside, she decided to keep scootering to Amy and Bennie's farm. She could help her friend fix supper and do the afternoon chores. Perhaps they'd even have time to talk.

There was a chill in the air, but Lois warmed as she flew down the highway. She passed the road that led to her family's old farm. A half mile later she crossed the highway and turned left onto a county road. A quarter mile later, she took a right and sped down the lane to Amy and Bennie's farm.

When she arrived, Bennie waved from his horse-drawn plow. The air smelled of soil and manure and the world starting anew, as it did each spring. It was the best smell in the world. Lois waved and continued on to the house. As she reached the back door, Ernest, the oldest at four, opened the screen door.

"Hallo, Lois!" he called out.

Amy appeared. "Lois?" She grinned. "What are you doing here?"

"I stopped by the post office to mail a letter to Teresa Schrock about the circle letter." Lois leaned her scooter against the back steps. "And figured I might as well keep coming." She started up the steps. "Do you need help with supper?"

Amy laughed. "Always. Although I mostly need help with the baby. Would you rock her?"

"Of course." Lois followed Amy into the kitchen and Ernie followed Lois.

"She's been fussy all day," Amy said. "I think she's teething."

Lois could hear the baby crying. "I'll get her." The baby, Maggie, was in a bassinet in the living room, and the middle two, Oliver and Deborah, who were two and half and eighteen months, were playing in what Amy referred to as the pasture —it was a fenced off area that kept them contained and Maggie safe. Ernie climbed over the fence and sat down next to Oliver.

Lois scooped up the baby. Deborah lifted her arms. Lois said, "After I rock Maggie I'll be back." She didn't know how Amy did it.

As Lois sat down in the rocker, Amy asked, "So did Moses buy the shop today?"

"Not today, but it seems to be imminent."

"You'll still have a job, right?"

"Supposedly." As she settled Maggie on her shoulder and began to rock, she told Amy how Scotty had made Moses promise to keep her on.

"That's good."

"He won't, though," Lois explained. "Sure, he will for a few months, probably until October, when Scotty and Barb move to Florida. Then he'll let me go."

"I don't think Moses would do that."

"You'll see. I won't have a job or a place to live."

Amy shook her head but said, "If that happens, you can move in with us."

Lois smiled at the thought. If she were going to be a mother's helper, it would *only* be for Amy. But her friend wouldn't be able to pay her, and it wouldn't be a good idea anyway. "I wouldn't do that to Bennie. It wouldn't be like our last year of school when he liked having me around." That was when Bennie and Amy had fallen in love, at fourteen. Truly. And Lois was their go-between. She adored Bennie almost as much as she adored Amy, but that didn't mean she should move in with them.

"You know Bennie thinks the world of you."

"I know," Lois said.

Amy turned the propane off and slid the pan of hamburger to the back burner.

Maggie relaxed against Lois's body. Slowing her rocking, Lois said, "Bishop Stephen asked me to think about moving back to Big Valley."

Amy wiped her hands on her apron as she asked, "Why?"

"I need to be under the authority of a man and if I don't have a husband, the man should be my brother." Most single adult Amish women did live with a relative, but it wasn't unheard of for one to live alone. But they were usually older than Lois.

"Then you need a husband in Lancaster County, preferably Paradise Township," Amy said. "And soon."

"I need to figure out this whole courting thing." She told Amy about the singing. "Why am I so bad at it?"

"There's nothing to figure out. You have to let it happen naturally."

Lois didn't believe her. "What do you think about John Miller?"

Amy's eyes grew large. "John Miller? Mark's little brother? That John Miller?"

Lois nodded.

Amy stirred the hamburger. "Wasn't he in the third grade when we were eighth graders?"

Lois's face grew warm. "Fourth grade. He's twenty-one."

"Four years is a lot. . . ."

"According to Bishop Stephen, John is mature for his age."

Amy rolled her eyes. "That's what bishops always say. John's going to take over the Miller farm, right?"

"Jah."

Amy turned the burner down. "What about Casey?"

Lois relaxed as she said, "I adore Casey. And I've always been thankful for his friendship, but I've never been romantically interested in him. Don't you think I would have been by now if he was the right one?"

"Jah." Amy cocked her head. "So that brings us back to Moses."

Lois's rocking came to an abrupt stop, causing Maggie to let out a cry. She started again.

Amy had a mischievous look in her eyes. "I've always thought you and Moses would get back together."

Lois started patting the baby's back again. "We weren't really together."

Amy scrunched her button nose, pushing her cheeks upward. "You were. You were even thinking about marriage, remember?"

"Believe me, I've tried to forget."

"He was in love with you, even after you'd been so mean to him." Amy stepped back to the counter.

Lois rocked faster. "I wasn't mean to him."

"You called him Goliath."

That was true.

Amy ran a dishcloth under the water. "Remember, you asked him one time why he was so tall when his parents were so short."

Lois's face grew warm. She remembered that too, much to her chagrin. "Well, he was tall. And his parents were very short. He was as tall as his mother by the time he was nine. As tall as his Dat by the time he was twelve. We all wondered."

"But you said it out loud and that hurt his feelings."

Lois did her best to be humble, but her defenses grew. "He used to call me Baby Bunting. Do you remember that?" He meant a baby bunting bird, not Baby Bunting from the poem.

"It's not the same. Baby buntings are cute." Amy leaned closer. "Have you forgiven him for acting like a normal boy?"

"He was fourteen by the end of our school days."

Amy turned off the water. "Has he forgiven you?"

"For what?"

"For being mean to him."

"I wasn't, not really."

"He was tall, taller than anyone." Amy lowered her voice. "Don't you think he already was self-conscious without you pointing out how big he was?"

Lois's face grew even warmer. Amy was right. That had been rude. Should she apologize to Moses now for something she'd said twelve years ago? Would apologizing just make it worse?

Amy began wiping down the counters. "How does Moses look now?"

"Even bigger."

"Meaning?" Deborah began to cry in the living room. Amy waited for Lois's answer.

"Taller. And very fit." Quite muscular in fact. But she wouldn't tell Amy that.

~

Lois and Amy hadn't had another chance to say a word to each other unless it had to do with preparing supper, the kinner, cleaning up, or bath time the rest of her visit. As Bennie put Ernie, Oliver, and Deborah to bed, Amy nursed the baby in the rocking chair in the kitchen.

"I better get going," Lois said.

"It will be dark soon. Bennie can give you a ride."

Lois glanced toward the staircase. Deborah was crying and Oliver was yelling. She turned her attention back to Amy. "I can scooter home. It's not dark yet—and I have my vest." She stepped to the door and picked up her backpack. Then she pulled out the flashing light she used at night. Turning it on and holding it up, she said, "And I have this."

Amy grinned. "That's awfully fancy." She pulled the baby away from her breast and refastened her dress. Then she put the baby up to her shoulder.

"Thank you for having me for supper," Lois said. "It's always good to be part of your—" she grinned—"chaotic household."

Amy faked an expression of shock. But then said, "Please come more often. I mean it. And if you need a place to stay, please come live with us. Bennie and I both want you to."

Lois stepped back toward the rocking chair. "Denki. For everything. You're the best friend ever."

"No." Amy continued patting the baby's back. "You are."

It was a conversation they'd had more than once.

"I'm praying for you." Amy gave her a sassy look. "And for Moses."

Lois laughed, gathered up her things, waved, and then slipped out the front door for her solitary ride home.

The next morning, as Lois ate breakfast, she thought of Amy praying for Moses. Could Lois do that? She swallowed a lump of oatmeal. Nee. She didn't think so.

As she stood to take her bowl to the sink, she caught a flash of neon out the window. She looked again. There were two men in the field behind the store close to the shed—near the loblolly pine. Surveyors wearing safety vests. Moses stood next to the shed.

Lois quickly finished getting ready for work, donned her cloak, and rushed down the steps. Then, instead of going into the shop, she marched through the wet grass toward Moses. When she neared him, she called out, "What's going on?"

He gave her a wry smile. "*Guder Mariye* to you too, Lois. How are you this fine day?"

She crossed her arms. "Fine, thank you very much. Fine and curious. Why do you have surveyors out here?"

"I need some measurements before I can negotiate with Scotty."

"For what plans?"

"I hope to put in a market on this part of the property. I want this place to be a tourist destination for—"

"I'm all for attracting more tourists, but you don't need to decimate the property to do so."

"I have to develop it to create a market. A foundation and then a building. And a sheltered area with a concrete pad. All for an Amish market."

"You're Mennonite."

His face reddened. "I grew up Amish. I want to provide

business opportunities for Amish people through a tourist destination."

"Even if it means paving over a pristine green space?"

"A market will bring more business into the shop and the township than this field."

Lois narrowed her eyes as she glared at him. "But it's practically a park."

"A park?"

"Jah. Sometimes local people walk around the property for exercise and to enjoy the woods. A few have even brought a picnic here in the summer. Scotty lets me host a Youngie wiener roast each summer, the first Friday of June. And—" she stared up at the pine tree—"the red-tailed hawks might still come back, plus multiple species of birds make their home in the woods."

He sighed. "I'm not going to do anything to the woods."

"You don't think construction and then a market will negatively impact the bird population around here?"

"Since when do you care about birds?"

"Everyone cares about birds." Lois glared at Moses and then muttered, "At least they should."

He shrugged. "I chose this property so I could build a market."

"Then don't put up a building and a concrete pad. Have the market on the grass."

"It wouldn't be safe," Moses answered. "The uneven ground would be a liability."

"Then level the ground."

"It wouldn't stay level."

Lois continued to glare at him for a long moment. Why did he have to be so logical? She spun away from him and marched toward the shop without saying goodbye. As she fumed, she chastised herself. What did she care? She wouldn't live or work on the property much longer.

But she did care. And she couldn't shake her fury. Moses, thankfully, didn't come into the shop, but he was still out back with the surveyors. Was he having every inch of the property measured? He'd probably change his mind about the woods when he became greedy for even more land to develop.

Lois waited on customers and stocked shelves, but put off doing inventory. No need to do that until Scotty told her to. He'd need the information for the sale, no doubt.

She was still fuming when her favorite customer, Isabelle Conley, came into the shop. Isabelle had been gone all winter, staying with friends in Arizona. She greeted Lois with a hug. After she told Lois about her time away, which included several weeks in Palm Springs and a week in San Diego, Lois told Isabelle how much she liked her outfit.

Isabelle beamed. "I picked up the necklace and bracelet at a shop in California." The jewelry had a nautical theme, which complemented her outfit—white capris, a navy shirt with a striped collar and cuffs, and white flats. Isabelle, who was in her fifties and glamorous—at least to Lois—had grown up in Lancaster County and then owned a gift shop in Philadelphia years ago. She sometimes offered helpful advice to Lois on displays and product placement.

Isabelle asked, "What's going on outside with the surveyors?"

"Have you talked with Barb or Scotty?"

"No. I just got home last night."

"They're selling the business, it seems to Moses Lantz."

Isabelle's hand flew to her chest. "They're selling?"

"Jah."

"Why didn't they tell me?"

Lois wrinkled her nose, fearing she'd said too much. "I think it all happened pretty fast."

Isabelle's hand fell to her side. "Tell me the name of the buyer again."

"Moses. Moses Lantz."

Isabelle hesitated and then said, "Doesn't he own the new café?"

Lois nodded.

"I'm flabbergasted." Isabelle shook her head as she spoke. "I told Scotty a year ago that I would buy this shop in a heartbeat. Why didn't he let me know?"

"Call him," Lois said, shocked at how quickly the words came out. "Do you have his number?"

"I have Barb's." Isabelle and Barb had been friends for years. "Could you give me Scotty's?" She pulled her phone from her purse.

Lois rattled off the number, and Isabelle placed the call as she stepped toward the birch tree display.

A moment later, she said, "Scotty! It's Isabelle Conley." After a pause, she added, "I'm home from Arizona." She laughed. "I'm mostly fine. I am a little disappointed you didn't offer to sell Paradise Found to me." Her voice took on a teasing tone. "Don't you remember? I told you I'd be interested in buying it last year." Lois was impressed with how light Isabelle's voice sounded. She could learn a lot from how Isabelle handled her emotions.

There was another pause, and then Isabelle said, "Of course I was serious. It's the best shop around."

Lois realized she was eavesdropping and busied herself by reshelving a candle. However, she could still hear Isabelle say, "I'd love the opportunity to make an offer on the shop, a serious one."

As Lois placed the candle on the shelf at the front of the shop, she let out a sigh of relief. Perhaps she wouldn't be home and job shopping after all.

8

Moses sat across from Scotty in the Paradise Café, his coffee mug suspended in midair. "Have I heard you correctly? You're considering another offer? After my letter of intent? After you already drafted a purchase agreement? Are you considering someone from out of the area?"

"No." Scotty leaned back in his seat. "And I appreciate the steps you've already gone through. I'm guessing this offer is more of a formality—one I need to at least consider. It's a local person."

Person. Why did he choose that word? Was he trying to conceal the possible buyer's identity? Moses put his mug down. Sara appeared with the coffeepot and filled it. Moses said, "Thank you." When she'd moved on, he added, "I'm surprised. Shocked, really. We're so far along in the process."

"We are. But it seems this person told me she—they—"

So it was a woman.

"They told me they were interested in buying the store over a year ago, but I hadn't remembered or perhaps thought they weren't serious." He rubbed his chin. "But I believe I should at least consider their offer."

"Will I have the opportunity to counter?"

"Yes. Of course."

"Does this person have a Plain background?" Could it be Lois? Perhaps she had an inheritance from her parents, although it seemed they didn't have much money. That was the thing about the Amish—it was hard to tell when everyone dressed alike and drove similar buggies.

"No, no Plain background as far as I know," Scotty said. "I just want to give this person a chance."

"When will you decide?"

"I should know if it's a legitimate offer soon. I'll give you a call."

"All right." Moses took a sip of coffee. "I can pay cash. There will be no waiting for financing."

"I'll keep that under consideration." Scotty scooted his chair back. "I need to get going."

Moses stood. "So do I."

Scotty pulled out his wallet.

"The coffee's on me," Moses said as a crash reverberated in the kitchen. Moses forced a chuckle. "It's always something, right?"

Scotty laughed. "I'll let you attend to business."

"Talk to you tomorrow." Moses took a couple of deep breaths. He hadn't expected a delay in purchasing Paradise Found. He'd thought he'd be signing the papers within a day. Instead he might be making a counteroffer. Perhaps he'd end up spending more than he'd planned. The grocery store was profitable. So was the Byler's Corner Market. That was why he wanted to get the market in Paradise going as soon as possible. The café hadn't made a penny yet and wouldn't for months.

He strode into the kitchen to find the man who washed the dishes kneeling on the floor, putting broken plates into a bus tub. Sara stood with her hands on her hips, tapping one foot.

Moses spoke softly. "Sara, go take a break. I'll help clean up."

An hour later Moses drove toward Paradise Found. He wanted to stop, but then he saw Scotty's Buick in the lot. No. He needed to keep going.

The next afternoon, when Scotty called, Moses was at the grocery store, speaking with the manager about a late delivery. He held his phone in his hand, let it ring five times, and then excused himself and stepped through the warehouse and out the back door onto the loading dock. He didn't want to seem too anxious. Finally, he answered it slowly, saying, "Hey, Scotty. How are you?"

After their greetings, Scotty cleared his throat. "The offer didn't turn out to be serious enough for consideration, although the other interested party would like to be notified if you back out of the deal or decide to sell the shop in the next few years. Of course, the latter would simply be a courtesy on your part."

"Of course," Moses said. There was no way he'd want to sell the shop in a few years. "Do you mind if I ask who the interested party is?"

"Isabelle Conley. Do you know her?"

"No." At least Moses didn't think he did.

"She used to own a shop in Philly and moved here about ten years ago. She's a childhood friend of my wife's and became close with Lois over the last two years."

That stung. Had Lois put Isabelle up to saying she wanted to make an offer to delay Moses's plan? If so, it hadn't worked.

"Anyway," Scotty said, "my lawyer has drawn up the papers between us. We can go over them as soon as you're ready. I'll email you a copy to forward to your lawyer."

Moses spoke slowly. "I'd still like to see the apartment above the shop before we finalize the deal."

"Lois's apartment?"

Moses nodded. "I think I have a right to see it. Sure, she's living there, but I would own it."

"Well, sure. But if you keep her on as you've promised and allow her to live in the apartment, it won't matter, right?"

"Except I'm buying the property."

"I don't feel comfortable showing you the apartment with Lois living there. Nor pressuring her to allow you to see it."

Moses's face grew warm even though it was an unusually cold day for late April. Had he come off as inappropriate to ask to see an apartment he was buying? Scotty was clearly protective of Lois.

"How about if we meet in the morning?" Scotty asked. "My lawyer has a ten o'clock appointment available. Does that work?"

"As long as my lawyer has a chance to preview the document by then, jah." Moses cringed. *Jah.* He tried not say the word anymore, especially not in a professional conversation. His face grew even warmer. "Yes, I can make that work."

~

Friday morning at nine, with the signed papers in his hand along with the canceled cashier's check from the bank for the entire amount, Moses unlocked the back door of the shop

The Shop Down the Lane

and stepped into the dark hallway. He quickly found the light switch. Obviously, Lois hadn't come down yet.

Once his lawyer had reviewed the contract, it had taken another day to work out the details. After they signed the paperwork and Moses turned over the cashier's check, Scotty handed him the keys, saying he'd already cleared out the office except for the computer and files, which were included in the sale.

Moses stepped to the office door, which was wide open, and entered. It was a little dusty, but in good shape.

He placed his satchel on the desk next to the monitor and sat in the chair. This was exactly what he'd wanted—a gift shop, a property for a market in Lancaster County, a living space on the property, and an office with a computer where he could consolidate all the paperwork for his, now, four businesses. So why did he feel so unsettled? As if he were trespassing? He'd never felt this way about any of the other businesses he'd bought.

Someone knocked on the back door. He'd been expecting Lois to arrive at any moment, but why would she knock? He stood.

Someone called out, "Moses? It's me!" *Sara.*

He stepped into the hallway. She walked toward him, carrying a cup holder with two coffees and a cinnamon roll on a paper plate. "I came so we could celebrate, and you could show me around."

He took one of the cups of coffee from her and the plate. "Denki." He nodded his head toward the cinnamon roll. "I'll put this down and then give you a tour."

As Moses led Sara around the shop, taking sips of his coffee, he felt not only unsettled but anxious. Lois would come through the back door any minute. He hadn't imagined his first morning in the shop to include Sara, but he was grateful she wanted to celebrate with him. She was good about marking special occasions, something he'd tried to avoid over the last few years because of his grief over his parents.

He showed her around the shop.

"It's cute," she said. "Of course, it needs a few updates. Several, in fact." She shot him a smile. "I'll help, starting with the window display. That will be my job." She smiled.

Moses shrugged. "That's fine by me." He returned her smile but it felt halfhearted. If she had time, he was fine with her doing the window display. But he didn't want Sara to remake the entire place. She was too busy with the café, plus he didn't want her to feel as if she were in charge of the shop too. "Let's go outside." He started toward the door. "I'll show you where the market will be."

As they reached the door, it flew open. Lois gasped. Why was he always scaring her?

"Sorry," she said. "I wasn't expecting you." She smiled. "Hallo, Sara."

"Hi," Sara said. "How's your leg?"

"*Gut*." Lois tilted her head back and met Sara's gaze. "Are you working here now?"

Sara sweetly answered, "No. I stopped by to celebrate Moses's new purchase. He's going to show me where the market will be."

"Have fun. Watch out for the mole holes." Lois breezed by them without saying anything more.

Sara stepped outside and Moses pulled the door closed behind them. "Maybe I should work here," she said. "Lois can manage the café."

"Why do you say that?"

"It doesn't seem appropriate for you two to be here alone."

Moses laughed, the first time he remembered doing so in months.

"What's so funny?"

"Lois despises me." He increased his stride and headed toward the pine tree. "The only thing you should worry about is my safety."

Early Saturday morning, Moses headed to Delaware for his weekly trip to the Byler's Corner Market. When he arrived, he parked his SUV and then walked to the locked mailbox at the edge of the parking lot. He had a couple of payments from vendors at the market and a thick envelope. The return address was Teresa Schrock's. He hadn't expected a circle letter so soon.

He put all the envelopes in his satchel—he'd deposit the checks later and read the circle letter when he had a chance.

He checked in with Joey first, who greeted him, jumping up and pouring him a cup of his wife's coffee. She greeted Moses too. "I have fresh doughnuts. Made this morning."

"I'll take an old-fashioned," Moses said. "Make it three." He'd give the other two to Casey and Walter.

When he reached their stall, Casey stood as soon as he saw him and then limped toward him with his right hand held high. Moses put the doughnuts down on the closest shelf, and Casey gave him a high five. As their hands connected in a loud slap, Casey said, "Congratulations on buying Paradise Found."

"Denki." Moses made his hand into a fist against the sting on his palm as he lowered it. "I'm grateful it all worked out."

Casey smiled. "Now you'll see Lois every day."

Moses ignored the comment. "How is business so far?"

"*Gut.* Better than last week."

"Where's Walter?"

"Helping a new vendor get their stall set up."

A customer approached and picked up a wooden train engine.

"I'll stop by in a little while," Moses said.

Casey waved.

An Amish woman selling jams, jellies, and peanut butter spread waved Moses over and then said, "One of the sinks in the women's restroom is clogged."

"Thank you for letting me know," Moses said. "I'll go take care of it." He had a shed at the back of the property full of tools. Some of them Moses even knew how to use. He liked to give Joey a break when possible. He retrieved a plumber's snake, a wrench, drain cleaner, and a bucket. He tried to work as quickly as possible and put the restroom back in use, but it took him longer than it should have.

The day continued with other problems. An older Englisch woman tripped and fell, bloodying her knee. An Amish horse on the road spooked and headed toward the market, scaring a group of tourists. Thankfully, the driver controlled the horse before anyone was injured. Then, just after noon, some unruly young Englisch men harassed a couple of Amish teenage girls selling cloth dolls. Moses planted himself at the edge of the stall, crossed his arms, and stared at the three Englischers. One of them said, "Nice suspenders," and then broke out laughing. Moses took a step toward him. The kid's smile disappeared. Moses took another step, squaring his shoulders.

The second boy said, "Let's go." They sauntered off, but Moses knew he'd spooked them.

"Denki," the older of the girls said.

"You're welcome. I'll stay close to make sure they don't come back." They didn't.

At four, as the market closed, he checked in with Sara at the café. When he didn't hear back from her, he decided to head home to Lancaster County. Before going to the café, he'd stop by the shop.

It was five forty-five by the time he arrived, right before closing. Six cars were parked in the lot. He let himself in through the back door and headed straight to the office. After he deposited the checks from Delaware using his phone, he stepped into the hall and then into the back of the shop.

"Hello!" A fiftyish Englisch woman wearing a pair of navy-blue pants and a white sweater waved at him. "Are you Moses?"

"Yes." He took a step toward her.

She wore hoop earrings and a gold necklace. "The new owner of the shop?"

"That's right."

"I'm Isabelle Conley." She extended her hand. Moses noted several rings, including one with a large diamond. Her nails were manicured and painted pink. They shook hands.

She said, "I hope Scotty mentioned me."

"He did." Moses let go of her hand. "I can assure you, I hope to own the store for decades."

She chuckled. "I'd be hoping the same thing if I'd managed to buy it. Unfortunately for me, but not for you, I didn't have enough time to come up with the financing. If you do decide to sell the shop, say in the next decade, I'd appreciate it if you would contact me first." She took a card from her purse and handed it to him.

He didn't take it. "Just the shop?"

"That's right."

He took the card. "I don't foresee changing my mind, but thank you just the same."

She smiled. "And yet you took my card."

"I did." He slipped it into his pocket.

As Isabelle left the shop, Moses approached Lois—but then the front door swung open and four Englisch women swept in. Five minutes before closing.

Lois stepped forward without acknowledging him.

"This is the cutest shop," one of the women said.

Another headed toward the linen rack.

A third toward the birdhouses.

Moses stepped backward, hesitated, and disappeared into the office. He could still hear Lois conversing with the women, suggesting different items.

The women didn't leave until a half hour later. Then Lois vacuumed. She didn't knock or acknowledge Moses in any way. Did she even know he was still there? Did she care?

Finally, at a few minutes past seven, she knocked on the office door.

"It's open," he said.

She pushed it a little bit and then stood in the small open space. She had a bank bag with her and handed it over the desk to him. "I'd put this in the safe if you weren't here, but since you are . . ."

He took it from her. "Thank you."

"Before I go," she said, "I wanted to check about Monday."

"Monday?"

"Typically it's my day off."

"Oh."

"However, I could work this Monday if needed."

"Yes, it's needed. If you don't mind. I'll get someone for next . . ." He thought through his staff at both the café and the grocery store. No one came to mind.

"I know of someone who might be interested. A young Amish woman named Evelyn. She stays with her grandmother in the next district over. I should be seeing her tomorrow."

If the grandmother lived in the next district over, she didn't go to Lois's church. Moses's old church group. Lois must know Evelyn from Youngie events—singings and volleyball games and outings.

"Should I ask her?" Lois sounded tired—and annoyed.

"Please," Moses said. "Ask her to come into the store on Monday and talk with me. I'll plan to be here from ten until noon."

"All right. I'll see you Monday."

She turned to go.

He said, "Lois?"

She turned. "Jah."

"You don't have to keep the shop open late like you did tonight."

"I don't have to? Or you don't want me to?"

"You don't have to." His face grew warm.

"Okay. Thank you for letting me know."

Honestly, he didn't want her to. The extra time added to her wages, especially when he was paying her overtime.

After he heard the back door shut, he opened up the bag

and went through the receipts. It had been a profitable day. He skimmed through the last half hour. The four women had spent over seven hundred dollars. He whistled. Paying Lois for an hour of overtime was certainly worth it. But that wouldn't always be the case. He opened the safe and put the bag inside.

He stood and stretched and stepped into the shop. Lois recorded her time on a card she kept on the shelf under the register. He pulled it out. She'd logged out at six thirty. She'd given him a half hour of free labor—for seven hundred dollars. He didn't like that either. Had she recorded her time before or after he'd said she didn't have to keep the shop open?

He stepped back into the office and took the circle letter from his satchel. He needed to get over to the café. His phone dinged. Sara.

Where are you?

Be there soon

He was tired and hungry. A salad and a bowl of soup at the café would hit the spot.

He picked up the circle letter to put it in his satchel and then stopped himself. It wouldn't hurt to read it. He'd answer it later.

Dear Fellow Birders,

One of my prayers for our circle of birders is that we learn more about nature, and therefore our Creator, as we observe our feathered friends over the next seven months. There are many, many things

we can learn from birds, including to <u>be confident</u>.
Think of how nestlings throw themselves out of the
nest, sometimes off cliffs, to forage and fly. I hope
you'll know when to throw yourself out of your nest,
whatever it might be, and have faith as intrinsic as
these chicks that Gott will care for you too.

Moses wasn't sure of what he thought of Teresa's plati-
tude. A percentage of nestlings threw themselves out of their
nests to their deaths. However, there was truth to what Teresa
wrote. He could relate—he felt as if he'd jumped off a cliff
after his Dat died. But did it take confidence? Or simply an
intense desire to survive?

Teresa explained that because birding season was in full
force, she was modifying the usual circle letter rules. Instead
of sending the letter around the circle and taking months and
months to hear from everyone, members would write about
their birding experiences each week and send their reports
to her. She wrote,

Include the type of bird, location, time of day, the
weather, and any other relevant information. Then I
will photocopy all the letters and mail a copy of the
reports to everyone. Be mindful of our songbirds, our
Little Brown Birds who are often overlooked but add
so much beauty to our world. Let us know who you
hear and see!

Teresa encouraged each member to respond to at least
one of the previous sightings each week. She also specified
everyone should put his or her name and address at the bottom

of his or her "letter," adding it wasn't unusual for members to communicate privately too. She listed eleven members—five couples and a woman named Mary, whom he knew. She managed a shop in Bird-in-Hand, was a widow, and, he guessed, was in her late thirties. He continued reading.

Before I close, I want to welcome our two newest members, Jane Weaver and Menno Stoltzfus!

It appeared Jane Weaver was single too. Perhaps she was fifty and single—but maybe not. Moses refolded the letter. He'd take time to do some birding the next day, so he'd have something to write about, to the circle and perhaps to Jane Weaver individually. Whether she was fifty or twenty, it might be nice to have a pen pal interested in birds. He wasn't looking for a romantic relationship—he had one with Sara. He was looking for a new friend—someone who didn't know about his past or that he'd sold his Amish father's farms and put his Amish mother in a care center. Or anything else about him.

But hopefully, the circle letter would get him thinking about nature again. Either way, it would be a good distraction from his current problem—Lois Yoder.

9

Lois sat in the middle of her bed with her back against a pillow and her other pillows and blankets arranged around her, trying not to scratch the scab that had formed and dried over her road rash injury. By the light of her battery-operated lamp, she read the letter from Teresa Schrock. She enjoyed her missive about learning from birds, about being confident in particular. It reminded her of Dat's bird lessons.

She smiled at the last line, which welcomed her. *Jane Weaver.* She liked the sound of it.

She recognized the name of one of the other members. Mary Schmidt, a widow without children who worked at a gift shop in Bird-in-Hand. Lois stopped at the shop occasionally to see what merchandise they carried and chat with Mary about the business.

Mary had stopped at Paradise Found a few times in the last two years too. If the group ever had an in-person event, Lois wouldn't attend. Otherwise she'd be exposed for using a pseudonym.

Menno Stoltzfus. That definitely wasn't a name she recognized. All of the other men in the group were obviously married. Perhaps Menno wasn't. Lois folded the letter and slipped it back into the envelope. She liked the idea of the weekly letters. She'd write one by Monday. It would only take a day or two to reach Teresa.

Thankfully she'd see Evelyn the next afternoon and could tell her about the position at Paradise Found. John had stopped by the shop earlier and said he'd found a ride to the volleyball tournament. She'd warned him she was an inadequate volleyball player at best. He said that was fine—she could sit and watch him. The tournament would have both team games and pick-up games.

She'd take her binoculars and birding notebook in her backpack. If she could sneak off by herself, it would be the perfect place to spot herons and loons—and imply Jane Weaver, even though her address was in Paradise, easily traveled to other places in the county.

Mark and Evelyn didn't ride with Lois and John, but John assured her they'd be at the tournament. "Mark went to church with her family near Marietta this morning," John said. "They'll meet us there." They rode in a sedan with one of John's teammates who hadn't joined the church yet.

John pointed at Lois's backpack, which sat at her feet. "What did you bring?"

"A water bottle." She reached down and felt her binoculars through the fabric of the backpack. "Things like that. I thought I might have time to walk along the river for a few minutes."

"I'll go with you," he said.

"All right." It wasn't what she'd planned, but she couldn't tell John not to take a walk with her.

When they arrived at the park, Lois didn't see Evelyn or Mark. "Want to go down to the river?" John asked.

"Sure," Lois answered. She led the way, hurrying down a pathway.

"We can't actually get to the riverbank, can we?" John asked.

"Jah, we can. There's a dirt path up here."

The pathway intersected with another one, heading northwest. The Riverfront Trail. Lois took it but then darted off to the left.

John followed, saying, "Is this a good idea?"

"Absolutely." Lois followed the path along the river and then stopped at a willow tree and slid her backpack off her shoulder. "Look." She pointed to a duck on the water.

John laughed. "It's a duck."

She stopped herself from taking out her binoculars. She was pretty sure the duck was a hooded merganser, a rare sight.

A bird flew by, and Lois forgot she wasn't going to act like the birder she was in front of John. "Oh, look! An eastern bluebird!"

John laughed again. "It's brown."

"It's a juvenile female. You can tell by her gray tail feathers. Her wings will have more blue soon, but never as much as the male birds."

John shrugged. "Whatever."

That stung. Lois directed her attention back to the Susquehanna River. Dat had told her it was a mile wide at Harrisburg. It wasn't that wide here, but downstream at Columbia it widened to a mile again.

Movement in the willow above caught Lois's attention. A female belted kingfisher. They were bigger and more brightly colored than the males, a rarity in the bird world. She didn't draw John's attention to the bird.

He glanced back up to the park. "I should go see if my team's arrived."

"All right," she said.

"Are you coming with me?"

"Oh." She thought of her binoculars in her backpack. "Jah, of course."

He led the way. She followed.

The sun warmed Lois's back as she sat on the grass. John was the best player on the team, which wasn't surprising. Her gaze drifted to the branches of the silver maple on the other side of the volleyball court. Something fluttered in a top branch. Again, she longed to take her binoculars out of her backpack but didn't. Instead she retrieved her notebook and began recording what she'd seen along the river.

"There you are!"

Lois turned, shading her eyes from the late afternoon sun. "Oh, hello! I've been waiting for you."

Evelyn sat down on the grass beside her, and Lois slipped her notebook into her backpack.

Mark had joined the game.

"Do you play?" Lois asked.

Evelyn shook her head. "Not with them."

There weren't any girls on the team.

"I was hoping I'd see you." Lois told her about the very part-time job opening up at Paradise Found, starting with

Mondays and maybe adding a few more hours once summer started.

Evelyn clapped her hands together. "I'm definitely interested. I'd love to work there, plus it will give me an excuse to stay with my *Mammi* more." She giggled. "And be close to Mark."

"Can you stop by the shop in the morning between ten and noon?"

Evelyn pursed her lips together. "I'll need to talk to my parents. Then ride back with you and Mark and John."

"I think that would work," Lois said.

Evelyn's plan did work, and the next morning she came by the shop at ten thirty. Lois directed her to the office door. After Evelyn chatted with Moses for ten minutes, the two came out. Moses told Lois she'd be training Evelyn on Thursday.

"All right," Lois said.

"Please make her a time card," Moses said, "and a list of duties she can reference."

At noon, after Moses left, Lois put a sign in the window saying she'd be back by twelve thirty and scootered to the post office with the report she'd written in her best penmanship the night before to the Flight of Doves birding circle. She wrote about seeing the hooded merganser, the belted kingfisher, and the female eastern bluebird along the Susquehanna River. She dropped it in the outgoing mail slot with a sense of satisfaction.

Moses wasn't around Tuesday or Wednesday. Surprisingly, on Wednesday afternoon, when Lois checked her mail during her lunch break, she already had a letter from Teresa that included a couple of reports, including her—Jane's—

106

account about birding on the Susquehanna River. One of the other two was from Mary, who had seen a Carolina wren outside The Country Store in Bird-in-Hand. The third was from Menno. He'd seen a great egret on the Delaware shore. Lois had never been to Delaware nor to the shore of any state.

Teresa ended the letter by writing,

> *Gott made you, just as He made every single bird, to be YOU. Let others see the beauty He created in you, both internal and external.*

Lois read the last two sentences several times. It went against the Amish teaching to emphasize outer beauty, and yet every bird—and human—was beautiful in their own way.

Moses was back on Thursday before the shop opened, along with two surveyors. However, he stayed out on the property instead of coming into the shop or office.

Evelyn showed up at nine thirty wearing a pink dress and a huge smile. Lois went through all the steps of opening the shop. "I wrote all of this down for you," she told Evelyn.

Evelyn followed Lois around as she did each task. Lights. Temperature. Clock in. Put away any deliveries that have been left by the back door in the storage room. Unpack, price, and stock if there's time—or work on those tasks during the day. Make sure the shop is tidy. Clean the restroom if it wasn't cleaned the night before. Wipe down the counter, even if it was cleaned the evening before, and the front door, especially the handle on both sides. Lois continued through each task, surprised at how many there were. She ended with "Flip the sign, and open the door if it's a nice day."

"Got it?" Lois asked.

Evelyn nodded.

"I'll go cut tulips from the flower bed," Lois said. "If anyone comes in, I'll be right back to show you how to use the register."

The day was busy but not overwhelming, perfect for training Evelyn. Lois remembered how kind Scotty and Barbara had been when they taught her, and she did everything she could to make Evelyn comfortable.

Around noon, the shop was empty, and Evelyn asked, "Does Moses actually come into the shop?"

"Jah," Lois answered. "He works in the office some of the time—I guess when he's not at his other businesses. He must be working on the logistics for the farmers market he wants to put in here. I think he's trying to get permits."

"Oh." Evelyn spoke softly. "Don't tell Mark this or anything—because I really do like him—but I think Moses is hot."

Lois suppressed a laugh. "Hot?"

Evelyn nodded. "He's tall and buff. And in charge. I like that."

"He's also Mennonite, and he already has a girlfriend."

Evelyn shrugged. "Minor details."

Lois laughed.

Evelyn grinned. "I'm surprised you're not interested in him."

"I'll repeat: He's Mennonite and has a girlfriend. Besides, we have a history."

Evelyn's eyes sparkled. "Oh?"

"Not a good one. We were in school together. We were frenemies. Is that what it's called?"

Evelyn nodded.

"Heavy on the enemies." That wasn't entirely true, but Lois didn't want to offer any more of an explanation.

Footsteps fell and then, "Lois?" It was Moses.

Her face warmed and she stepped toward the back of the shop. "Jah?"

His golden hair curled a little at the ends, and his brown eyes shone. Evelyn was right. Moses was hot. "Can you call Scotty's home phone? He's not returning my texts." He pushed the rolled sleeves of his shirt above his elbows, exposing his biceps.

"I'll give it a try." She stepped back to the counter and called Scotty and Barb's number while Moses hovered nearby. No one answered, so she left a message, ending it with "Call me back at the shop. We have a business-related question."

Moses gave her a nod as she hung up. "The surveyors have some questions about the north boundary. I can't file for the permit until it's settled." As he walked away he muttered, "This better work out."

Lois suppressed another smile. Hopefully Isabelle would come in before long. She said she wouldn't stop working on her financing, just in case Moses decided to sell soon.

But Lois couldn't count on that. When Moses fired her—unless she quit first—he'd have Evelyn to take her place. Unless she wanted to return to Big Valley or move in with Amy and Bennie, she needed to have a plan.

Out of the blue, Evelyn said, "Moses Lantz might be hot, but I'm still aiming for Mark." She met Lois's gaze. "And I'm guessing you have your sights set on John."

Unsettled, Lois smiled demurely.

Evelyn stepped away from the counter and grinned. "John Miller is definitely the next best thing to Moses Lantz."

Lois didn't respond. She couldn't agree—or disagree. Which unsettled her even more.

10

On Friday Lois was standing under the birch tree when Moses arrived at the shop just after noon. He'd rolled the sleeves of his white shirt to his elbows, but they were pushed up over his biceps now. And his hair curled more at his collar than usual. He glanced down at the mail in his hand and then handed Lois one of the envelopes—the return address was her brother's. Thankfully his name wasn't included. If she wrote him back, she needed to use her new post office box address. She didn't want Moses knowing even a hint of her business. She slipped it into her apron pocket as she said, "Do you have time for a question?"

"I have a couple of minutes."

"Would you consider having Evelyn come in on Saturdays from eleven to four?" She explained that starting the first of May, Barbara had worked on Saturdays too. "If Evelyn can do the same, it would give me a few hours working with her each week to provide more training."

After a long pause, he answered, "How about from noon to two?"

"Two hours hardly seems worth it for her," Lois said.

Moses hesitated again. "That's fair. Let's give it a try from eleven to three and reevaluate it in a couple of weeks."

"I'll give her a call." No doubt, in light of her relationship with Mark Miller, Evelyn checked the message machine in her Mammi's phone shanty several times a day.

After Moses left, Lois read the letter from her brother, which was actually from her sister-in-law. It was full of news about their children—Jonas, Miles, Rebecca, and Lottie. The oldest was twenty-three and the youngest was seventeen. At the end of the letter, Deanna wrote,

> *Randy had a letter from your bishop, who, as you know, is concerned you don't have enough supervision. He says you weren't clear about who you were living with, or not living with, when you first returned to Paradise Township. Nor were you clear with us, implying you would be living with Amy and her husband.*

That wasn't true. She'd implied no such thing to anyone. They'd all assumed.

She continued reading.

> *Since you are still unmarried, Randy believes you must live under the authority of a male, preferably a relative—which would be him. You need to move back to the family farm and, of course, live under our rules.*

Lois folded the letter and put it back into the envelope. What exactly did Deanna mean by their rules? Did that include marrying who they wanted her to marry? She missed her nieces and nephews, but not enough to move back. Paradise was home. Big Valley wasn't and would never be.

Evelyn called back a half hour later, excited to be needed more already. "See you at eleven tomorrow!"

She showed up fifteen minutes early.

By one, Evelyn was running the register entirely on her own. By one thirty, there weren't any customers in the shop. Lois said she'd take her break and be back in a half hour—but instead of going to her apartment to eat, she scootered to the post office and retrieved her mail. She had one letter—from Menno Stoltzfus. She put the letter in her backpack, fighting her curiosity to read it immediately. But she didn't have time. She scootered back as fast as she could.

After she tucked the scooter away around the back of the building, she hurried up to her apartment, slipped the letter into her apron pocket, wiped the sweat off her brow, grabbed an apple, and hurried back to the shop.

Moses stood at the counter, chatting with Evelyn. Lois held up her apple and said, "I just grabbed some lunch." Then she headed to the storeroom.

When she returned, Moses was gone.

"He just stopped by on his way to the café," Evelyn said. "He said he'll be back later."

When the phone rang, Evelyn answered it but after a moment, she handed the receiver to Lois. "It's for you."

Lois took the phone. "This is Lois. How may I help you?"

"It's Scotty. Sorry I took so long to return your call. We went to visit my sister in Virginia. My cell phone stopped working."

"Moses has some questions about the property line."

"I thought I left it for him with the files. I must have it here at the house. I'll bring it in Monday morning."

"Thank you." Lois wanted to tell him there wasn't a hurry, but she knew that wasn't true.

He asked, "How's everything going?"

"Good," she answered. "Busy."

"Glad to hear it. I'll see you soon."

Lois hung up with a pang of sadness. Life had been so easy when Scotty owned the shop.

Evelyn left a half hour later. Lois dusted the merchandise between customers, the letter in her pocket calling to her as she worked. She'd thought of writing Menno but believed it was too forward. Yet, he'd written her. Had she included something in her letter to the group about the birds on the Susquehanna that caught his attention? Perhaps he guessed she was single since all of the other members of the group were part of a couple, except for Mary.

Her heart skipped a beat.

She didn't think John *didn't* like the outdoors—he was a farmer, after all—but he didn't seem that interested in nature in general. What would it be like to find someone who loved birds as much as she did?

There were no customers in the store and Lois had caught up on her tasks, so she finally took the envelope from her apron pocket.

A customer opened the front door, and Lois casually put the envelope back into her pocket. "Willkumm to Paradise Found," she said. Customer after customer arrived, browsed, bought, and left. She didn't have another break until five thirty, when she pulled the letter from Menno Stoltzfus out again. He'd printed the entire letter. It began,

Dear Jane,

I hope you don't mind me writing to you directly. If so, please don't feel obliged to write back—or do write back and let me know you <u>do</u>—

"Lois!" The voice came from the back of the building.

She quickly folded the letter and stuffed it into her apron pocket.

"Jah." She stepped out from behind the counter as Moses entered the shop.

"How did it work out with Evelyn?"

"Wunderbar." Lois pressed her hand against her pocket, trying to flatten the letter. "She caught on quickly. She'll be a real asset to the shop."

He smiled a little. "*Gut.*" And then, as if correcting himself, he said, "Good. We'll see how she does on her own."

Lois told him about Scotty's phone call. "He thinks he has the information you need. He'll bring it in on Monday."

"Denki." He took a step backward. "I'm going to work in my office for the evening. No need to let me know when you leave."

Lois busied herself with tidying up the shop and waiting on one last customer. She didn't dare read the rest of Menno's letter with Moses so close. At six on the dot, she collected the two sandwich boards and then turned the sign to Closed and locked the front door. After she vacuumed, cleaned the restroom, and wiped down the counter, she left through the back, locking the door behind her.

Once she settled on her bed with a peanut butter and grape jelly sandwich and an apple, Lois pulled the letter from her pocket again and started from the beginning. When she got to the part where Menno explained why he'd chosen to write to her, she read it twice.

> *Your account of the eastern bluebird reminded me of one of my fondest memories. I saw a pair of eastern bluebirds, also along the Susquehanna, when I was a boy. The two had a nest in a woodpecker's hole in an old pine tree. They must have had fledglings in it because they both fluttered around, trying to scare me away. I complied—not because I was scared but because I was enthralled. At a safe distance, I saw them foraging for insects on the ground around the tree.*
>
> *Anyway, your sighting of the bluebird brought all of that back. Thank you.*
>
> *I'll be honest, it also seems—please correct me if I'm wrong—you may be unattached. I've been thinking a pen pal would be nice but don't want to propose corresponding with someone who is courting or, forgive me, married.*

Was she attached? She'd gone to a singing and a volleyball tournament with John. Did that mean they were courting? She'd have to ask Amy. John hadn't stopped by the shop all week, and he hadn't asked her to the singing the next day, which was fine with her—until she remembered she needed to find a new job and a new place to live.

In the meantime she'd write Menno back.

He ended the letter without sharing anything more about himself, such as what he did in Delaware, where it seemed he lived. That was his return address. Was he a farmer? Or perhaps a craftsman? He hadn't asked, thankfully, what she did. Perhaps it didn't matter. He wanted a pen pal. The idea sounded fun.

The next morning at church, Lois avoided John and instead of staying for the meal, scootered to Amy's house, hoping no one would notice she'd slipped away. Especially Bishop Stephen. It was Amy's district's off Sunday.

When she arrived, Amy and Bennie were sitting on their front porch. He was holding the baby and Amy was tying Oliver's shoes. Deborah was sitting at her feet. Ernie yelled, "It's Lois!"

Amy waved. As Lois reached the steps, Amy asked, "Did you skip church?"

"No." Lois leaned the scooter up against the side of the steps. "Just the meal."

Amy said, "You can eat with us."

"Denki." Lois shot her friend a smile. "I was hoping for an invitation."

"Come on into the kitchen." Amy opened the screen door. "You can help me get dinner on the table."

Bennie stood. "Take Maggie in case I have to chase two kids at once."

Lois took the baby with one arm and then reached down and tousled Ernie's hair with her free hand.

"May I set the table?" he asked Amy.

"Of course."

Oliver stomped his feet. "I help!"

"Let's go check on the baby chicks," Bennie said to Oliver, quickly sweeping him off his feet. "Come on, Deborah." He scooped her up too.

As Lois opened the screen door, she said, "Yum." Roasted chicken. Lois hoped she still remembered how to cook by the time she married. If she ever married.

Amy whispered, "If you rock Maggie for a few minutes, she should go down for a nap."

Lois did as Amy said. Sure enough, in a couple of minutes Maggie was asleep. Lois tiptoed into Amy and Bennie's room and gently put her in the bassinet. When she returned Amy was putting the plates on the table and Ernie was putting a fork next to each plate.

"What's up?" Amy asked Lois, speaking in a normal voice now.

Lois laughed. "Am I that easy to read?"

"Absolutely," Amy answered.

Lois told her about the letter from Menno. "So I'm not courting John, right? He didn't ask me to the singing tonight. Do you think it's all right if I write Menno back?"

"Jah," Amy answered. "But do you want to be courting John?"

"Honestly?"

Amy nodded.

"I want a home and some sort of work that doesn't include having to see Moses." She shrugged. "Would I know by now if I could *liebe* John Miller?"

Amy rubbed the back of her neck. "Jah. Maybe. Nee." She laughed. "I don't know. Only you can figure out if you could love him."

Lois groaned. "What should I do?"

"Write Menno back. See what happens. But figure out how you feel about John—"

"If he asks me to another—"

"Before you fall for Menno." Amy gave Ernie a handful of spoons. "Oh, and make sure and meet Menno as soon as you can. You don't want it to turn into one of those creepy stalker situations, right?"

Lois shoved her hands into her apron pockets. "I'm nowhere near ready to meet him. I haven't even written him back."

"Well, don't let it go too long. Those circle letters can be like social media. People aren't always who they say they are."

As Ernie put the last spoon on the table, he asked, "Who is Menno?"

Amy laughed and then put both hands over Ernie's ears, but Lois answered, saying, "A friend of mine. At least I hope so."

Lois popped into the store on Monday at noon to check on Evelyn, but the young woman didn't need any help. "Everything's fine. The previous owner came by with some documents. I put them in the office," she said. "Do you think Moses will stop by today?"

"Most likely," Lois answered. "I'm going into town. I'll check in when I return."

The day was bright and warm. The cherry trees swayed and white blossoms floated down as Lois scootered toward the highway. A northern flicker made its loud, rolling rattle. Lois playfully turned her scooter to the right and then the left and did it again. She was feeling a measure of joy. Why?

She turned onto the highway and scootered on toward the park. Ten minutes later as she stood on the edge of the run, watching for the Cooper's hawk, she thought of Menno again. Perhaps she wouldn't write to the entire group if she saw the hawk—perhaps she'd save it for Menno.

Five minutes later, the hawk soared above the trees, tilting to the left and then to the right. She smiled. Was he showing off for her?

She sat at a picnic table and pulled her notebook from her backpack, flipped to an empty page, and paused. Should she write *Dear Menno* or just *Menno*? He'd written *Dear Jane* in the letter to her. She finally settled on *Hallo, Menno*. She only wrote two paragraphs in her very best penmanship. She wasn't married or courting and yes, she would like to correspond with him. Then she wrote about the Cooper's hawk with its black cap and red eyes. Amy had suggested meeting Menno as soon as possible, but she didn't want to meet him too soon. And she especially didn't want him showing up at the shop unannounced. But he lived in Delaware. It wasn't as if he'd come to Paradise looking for her.

She signed the letter *Looking forward to your next letter, Jane Weaver*. Next she wrote a response to the circle letter she'd received Wednesday, following Teresa's prompt to write about songbirds, little brown birds in particular. She'd always felt like a little brown bird herself. Extra small. Brown hair. Nondescript features. Little brown birds never got the attention they deserved even though their music made the world go round. She got it—bald eagles and Cooper's hawks and even red-tailed hawks were powerful and stunning. Of course everyone wanted to see them.

She wrote about how the chipping sparrows perched on the fence posts near the house and serenaded her while she worked in the kitchen garden. It was a memory from eight years ago, but it would do. Next she sent a short note to her brother to inform him she had a new mailing address. She didn't acknowledge Deanna's letter nor did she give a reason for having a PO box. The less information she shared with him, the better. After she addressed and put stamps on all three envelopes, she scootered back to the post office and mailed the letters.

The week sped by. Each day, Lois would close the shop for a half hour and check her mailbox at the Paradise post office. Only Randy, Deanna, Teresa, and Menno would use the address. She didn't want another letter from Deanna, but a letter from Menno would make her day. None arrived.

Friday, Bishop Stephen came into the shop. Lois put on her cheerful face and said, "Bishop Stephen! Willkumm!"

He took off his straw hat and said, "We missed you last Sunday."

"I was at the service," she said. "I left before the meal."

"Oh."

"What can I help you with?" Lois asked.

"I'm looking for a Mother's Day card. For my Mamm."

Lois directed him to the cards. "The first rack is all Mother's Day cards."

"Denki," he said. A few minutes later he approached the counter empty-handed. "Do you mind if I ask why you didn't stay for the meal last Sunday?"

She didn't want to lie and say she was ill. "I didn't feel up to it."

"Meaning?"

"I had dinner with Amy and Bennie and their family."

"Because?"

Lois shrugged.

"Were you feeling lonely? As if you wanted to be with a family?"

Lois kept her face neutral.

"Because I'd take that as a sign you should be with *your* family."

Lois rubbed her brow, careful not to bump her Kapp, just as Moses stepped into the shop. "Stephen," he said. "It's good to see you."

Bishop Stephen frowned. "Moses. I heard you bought this place."

"You heard correctly."

"It seems a little worldly, doesn't it, to spend your inheritance on a gift shop?"

Moses smiled wryly. "It's good to see you too, Stephen." He nodded at Lois and said, "I'll be in the office if you need me."

Lois gave him a nod of acknowledgment. Had Moses Lantz come to her rescue? It was hard to believe.

Bishop Stephen left without buying anything, and Lois busied herself with restocking the card racks. A few of the Amish who shopped at Paradise Found bought Mother's Day cards, but it was more likely most would make them rather than buy them. Lois always used to make her parents cards. And she would make them gifts—often something that had to do with birds, such as a calendar with a drawing of a different bird for each month. Those gifts were never well-done, but her parents always cherished them.

An hour later, Moses appeared in the shop again and watched as she waited on a customer. After she finished the transaction and the customer left, Moses was still standing by the birch tree.

"May I help you?" she asked.

"I wanted to talk about the front window display. It needs to be updated."

"I agree," Lois said. "I'll come in Monday morning before we open."

"I don't want to pay you overtime."

Lois crossed her arms. "I know."

"It would have been good to update the window before Mother's Day."

She nearly laughed. He should have said something earlier—it was too late for that now. There was a tea set, a toy bunny, and several "potted" silk tulip bouquets in the current display. Lois had designed it to cover both Easter and Mother's Day, but perhaps she should have taken the bunny out. Even a teddy bear would work better. She'd simply change it out and call it good for now.

She used to do the window displays on her off time for Scotty, and she'd planned to do it on Monday without recording her hours—but she wouldn't tell Moses that. Lois turned away. Why was he meddling in the operation of the gift shop? She knew what she was doing.

The door buzzed. Lois tried to plaster a smile on her face as she turned toward it.

"Isabelle." She greeted her friend with a hug.

Moses walked—slinked—back toward the office.

"How's it going?" Isabelle asked.

"I wish you could have bought the store." Lois kept her voice low.

Isabelle patted Lois's hand. "So do I."

After purchasing a candle for a friend with an upcoming birthday, Isabelle said, "I'll see you soon."

Lois waved as Isabelle left, resisting the urge to resent Moses, trying not to want him to fail at owning the store. If he failed, then she had failed. Besides, it would go against her faith to try to sabotage his business. Or pray that he would fail.

She felt unsettled. She needed to think about what she had to look forward to. Mother's Day—not. She shuddered.

A second letter from Menno. That was what she would look forward to.

11

Saturday morning, Moses sat at a picnic table at the Byler's Corner Market and read the last circle letter from Teresa. He hadn't received a response from Jane to his letter, but it was probably too early to expect one.

He read Teresa's introduction from her last letter. She'd written,

> *Another thing we can learn from birds is to let our colors shine. As Plain people, you may be asking, What colors? Stay with me on this one. We might dress alike in clothes made from the same bolts of fabric, and we've been taught our entire lives not to be prideful, but each of us has a colorful inner life, unique to us and the way Gott made us. Don't be afraid to let your inner light shine. You can be honest about who you are and your gifts without being prideful.*

Moses had finally grown into his body, but for years he'd felt like a freak. As if there were something inherently wrong with him, perhaps even dangerous, being so tall. Being called Goliath hadn't helped, although he'd certainly forgiven Lois for that. He wished he'd heard Teresa's advice when he was small—er, young.

He'd write a birding report to the group about another recent trip to the Delaware shore after he went through the rest of his mail. As he thumbed through the stack, he realized he did have a letter from Jane in a small envelope, wedged into the seam of a large manila envelope. He'd missed it the first time he'd gone through the mail. He quickly opened the envelope, read the letter—which was short—and read it again. No, she wasn't married or courting.

He paused. How would Sara feel about him writing to Jane?

Moses put the thought aside and kept reading. Jane wrote about seeing a Cooper's hawk, one of his favorite birds. Her account of the hawk confirmed it had been a good idea to propose corresponding with her. He kept reading. She wanted to correspond with him too. He envisioned Jane being in her twenties—not her fifties. He scooted thoughts of Sara out of his mind again and smiled at the good news from Jane. Then he read her letter again.

He hadn't thought about his letters needing a Delaware postmark in addition to the Delaware return address. If he didn't drive to Delaware to mail the letters early in the week instead of waiting until Friday or Saturday, the envelopes wouldn't have a Delaware postmark. If he did wait, he'd always be a week behind. If he mailed the letters from Lancaster County, someone might notice. If it was only occasionally, perhaps no one would think anything of it. The only solution was to mail the letters on Saturdays—or drive to Delaware on Monday or Tuesday. Thankfully, he enjoyed driving, and the ninety-minute trip always passed quickly.

He drafted the letters, printing so people could actually read his penmanship. In the circle letter, he wrote about birding at Bombay Hook, on the western shore of Delaware Bay, detailing the wading birds, waterfowl, and shorebirds he'd seen. He wrote to Jane, saying he was happy to hear from her and that she wanted to correspond. Then he wrote about observing a downy woodpecker's futile efforts to drill a hole into a treated telephone pole.

Once he'd finished, Moses walked across the street to The Country Store and deposited the letters in the old-fashioned mailbox that sat just inside the door. Then he returned to the market and bought a card and a box of chocolates for his mother.

When he was little, Moses and his family celebrated Mother's Day with a picnic at Paradise Park, along with other families, both Amish and Englisch. They'd eat sandwiches Dat and he made, along with carrot and celery sticks and chocolate cupcakes. Then they'd spend time along the run, birding. When they started home in the buggy, Mamm would always say, "Each day with my family is the best day of my life."

He thought about that as he parked his SUV in front of the Green Hills Care Center after church. He wished he could give Mamm more best days of her life.

"Ready?" He glanced at Sara and then opened his door.

"Jah." She hesitated but then opened her door too.

It was the first time Sara had come with him to visit

Mamm. He couldn't imagine Sara really wanted to spend time visiting an Alzheimer's patient, but it did seem she wanted to spend more time with him.

Moses grabbed his satchel and then hurried around to hold Sara's door. When they reached the entrance, Moses opened the door. Sara smiled at him and walked in. He quickly stepped to her side and then pointed to the hall to the left. "Mamm's down this corridor."

When they entered the room, Mamm was sitting at the window in a chair watching a yellow warbler in the new bird feeder Moses had installed. Softly, Moses said, "Happy Mother's Day, Mamm."

She turned toward him with a smile on her face, but then it fell. "Where's Lois?"

It had been a mistake to bring Sara, but he returned his mother's smile and said, "Do you remember Sara Fisher? She wanted to visit with you today too."

"Sara." Mamm pursed her lips together. "Have I met you before?"

"Jah," Sara answered. "Several times, but it's been a few years since I've seen you. I went to school with Moses." She stepped close and took Mamm's hand.

"And Lois?"

Sara nodded. "We were all in school together."

Moses opened his satchel and pulled out the card and box of chocolates he'd brought.

Her eyes lit up as he handed them to her. "For me?"

"Jah, for you."

She fumbled with the envelope. Moses opened it for her and pulled out the card. She handed it to him to read.

"To my mother . . ." He choked up a little as he read the

128

card. By the time he finished, Mamm had her nose up against the window.

Without looking at him, Mamm said, "Paul, remember the robin that used to build a nest on our porch year after year, and how protective Mamm was of it?"

Sara gave Moses a questioning look and whispered, "Who is Paul?"

He whispered back, "Her little brother." In a normal voice, he said, "Tell me about it."

"Mamm always had a heart for the little ones—and little birds." Mamm opened the box of chocolates.

"Don't let her eat too many," Sara whispered.

Moses ignored her.

Mamm ate one. And then another.

"Your wife certainly was tall for a woman." Mamm's eyes clouded.

"My wife?"

"Jah. Faith."

Moses had never heard anything about Paul's wife. In fact, he didn't even know Paul had been married.

"I felt badly about the way our parents treated you after you and Faith married. You hadn't joined the church yet. They didn't need to shun you." Mamm sighed and then stood. "I need to go feed the chickens."

Moses quickly said, "I already did that. You should rest."

Mamm stared at him a moment and then her eyes brightened. "You're tall like Faith's brother. He was over six-five."

Moses tilted his head. She wasn't making sense. And he shouldn't try to make it make sense. Mamm talked nonsense sometimes and often went from thinking he was Paul to knowing he was her son. There was no way his height came from Faith's family. Somewhere in Mamm or Dat's families—or maybe both—there was a gene for height. It had skipped a couple of generations was all. He'd gotten the golden hair gene too.

The next morning Moses arrived at the shop at seven and holed up in his office, turning his attention to his work. Since he had the property line sorted out and the dimensions for the market building, he needed to sift through his plans and then apply for his Paradise Township zoning permit, which he could do online. On Friday he'd spoken with a councilman, who wasn't as enthusiastic as Moses had hoped. Then later at the grocery store, Bishop Stephen's father had approached him with concerns about a market.

Moses had listened to Amos intently, not surprised by his concerns. More tourists. More traffic. More distractions. When Amos finished, Moses said he'd take all of those issues into consideration. And he would. But he didn't plan on changing his mind. Instead, he hoped to come up with a plan to alleviate Amos's concerns and the concerns of others too. Somehow, he hoped to make the market worthwhile to all of them, Amish and Englisch alike. And Mennonite. He knew people had been talking behind his back, dishing dirt about him since he'd sold Dat's farms and hadn't joined the church. He couldn't stop the talk, but he hoped he could still help his community.

After he jotted down more ideas and then organized all his plans, he opened the Paradise Township site, downloaded the form, and then began filling in the needed information. He heard someone come through the back door at eight. Much too early for Evelyn. He stood and opened the office door. Someone was in the storeroom. He waited. Lois stepped out carrying a box with several paper flowers and tubes of paper and a large bumblebee.

"I'm going to change the window display."

"But it's your day off."

She shrugged. "I did it on my day off for Barb and Scotty."

He hesitated. He remembered Sara had said she'd do it, but not when.

"Is there a problem?" Lois asked.

"No." Moses motioned toward the front of the shop. "Have at it."

Lois continued on, bumping his arm with the box as she passed by. "Sorry," she mumbled.

He returned to his office. A half hour later, his door slowly opened. Then Sara stepped inside. "Hi," she whispered.

Moses suppressed a groan at her timing as he swiveled toward her. "What's up?"

"What is Lois doing?"

"About that—I wasn't sure if you intended to do the window display and if you did, when. I hadn't told her you planned to, and she came in this morning with everything ready to go." He leaned toward her. "You can go help her now or do the next one."

"Oh." Sara stepped back toward the door. "I'll go take a closer look."

She returned a few minutes later. "It's not bad. How about if I come up with a new one in a few weeks?"

He nodded.

She hesitated.

"Is there something else?" He needed to get payroll done for all his businesses. Plus he heard footsteps in the hall. Could Lois hear their conversation?

"What do you think your mom was talking about yesterday?" Sara asked. "When she said you take after the brother of her sister-in-law?"

"She was confused, is all."

"But don't you think it was a weird thing to say?"

Moses shrugged. "Believe me, she's said weirder. Plus, as far as I know, Uncle Paul never had a wife."

Sara gave him a funny look.

"What?"

"Do you think you might have been adopted?"

After Sara left, Moses stared at the computer screen for several minutes, completely lost. The permit application was only half completed.

He needed to clear his head. A walk around the property would help. He stepped out the back door into sunshine and warmth. It was going to be a perfect day—weatherwise. Someone called his name. Coming toward him was Isabelle.

Moses groaned inside but smiled on the outside, remembering Teresa's advice about letting one's colors shine. "Good morning!" he called out.

"It is a good morning," she responded a little out of breath. As she grew closer, she said, "I hope you don't mind if I walk the property in the mornings. Scotty never did. I usually do five or six laps."

"That's fine," Moses said. "Until construction starts."

"Aah, for the Paradise Amish Market. You know, this

Amish market thing might really take off. So much so that you'll want to concentrate on it and not the shop. I'd prefer to buy just the shop and not the entire property."

Moses tried to contain his irritation. "I intend to keep the shop."

She gave him a smile. "Time will tell." Then she pumped her arms a few times, gave him a wave, and took off walking at a brisk pace.

He certainly didn't want to follow her—or go the other way and bump into her in a few minutes. Instead he walked around the building to the front. He'd take a look at what Lois had done to the display window.

He stepped around the corner and then stopped in a patch of sunlight. Lois was standing with her hands on her hips, staring at the window display. She took a step closer and then several feet back. She held up her hands like a frame.

"How does it look?" Moses called out.

Lois didn't turn toward him as she said, "I like it. What do you think?"

He stepped to her side. She'd left the white wrought iron table and two chairs and surrounded them with the paper flowers—daisies, dahlias, and cosmos. All the flowers his mother loved. The bee was suspended by a string. Two fine china cups and a teapot sat on the table. "Nice. It's very whimsical." He stole a glance at her as she stared straight ahead, looking rather whimsical herself in a lavender dress and white Kapp and apron with a faraway look in her bright blue eyes. Whimsical and beautiful.

He exhaled slowly.

"Denki," she answered. "I appreciate the feedback." Then

she said, "It's such a nice day. I think I'll go for a long ride on my scooter."

"Have fun."

"I will." She shot him a smile and then took off for the door, most likely to put away the things she'd left in the front of the shop. He took his phone out of his pocket. *9:45.* Evelyn would arrive any minute. He headed for his office—Evelyn was much chattier than Lois. He didn't have time for that.

When he stepped through the front door, Lois was already gone. He heard the storeroom door close and then the back door. She'd seemed a little nicer. Was it because he'd given her feedback—positive at that? Or was it because she'd overheard Sara ask Moses if he'd been adopted?

12

Lois scootered past the café and Paradise Park to the far side of town to the post office. She hadn't had time to check her mail on Saturday. She hurried through the glass front door and to the boxes, kneeling in front of hers. She unlocked it and pulled out the Flight of Doves letter, which she put in her backpack. There was one more envelope in the box, a letter from Menno. She smiled as she slipped it into her backpack too. She'd read it once she had time to savor his words.

She kept going down the highway, past the left-hand turn to Amy's house, and then right onto Meadow Lane. A whistle blew as the Amtrak train flew through town. Jah, Paradise was a train town.

She passed the marsh, where she'd spent hours watching birds as a child, and kept scootering. The lane crossed over the creek, which fed the marshy area, and next was the Harris farm. She slowed. Was that a For Sale sign up already? Scotty wasn't exaggerating when he said he and Barb wanted to be in Florida by October. She slowed as she approached the driveway and stopped by the sign. There weren't any cars in the driveway, but there was a pickup between the barn and the silos. It probably belonged to the farmer who leased the land. Perhaps Barb and Scotty were off on another trip.

The day Mamm, Dat, and she had moved into the house, seventeen years ago, Lois had skipped through each room. The builder wasn't Amish, so the house was much fancier than she was used to with a built-in hutch, built-in closets, and a big built-in pantry. The house was new compared to her grandfather's house in Big Valley—built in the 1990s rather than the 1890s.

Lois had been sad to leave Big Valley and her nieces and nephews. But she wouldn't miss the arguments her father and brother used to have, nor the way her brother treated her mother.

Even as an eight-year-old, Lois understood why her parents wanted to move to Paradise.

The next day, Dat and Mamm took her to school a half mile down the road. She noticed Amy, with her bright eyes, dimples, and dark hair, immediately. Lois smiled shyly at her—Amy responded with a big, welcoming grin. They'd been best friends ever since.

When Lois returned to Big Valley after Mamm died it was Amy she missed the most. And when Randy, even though it wasn't customary for the Amish to arrange a marriage, insisted she court his best friend, Nathan Hertzler, she missed Amy even more.

As she scootered along, she involuntarily shuddered at the thought of Nathan. He was eighteen years older than Lois and a widower with five children. He was harsh and demanding, nothing like her father, nothing like who Lois had imagined marrying.

Which made Nathan—and Randy—angry. Randy said he wouldn't spoil her the way Mamm and Dat had, and he certainly couldn't be expected to support her forever. Lois had always believed God intended her to have free will when it came to marriage, but Randy clearly thought differently.

After Lois wrote Amy, trying to be as positive as possible, Amy read between the lines, asked Scotty to give Lois her job back and let her live in the apartment again, and hired an Englisch driver to take her to Big Valley. Even with Amy standing beside her, ready to grab her by the hand and drag her away, Lois had a hard time telling Randy goodbye. But then she thought of Nathan and how he bullied his children and how he bullied her and how he said he wanted to marry within the next month, and she simply said, "I'm going home."

She hurried to her room, packed a bag, and returned to the porch, where Randy and Deanna sat in silence, staring at Amy. Lois grabbed her friend's hand and said, "Let's go."

As they hurried down the stairs, Randy called out, "Don't come back!"

The one person Amy hadn't thought to speak with before she rescued Lois was Bishop Stephen. Lois wasn't one to draw attention to herself, so she'd never explained what had happened in Big Valley or that she was living in the apartment over Paradise Found. She had no idea Bishop Stephen assumed she'd lived with Amy and Bennie for the last two years.

Lois scootered along the fence line. Cattle grazed in the pasture—beef, not dairy. Dat had run a dairy but the profits were falling, and she'd heard the current farmer had switched to beef. The pasture was green. Alfalfa grew in the fields. She couldn't see anyone around. Would the current tenants try to buy the property? They'd have to have a fair amount of money to do so.

A shadow passed over her. Lois tipped her face upward, swerving as she did so. She stumbled and then hopped off the scooter, bringing it to a stop. She didn't want another case of road rash. She turned her eyes up to the sky. A red-tailed hawk, with its cinnamon-colored tail feathers, flew toward the covered bridge.

She shaded her eyes. Based on its large size, she guessed it was a female. The bird soared higher. Perhaps the pair that had lived in the loblolly pine had relocated.

The hawk made her think of Moses, which made her wince. She'd overheard Sara ask him if he was adopted on her way out of the storeroom but hadn't heard his answer.

It made sense. She'd seen the clues as a child, although she had no idea he might be adopted. He was nothing like his parents, not in size, coloring, or behavior. Well, she couldn't be sure about behavior. She'd only known his parents as old people. And she didn't know Moses, not even now, as an adult. She'd known him as a busy boy and then as an appealing young man, or so she'd thought at the time. But she'd been wrong. Perhaps she'd never really known him at all.

If he had been adopted, who were his biological parents? Some Amish families took in foster children. Perhaps that had been Moses's case.

Lois winced again. Her bluntness about Moses's size when they were young now seemed horribly insensitive. In fact, she felt downright mortified about it if he was adopted.

She exhaled. She was beginning to feel mortified by her behavior even if he hadn't been adopted. She knew what it was like to be teased about her small size. And yet she'd

138

done the same to him, except she hadn't teased him. She'd been mean to him about it.

She watched the hawk until it disappeared, and then scootered on toward the covered bridge. Ahead, a horse and buggy clopped and rolled over the wooden planks, creating a drum-like rhythm. Lois rolled onto the bridge, and the pushing of her foot and the wheels of her scooter on the planks made their own rhythm. She stopped in the middle. A mother duck with five ducklings trailing her quacked at the sixth baby duck, who stood on the bank of the creek. It toddled into the murky water. A blue heron stood on one leg in the middle of the creek. Then a bittern, with its short neck bobbing up and down, poked out of the reeds.

Her heart ached. She'd spent hours by herself in the marsh, but it was here that she'd often walked with her parents and then taken the path on the other side down to the creek. She'd already lost so much—and what she still had might soon be gone for good too.

But she hadn't lost Amy. She was meeting her at the café at eleven thirty. It had been Bennie's idea. He said Amy needed a break. Lunch would be Lois's late Mother's Day gift to her friend.

At least Moses was at the shop and not the café.

She kept going on the scooter, looping back to the highway and the café.

Amy was waiting on a bench inside the entrance when Lois arrived. "There you are!" Amy stood and gave her a hug. Lois returned the hug and then pulled away, took off her safety vest, rolled it, and put it in her backpack.

Sara approached, holding two menus. Her face went slack and then she smiled. "Amy. Lois. How nice to see the two of you. Anyone else joining you?"

"Hallo, Sara," Amy said. "It's just us."

As they followed Sara to their table, she asked Lois how the window display turned out. Lois knew she should be humble about it, better yet self-deprecating. But she remembered Teresa's advice about God making each bird—and each person—to be exactly who they were. Why not show it? Lois said, "The display turned out great! Moses really likes it." Sara gave her a sideways glance. Lois responded with a sweet smile.

Jah, Lois knew she was on her way out of Paradise Found. It was inevitable. But she wouldn't go quietly, without showing Moses and Sara her true self.

She glanced around the café as she walked behind Amy. Twenty tables. Nearly full. Booths on three sides with tables in the middle. Half of the front was a garage door that was open to let in fresh air and sunshine.

Sara directed them to a booth near the door to a hallway, which most likely led to the kitchen. As she handed them their menus, Amy asked, "How do you like working at the café?"

Sara folded her hands. "It's been a lot of fun. Moses is a good man to work for." She gave Lois a pointed glance.

Amy held the menu up a little. "What do you recommend?"

"Our special today is tomato-basil soup and a tuna melt. Both are good. And our arugula, walnut, and cranberry salad is excellent. You can add chicken to it. Or we have country fare too. Meatloaf and mashed potatoes. That sort of thing." She smiled again. "Have a nice lunch."

"Thank you," Lois said.

When Sara had returned to the hostess station, Amy whispered, "She's intimidated by you."

Lois shook her head. "She doesn't like me. Probably because Moses doesn't like me." Lois leaned over the table a little. "Speaking of, have you ever thought Moses might be adopted?"

Amy's face contorted a little as if she were trying to process the question. "No. I've never thought that. . . ."

Lois interjected, "But . . ."

Amy wrinkled her nose. "Why do you ask?"

"I overheard Sara ask Moses if he was this morning."

"What was his answer?"

"I didn't hear it." Lois leaned back but still whispered. "Could you ask your parents and see if they ever heard that?"

"I don't know that I could without gossiping."

Lois put her hand to her chest. "Ouch."

Amy laughed. "You know what I mean. It's not gossip between us—but it would be out of the blue to bring it up with my parents. I never talk with them about Moses."

"I understand," Lois said.

"Does it matter if he is?" Amy asked.

"Of course not. I just want to know how badly I should feel about pointing out, so many times, how little he looked like his parents when we were young."

Amy grimaced. "Jah."

"You're not making me feel any better."

Amy wrinkled her nose. "Sorry."

A couple of minutes later a young Englisch woman approached with two glasses of water. "Ready to order?"

They both ordered the soup and tuna melt. After the waitress left, Amy asked if Lois had another letter from Menno.

"Jah." She smiled. "But I haven't read it yet. . . ."

"Read it now."

Lois laughed. "Sorry. I'm going to read it in private. Later."

"And deprive me?"

"Absolutely," Lois answered.

Amy rolled her eyes in a playful manner. "I haven't seen you this taken with someone, well, at least not since Moses."

"I'm not taken with Menno. And, as I already told you, I was *not* taken with Moses." Lois spotted Sara across the room, relieved she was out of hearing distance.

Amy sighed. "I thought you two were perfect for each other. I thought you'd get married, and we could have babies at the same time. And Moses would take care of you and your Mamm and you wouldn't have to worry about money anymore."

Unexpected tears stung Lois's eyes.

"I'm sorry," Amy said. "I shouldn't have said that."

Lois blinked rapidly. "I miss Mamm. I'm not teary about Moses, believe me."

Amy nodded. "I know."

Lois could declare she wasn't teary about Moses, but the truth was she was teary about all of it. The abrupt end to her relationship with Moses. Her mother dying. Her trying time in Big Valley. It had all left her numb and fearful to trust anyone again—except for Amy.

Sara led an older couple to the booth behind them. Then the waitress arrived with their food. Once the waitress left, they each said a silent prayer and began to eat. Lois figured the conversation about Moses was over.

They ate in silence for a long moment and then Amy said, "Change of subject."

Relieved, Lois said, "What do you want to talk about?"

Amy glanced around the room until she saw Sara seating two men at a table near the hostess station. "Moses."

Lois suppressed a groan. "We were just talking about him."

"This has to do with his Paradise Amish Market," Amy said. "I'm going to make soap and candles after the kinner are in bed and sell them in a booth at the market. Mamm said she'd watch the children on Fridays and Bennie said he'd make do on Saturdays, although I'll need to take the baby."

Lois slouched a little. She wanted Moses to fail enough to have to sell the business, but the market would help Amy and her family. Lois took a bite of her sandwich.

"I'm excited about it," Amy said. "I hope he can open it soon."

Lois swallowed and said, "Sounds like a good opportunity."

"I hope you'll figure things out with him and keep working at Paradise Found. It would be so fun to have you in the shop while I'm selling things at the market."

Lois gave her friend a nod. "That would be fun. I could come hang out with you during my lunch break."

"Moses is doing a lot of good for our community," Amy said. "I know you think he's an ogre."

They'd watched the movie *Shrek*, which she'd loved, on Amy's phone when they were seventeen, during their Rumspringa. And jah, *Shrek* had made Lois think of Moses.

"A Goliath," Amy corrected herself.

"I regret calling him that, truly—but, like I said before, he used to call me Baby Bunting."

"Like I said before, it's not the same." Amy widened her eyes as if exasperated. "Goliath was the villain. A baby bunting, in the way he was referring to it, is a fledgling bird. Not the same at all."

Amy was right. "You're . . ." Lois coughed into her elbow. "You're correct."

Amy leaned in a little. "We wouldn't have our farm if it wasn't for Moses. Please don't tell anyone this—it's not anyone's business but ours. But Moses financed the farm so we could make payments directly to him. Our parents couldn't help us—Moses made it so we didn't have to get a bank loan, which we wouldn't have qualified for. We never could have afforded it without Moses's kindness. And generosity."

Lois's eyebrows shot upward. She had no idea.

"I wish you'd give him a chance." Amy gave Lois a pleading look. "At least as a friend."

After Amy left, Lois stayed in the booth, ordered a cup of coffee, and took out Teresa's letter, saving Menno's for last.

Teresa wrote about birds letting their colors, whether bold or muted, shine in modest ways, and that even as Plain people all of them should do the same.

Lois squared her shoulders and sat straighter. Birds, no matter their size, were confident and colorful. Even the brown ones had beautiful patterns and markings. She liked Teresa more every time she read one of the Flight of Doves letters.

Finally, as she inhaled, she opened Moses's letter. He wrote,

> *Thank you so much for your letter. I'm relieved you are, indeed, single, and thrilled you want to correspond. I hope you won't grow tired of me soon. Or worse, bored.*

He went on to write about the birds he'd seen recently near Dover, Delaware. She read,

*I saw a male downy woodpecker on a telephone pole.
They are distinct with their black-and-white bodies and
red patch on the back of their heads. This one was very
persistent, determined to peck a hole into the creosote-
treated pole. I'm fascinated by the decisions birds make
based on the information they have. They intrinsically
know how to migrate, build a nest, and raise their young,
and yet they can't seem to determine what "tree" to drill a
hole into. When I walked by the pole a few hours later, he
was still at it.*

He added that he'd been going through a challenging time
in his life and the bird reminded him of himself, relentlessly
trying to make progress but changing nothing. He wrote that
he laughed when he saw the woodpecker the second time.

*No doubt Gott is trying to teach me something,
probably to find hope in the midst of uncertainty.*

He closed the letter with,

*I look forward to your next letter and to learning more
about you and what is currently bringing you hope in
your life.*

Lois held the letter to her chest for a moment. Menno had
been vulnerable with her. He had challenges too. She wasn't
alone. She slipped his letter under Teresa's, which she decided
she'd answer first. She wrote in her best penmanship about
seeing the blue heron in Pequea Creek. As she finished, her
thoughts shifted to what Amy said about the Amish market
Moses planned to develop and operate. She'd been tempted to

shirk her duties when it came to her job. Moses was a pain. Sara was arrogant. There was no way she'd be able to keep the job for long. Why should she put her heart into it? But not doing her best could hurt Amy and Bennie. And their little family.

She sighed. Besides, it went against her values.

"Penny for your thoughts."

Lois jumped. Sara stood beside the table, looking down at her. In a panic, Lois glanced down at her notebook.

"Oh, I'm just thinking about, you know, life."

"What in particular?"

Lois panicked again and then laughed nervously. "I don't want to bore you."

Sara hugged a stack of menus to her chest. She was so tall. And so gorgeous. And so poised. But she had a concerned look on her face.

Lois quickly looked around. The café was almost full. "Do you need this table?"

"Not yet," Sara answered. "I'll let you know when I do." She continued on to her hostess station.

Lois felt more unsettled. She *had* been mean to Moses when they were young. And she'd justified it because of the way he'd treated her. She'd never taken responsibility for her behavior. She twirled her pen again and then tapped it on the table. Perhaps if she'd apologized when they were twenty he wouldn't have disappeared the way he had.

Surely Moses had long forgotten her saying he'd been adopted. Surely he'd forgotten she used to call him Goliath. He hadn't thought of her in years. He'd pretended he didn't even know her when Scotty introduced them to each other in the shop. Besides, what he'd done was far worse. He'd asked to drive her home after the party on the river and then dumped her for Sara Fisher.

What she couldn't understand was why the two hadn't married already. Wasn't that why Moses dumped her? Why he never came after her when she was forced back to Big Valley? She assumed he'd joined the Mennonites because Sara already had.

Yet if Moses hadn't forgiven Lois for the things she'd said when they were young, he wouldn't have pursued her five years ago. He wouldn't have asked to drive her home that night.

The tension now between them was his fault—not hers. He was the one who'd treated her badly.

She addressed the letter to Teresa and the birding group and tore the piece of paper from her notebook, folded it, and slid it into the envelope. Then she stared down at the blank piece of paper. What should she write to Menno? Something about birding, but also something with a deeper meaning, that she faced challenges too and also sought to find hope in the world around her. Using the same meticulous handwriting she used for the Flight of Doves report, she wrote an introduction that acknowledged his challenges, whatever they were. She was definitely empathetic. Then she wrote about the *bevy*—she loved the word—of swans she'd seen at the Middle Creek Wildlife Management Area when she was fifteen. It had been in early March. Her parents had hired a driver, and they'd made an outing of the day, all bundled up against the late winter cold. They'd seen many birds that day—many that had just arrived from warmer climates and others, like the swans, that had wintered somewhere close by and were heading back to their northern home.

The sight of them taking off to continue their journey

had thrilled Lois. She'd never seen such majesty. She closed the letter by writing,

> *The day was amazing because my family was sharing the experience of seeing grace in flight— God's grace at gifting us images of His imagination, the grace of the pairs of swans taking off together two-by-two, and the graceful harmony of their flight as they gained altitude and disappeared into the late-winter sky. It's the most majestic thing I've ever seen—it seemed they could have been a flock of angels disguised as swans. It took my breath away. And it still does every time I recall the memory. I'd loved birding before, but I became hooked that day. It's a sight I'll treasure for the rest of my life.*
>
> *To answer your question, God's creation is what gives me hope. There's so much beauty and joy, tragedy and trauma, harmony and hope. No matter how difficult life is, I feel at peace when I'm birding.*

She took a stamped envelope, which she'd already addressed to Menno, from the back of her notebook and slipped the letter inside. She'd mail both letters on her way home.

"Hallo." A deeper voice said her name. It was Bishop Stephen.

She placed her notebook over the envelopes.

"Are you here by yourself?" He glanced around.

He really did think she was an odd duck. No doubt he was right. "Amy just left."

"I'm looking for Moses. Have you seen him?"

"I haven't, but check with Sara," Lois answered. "He was at the shop earlier today."

"All right," Bishop Stephen said. "I need to speak with

him about a different matter, but do you mind if I speak with him about your work?"

Lois inhaled and leaned back in the booth. Jah, she did. She didn't want Bishop Stephen talking about her with anyone, especially not Moses Lantz. But could she say that to a bishop without making things worse? "I'd rather you not," she managed to say.

"I might anyway."

"No doubt." She gathered her things and slipped them into her backpack. Why had he asked her? She took a last drink of coffee as he waited.

When he didn't move, she said, "Excuse me," scooted out of the booth, and headed for the exit. She didn't like the person she was around Moses when they were young. She didn't like the person she was around him now. She didn't like that she'd considered sabotaging the shop when it would have hurt Amy and her family and others too. She didn't like the person she was around Bishop Stephen either. She knew he was simply doing his job as expected by the community. A very hard job. She had no right to resent him for it.

Lately, the only time she'd felt like herself had been, including just now, when she wrote to Menno. Was she that desperate for affirmation that someone she didn't know made her feel better, simply by paying attention to her?

She felt unsettled the next day, avoiding Moses as much as she could in the morning and answering his questions with as few words as possible. He disappeared before noon. On Wednesday, when he hadn't shown up by one, she put a Be Back at 1:30 sign in the window and scootered to the post office. When she arrived, Amy was climbing down from her buggy.

Lois waved as she stopped her scooter. "Guder Nummidag!"

Amy hitched her horse to the post. "What are you doing here?"

"Checking my mail."

Amy blinked several times. "You have a PO box?"

"Jah. What are you doing here? Where are the kids?"

"The good news is, all four kids are napping. Even Ernie. And Bennie's in the house doing paperwork." She pulled a few envelopes from the pocket of her apron. "The bad news is, I didn't get these bills out to the mailbox in time this morning, so I brought them now."

They walked up the steps together and into the building. Lois checked her box while Amy put her letters through the slot. Relief swept through her. She had another letter from Menno. She quickly slipped it into her apron. As they met at the exit, Amy asked, "Who's your letter from?"

Lois smiled. "Menno."

"Ooh, will you read this one to me?"

Lois laughed. "Jah."

Amy pointed toward her buggy. "I can hang out for a few minutes. Can you?"

"Maybe five," Lois answered.

Once they were both seated on the bench, Lois opened the letter and read through it, pleased. "Do you really want me to read it to you?"

"Of course, silly," Amy said.

"It starts out with, 'Dear Jane—'"

"Wait. What? Jane?"

Lois's face grew warm. "I decided to use my middle name for the circle letter." She explained she didn't want anyone coming into the shop looking for her.

"But what if you and Menno meet? Won't that be awkward that you deceived him?"

Lois shrugged. "I'll explain things then." But the truth was, Amy had a point, and Lois didn't feel as at ease about it as she pretended. It would be awkward.

Amy sighed and said, "Keep reading."

"I felt as if I was with you and your family as I read about the bevy of swans taking flight. I loved that you compared the swans to a flock of angels and the sight of them is what hooked you on birding. I could imagine the scene because you described it so vividly. So perfectly.

Your description rang true—what an image of grace. Your words about what brings you hope also resonated with me—and gave me hope. I'm more determined than before to spend time in nature, reveling in God's glory."

He then wrote a follow-up to his account about the woodpecker.

"Proving himself to be a resourceful sort, he finally gave up on the telephone pole and moved on to a sycamore tree. Still hard but at least a better choice."

Lois glanced up at Amy.

"Get on to the part that's not about birds."

"That's it."

"Oh," Amy said.

"Well, at the bottom he did write, 'Thank you again for agreeing to correspond. It's been a while since I've had anyone to share bird sightings with—I'm enjoying the circle letter, but a one-on-one interaction with you is even better. Sincerely, Menno.'"

151

"I thought he'd write something significant." Amy was clearly disappointed.

"You don't think this is?"

Amy gave Lois a playful scowl. "Am I missing something? Is there some hidden meaning in his words?"

Lois smiled a little. "I may be reading into what Menno wrote, but I believe he found my account of the swans romantic. They mate for life. He would know that."

"Oh . . ." Amy smiled sheepishly. "Did you write about the swans because of that?"

Lois laughed. "Not on purpose."

Amy lifted her eyebrows as she said, "I hope something works out with Menno. I think you might be two peas in a pod. Or two birds in a hedge."

Lois put the letter back in the envelope. "Isn't one bird in hand better than two in the bush?" The saying was reportedly how the village of Bird-in-Hand got its name.

"Something like that," Amy said. "From a human point of view."

"Right." Lois gave Amy a wave and slid toward the door. "I'm definitely taking the bird's point of view of being in the bush, or hedge."

Amy nodded. "You deserve to. Seriously, I hope this thing with Menno works out—unless he's like an internet stalker or something."

Lois laughed at the thought as she climbed down from the buggy. She would write Menno back and mail the letter before she returned to the shop. She trusted Menno was legitimate—especially after receiving another letter. "You'll be the first to know," she called out to Amy as she closed the door.

13

On Friday Moses sat at his office desk, wishing it were Saturday and he had Jane's next letter in his hands. Instead he reread the email from Paradise Township asking for several revisions to the permit application he'd submitted earlier in the week.

Over the years, Dat had overseen several building projects on the farms he owned and never complained about the process. Moses had assumed he could handle the paperwork, but maybe he was wrong. Maybe he needed help.

He left the email open and clicked on the application. After he read it a third time, he dialed the number for his contractor. It went straight to voicemail. "J&R Contractors. We're out of the office for a week. Leave a message."

Moses hoped it wasn't an emergency. The phone beeped. He said, "Moses Lantz here. I'm filling out the Paradise Township building permit form and have a few questions. Please contact me as soon as possible." He left his phone number and added, "I hope everything is all right," and ended the call. He stared at the screen for another couple of minutes and then finally moved the mouse. Nothing happened. The screen had frozen.

He moved the mouse again, but the computer was as stuck as he felt. He rebooted, wishing he could reboot himself.

He'd felt unsettled since Mamm had alluded to his getting his height from Faith's brother. And even more so when Sara asked if he was adopted. Up until she asked, he'd been doing his best to ignore what Mamm had said—and how it made him feel. But he couldn't ignore it anymore.

If he was adopted, who else knew? When Lois had asked if he was adopted when they were children, had she known something he didn't? Mamm and Lois's mother, Beth Yoder, had been close. Had Mamm said something to Beth that Lois overheard?

He wasn't sure whom to ask if there was a possibility he was adopted. Mamm had grown up north of Gordonville but didn't have any siblings left in the area. Dat had grown up in Ohio.

Moses would need to go back to an Amish church service to ask if anyone knew if he was adopted. He went through a list of possible people. Wanda and Silas Miller might know. Perhaps Bishop Stephen. It seemed Mamm and Dat had moved to Paradise Township from Gordonville, where Dat's first farm in the area was located, after Moses was born. Perhaps they moved after they adopted him, and everyone assumed he was their birth child.

He ran his hands over his face, annoyed he had something else to worry about. As if he didn't have enough already.

The computer screen came back to life, but he had no motivation to keep working.

He rolled back from the desk. Did a letter from Jane

await him in his Delaware mailbox? He hoped so. He had the feeling Jane was an only child too—she never mentioned siblings.

Jane's address was a post office box in Paradise and yet she wrote about birding all around Lancaster County. Had she come into the café or shop or grocery store? Had he seen her before? He didn't know anyone named Jane.

He heard voices and glanced at the clock on the computer. *10:05.* The first customer of the day must have arrived.

He had to admit Lois did a good job with the shop. Sales were good. There were lots of regulars who came in—Amish, Mennonite, and Englisch. He believed it was unusual for a gift shop to have regular customers. He'd overheard several Englisch tourists say they stopped by Paradise Found every time they visited Lancaster County. He got the idea Lois was part of the draw.

He wished she'd be half as kind to him as she was to everyone else. She always met customers with a smile and a greeting. She was never pushy, but still made sale after sale by simply suggesting a certain item, from something as small as a card to something as large as a garden bench.

Now there was laughter out in the shop. Perhaps it wasn't a customer. Maybe it was someone Lois knew. Casey told him John Miller had taken Lois to a singing recently. John was in the shop at least once a week when Moses was around. Chances were, he came by much more often than that. His family farm wasn't far away. Moses couldn't imagine Lois as a farmer's wife, but it appeared she'd be one sometime soon. John was a good person, though. Lois wouldn't want for anything.

Moses stepped to the door, which was halfway open.

There was more laughter. It was Isabelle. Perhaps she'd been walking the property again and stopped in after she finished.

"Is Moses here?" Isabelle asked.

Lois responded, "In his office."

Moses scurried back to his chair, bumping his leg against the desk as he sat.

A knock fell on the door. "Moses?"

"Come in."

Isabelle pushed the door open. She held a plate in one hand. She smiled at him. "I made you cookies." Snickerdoodles. His mother used to make them.

"Thank you." He stood and smiled at her. "Any special reason?"

"Oh, you know, just to butter you up and try to convince you to sell the shop to me. What do you think? You keep the land—you'll have your market while I own and operate Paradise Found."

Isabelle certainly was persistent. He laughed. Dat always said to keep your humor when it came to business, to never burn any bridges, and to always be kind. "You're very determined," he said, "which makes me question whether I should accept food from you."

Isabelle put the cookies down on the desk. "Are you afraid I might try to harm you?"

He feigned surprise. "Poison me?"

Now she laughed.

"I'm not afraid you'd try to harm me, but I don't want to take advantage of your baking skills. I don't plan to sell."

She brushed her hands. "I'll keep trying."

He smiled. "I'm all for that." For a moment, Moses was

tempted to take Isabelle up on her offer, but then Lois would win. He couldn't fail.

As Isabelle waved and left the office, Moses wished he and Lois could laugh and joke. He imagined he could with Jane.

Whoever she was. Perhaps she was just a distraction from running his businesses. From Lois. From whether he was adopted. Was he hoping she'd be something more?

The next day, Moses drove toward Delaware with his windows down, breathing in the scent of the soil, pastures, and new crops. The cool breeze blew through his hair and stung his eyes. He blinked and kept driving with a smile on his face. He was feeling happy. Why?

Because he expected a letter from Jane.

Her words about finding hope in nature, even in the midst of trials, inspired him. He'd been more conscious of the world around him. Jah, birds had always interested him, but he was noting trees and flowers and the clouds in the spring sky.

He parked in his usual spot. Vendors were raising canopies and organizing booths. The rich scents of coffee, doughnuts, and freshly baked bread filled the air.

He headed to the mailbox at the edge of the parking lot to collect his mail. He had the usual Flight of Doves letter from Teresa, several bills and payments, and a letter from Jane. He put the bills and payments in his satchel and opened the letter from Teresa first, anticipating her latest contribution about what the group could learn from birds.

Show up early and often. The adage "the early bird catches the worm" is true. The early bird is more likely to survive, keep or find a partner, and complete their pre-dawn vocal exercises. Getting up early may (or may not) be less crucial for us. Regardless, forming good habits can lead to a more well-rounded life.

Moses read what Teresa wrote a second time as a wave of loneliness swept through him. Was his life really as un-balanced as it felt? No doubt it was even more so. He longed for a home, for a family. He longed for more of a routine. He longed for someone to share his life with.

He skimmed through the reports. Jane wrote about seeing a blue heron on Pequea Creek, which ran through Paradise Township, just north of town. It was a long creek, flowing from the border with Chester County all the way to the Susquehanna River.

Next he opened Jane's letter to Menno. This time, instead of writing about birds, she responded to his statement about being grateful to be able to discuss birds with her.

I had a male relative tell me not to let possible suitors know I liked birding, that they might think I was frivolous and wouldn't see to my household duties; this male relative believes birding is a waste of time, especially for women. He believes a man, while farming, might be interested in birds, but women—who hang the wash, tend to the garden and the yard, help with the farmwork, and oversee the children while they play—don't spend enough time outside to warrant studying birds.

His opinion never made sense to me.

It didn't make sense to Moses either, but he was thankful Jane shared her experience with him. That was brave. She'd trusted him with a painful story. He wondered who the male relative was. Her father? Grandfather? It had to be someone close. He folded Jane's letter. He'd assure her not all men felt that way. He put both Teresa's and Jane's letters in his satchel.

He headed to Walter and Casey's booth first. Only Casey was there. "Walter's helping set up a new stall," Casey said. "They couldn't make it yesterday—so they don't have it all figured out yet. It's another woodworking business." Casey grinned. "We have competition."

Moses shrugged. "Sorry. They've been asking for the last year if I had an opening. The jam lady left, so I offered the spot to them. Competition is good, though, right?"

"That's what they say." Casey lowered his voice. "Which is why Walter went to help them set up."

Moses knew that wasn't true. Casey and Walter were two of the nicest people he knew. But it never hurt to get an idea of how similar businesses operated.

"How's the Paradise market coming along?" Casey asked.

"Slowly." Moses picked up a birdhouse made to look like a log cabin. "I don't even have the permits yet."

"Ouch."

"Jah. At this rate summer will be half over before construction begins." He held the birdhouse. "This is nice. I'd tell you to bring it into Paradise Found, but I think Lois has over-ordered bird stuff as it is."

"What a shame." Casey stood. "Maybe I can sell them at the market."

"Good idea." That was another reason for Lois to cut back on bird-related merchandise in the store. Some competition would be good between the market and the store—but not too much.

"Speaking of the Paradise market, what do you think about managing it for me?"

"Really?" Casey took a step backward and bumped into his chair. He grabbed it before it fell over.

Moses put the birdhouse back on the shelf. "Really."

Casey grinned. "Walter could work here while I'd get to see Lois every Friday and Saturday?"

Moses suppressed a fleeting moment of jealousy, which surprised him. "If you wanted to, yes." If Lois didn't leave first.

"Jah, I'd love to be part of your new venture."

As Moses checked in with each of the vendors, he puzzled over why he'd care if Casey was interested in Lois as more than a friend. He shouldn't. Lois would be good for Casey. Clearly she adored him. Again, he felt a pang of jealousy. He'd been so happy for the short time that Lois adored him.

He spent a half hour talking with Joey and then checked the restrooms and parking lot. Everything was running smoothly. It was only eleven fifteen, so things could still take a turn, but it seemed he had some free time. He told Joey to call him if needed.

And then he headed for the Delaware shore. He needed something to write about—to both the group and Jane.

The day had turned warm but not hot. Perfect for being near the water. He pulled his rubber boots out of the back of his SUV, took off his shoes, and slipped on the boots. Then he walked from the parking lot down a trail along a marshy area. A marsh wren poked her head out between two cattails and then darted back. He took a few pictures on his phone and then kept walking until he reached a small beach. Shorebirds—plovers and killdeers—scurried over the sand, stopped to peck at insects, and then hurried along again. A couple of black-necked stilts swooped down. At least that's what he thought they were. He snapped a few pictures of them too.

Then he sat down and took his boots and socks off, digging his toes into the sand. He'd come to the Delaware shore a few times with Mamm and Dat. One time Dat had rented a cabin for a few days—it was the one vacation they'd had as a family. A *family*. They had been a family.

Casey and Walter lived a half mile away when they were all growing up, which gave Moses friends who were nearly as close as brothers: Looking back, he was more grateful than ever for them.

Had he been adopted? Did it matter? All he'd ever heard about his Uncle Paul was he'd died in an accident years ago. He'd always assumed it was a farming accident, but he didn't know for sure. If he had been adopted, why wouldn't his parents have told him? He couldn't believe they'd keep that from him.

He lay back on the sand. Knowing whether he was adopted wouldn't change anything. Mamm and Dat were his parents. That was what mattered. The sun was high. Cirrus clouds swept across the sky. The natural world provided wonders each and every day. He loved that Jane found hope—God's faithfulness, really—in creation and had shared that with him.

His stomach growled. He should get something to eat and then head back to Paradise. But for the moment he'd soak up the sun, breathe deeply, and take a minute for himself.

Dat used to say one had to take time to listen to the Lord. And to talk to Him. Dat used to say he'd talk through each of his businesses in silent prayer with the Lord. And he'd talk through his relationships with Mamm, Moses, and other people too.

How long had it been since Moses had prayed?

He sat up. He had an urge to pray for Jane, but then silently scolded himself for being foolish. He pulled on his socks and then his boots. What sort of fantasy was he falling into? Just because Jane liked birds didn't mean she was someone he could have a relationship with.

He could barely maintain relationships with people he'd known for years, let alone someone he'd never met. Still, when he reached his SUV, he dug his notebook out of his satchel and sat in the driver's seat, propping his notebook against the steering wheel. He began his letter to Jane by assuring her not all men believed the way her relative did about birding and women. He wrote,

> *God gave all humans special interests for a reason and I agree with you—learning about nature brings us closer to the Creator.*

He continued,

> *I can't stop thinking about the bevy of swans you saw and described in a previous letter. Such hope. Such beauty. Tell me more about the swans. Please tell me every detail you can recall. Tell me about other birds you've seen. Tell me about anything you want to tell me. I want to listen.*

In the next paragraph he wrote,

> *Would you be willing to meet in person at some point?*

He stared at the last line. Was it too early to ask to meet Jane? Would his request alarm her?

He was willing to take the risk.

⁓

Jeremy from J&R Contractors left a voicemail for Moses on Tuesday morning, saying his father-in-law had passed away. He was back at work and ready to take over the permit process. "Email me what you have," he said.

An hour later, Moses sat in his office at the shop. There was no way the Paradise Amish Market would be ready by the first of June. Most likely not even by the first of July. He'd been contacting vendors and had nearly enough interested, but he would need to call them and let them know about the delay. No doubt he would lose many to other markets.

He heard Lois in the shop, getting ready for the day. It sounded as if she were opening a box. Had a shipment of merchandise arrived? What had she ordered? He opened his office door and stepped into the hallway. She stood by the birch tree—the one he needed to get rid of—pulling another birdhouse out of a box.

Without even saying "Good morning," he said, "Do not buy any more birdhouses. Start pushing the ones we already have. We should change the front window display to birdhouses. Let's see if we can move the majority of these out. They take up too much room."

Lois gave him a blank stare and then turned her attention back to the box.

Feeling flustered, he reentered his office, closed the door, and returned to his desk. She was getting on his nerves. He began making calls to vendors, beginning with Casey.

An hour later, there was a knock on his office door. Expecting Lois, he barked, "Come in."

The door swung open, and Sara came in. "Feeling grumpy?"

He forced a smile. "A little. How are you?"

"Good. But feeling neglected. You hardly come by the café now that you have this office."

"I'm coming over in a half hour or so. I need to do inventory and place an order."

"Good. We can have lunch." She sat down in the chair on the other side of the desk. "Mind if I ask you something?"

She sounded serious. He turned his chair toward her. "Sure."

"How could you not know you're adopted?"

"What do you mean? I don't know I *am* adopted. The only indication I have is the ramblings of my mother, who has Alzheimer's."

"And that you look nothing like your parents."

He shrugged. "Genetics are weird."

Sara gripped the arms of the chair. "Don't you want to know the truth?"

"What difference would it make?"

"Don't you want to know your medical history? If your birth parents are alive? If not, what happened to them? Especially if your birth parents were your maternal uncle and his wife."

If that was the case, he still shared part of his DNA with Mamm.

"Moses?" Sara stared at him, her hazel eyes intense.

"Who would I ask?" He shrugged. "It doesn't matter much to me. Mamm and Dat were my parents. Mamm is still my mother."

Sara leaned back in the chair and crossed her arms. "I would like to know."

"Why?"

"Your medical history matters."

He wrinkled his nose. "It matters to you?"

"Jah." Her face reddened. "Don't you think I have a right to know your background before . . ." Her voice trailed off.

Oh. He was beginning to understand. Before they got married. Before they had children. "So, like, you want to know if there's heart disease."

She nodded.

"Or perhaps mental illness. That sort of thing."

"It might sound a little harsh, but yes. And I also would like to know why a married couple would give up a child."

Moses shook his head. "That's a lot of speculating."

"That's why you need to find out the truth."

"Who could I . . ." Maybe he should ask Bishop Stephen. He was Mamm and Dat's age. He'd known them the entire time they'd been in Paradise Township.

The office phone rang and Moses answered it.

"This is Jennifer at the café. Is Sara there?"

"Yes. She's right here." Moses handed her the phone.

After a moment Sara said, "I'll head back right now." She handed Moses the receiver and said, "I'd better get going. See you soon."

A few minutes later Lois knocked on the door. "I need to run an errand. Would you watch the counter?"

"Has it been busy?"

"No," she answered. "I won't be long."

Zero customers came into the shop while Lois was gone. When she returned, her face was red, she was winded, and a strand of hair had fallen out of her bun. Obviously she'd scootered to wherever she needed to go. She opened up her backpack and pulled out a stack of envelopes. "I got the mail," she said.

He kept intending to get a PO box for the shop instead of the mailbox at the end of the lane. Maybe he'd wait until Lois quit since she received mail at the shop too. Although she didn't very often.

She handed him several envelopes and kept a few—two or maybe even three in her hand.

"You got some too?" he asked.

"Jah," she answered. "From my brother."

"I didn't know you had a brother."

She nodded. "He's a lot older and lives in Big Valley."

He remembered she moved to Big Valley after her mother died. It made sense that she had a brother there. He wondered what else he'd been oblivious to when he was younger.

She slipped the letters into her apron pocket.

He shuffled through his bills as he walked back to the office and then put them on the desk. He needed to get to the café—but first he'd go by Bishop Stephen's buggy-making business.

He crossed over the covered bridge, turned right, parked his SUV to the side of three buggies, and then approached the open garage door. Inside, several men were working. He didn't see Bishop Stephen and entered the office through the side door.

"Hallo." Stephen stood behind the counter. "What can I help you with?" He laughed. "Not a buggy, I presume."

Moses forced a smile.

"Seriously, I'll always be sad you didn't join the Amish. Your father expected it."

"Which father?" Moses asked.

Stephen took off his hat, opened his mouth, and then shut it.

Moses crossed his arms. "Tell me about my birth parents."

"It's not my place," Stephen said.

Moses had his answer. His heart lurched. He was adopted.

14

Sometimes Moses would leave and then come back to the office for something he forgot, so Lois waited to examine the envelope from Menno until he'd been gone an hour. The last thing she wanted was for Moses to look over her shoulder and read a letter from the only person, besides Amy, who was keeping her afloat.

But first she read the letter from her brother—which was actually from Deanna, reiterating what she'd written before. Lois slipped the letter back into the envelope. She needed to respond—or the letters would keep coming. On the other hand, there was probably nothing she could write that would satisfy her brother and sister-in-law enough to stop their letters. Except to tell them she was returning to Big Valley, which she would never do.

She sighed and opened the circle letter, skimming through Teresa's missive and then down to Menno's entry. He wrote about seeing an American oystercatcher, a large bird with red rings around its eyes and a red-orange beak, on the Delaware shore. Lois longed to see coastal birds. Her parents had gone to the eastern shore of Maryland after they married and had always wanted to return with Lois, but they never did.

She moved on to Menno's letter. The envelope was post-marked last Saturday. She read her address on the envelope, printed like always. The stamp had swans on it. She slid her finger under the seal of the envelope and took out the letter, and then spread it on the counter.

Menno responded to her story about her male relative in a way that made her feel heard, made her feel like she mattered. He wrote that God gave all humans special interests for a reason.

She kept reading. Menno said her description of where she found hope resonated with him. That made her smile—and made her want to be more conscious about finding hope every day.

He requested that she tell him more about the bevy of swans she'd written about before. She smiled at how much he'd enjoyed her description. She could feel the passion in his words. He'd experienced the beauty of the swans—because she'd shared it with him.

As she read the last paragraph of the letter, *Would you be willing to meet in person at some point?* the door buzzed.

"Lois. What are you reading?" John asked.

She raised her head. "Oh, hallo." She slipped Menno's letter into its envelope. "I received a letter from a relative in Big Valley." She cringed at the white lie. It was true she'd received a letter from Deanna, but it wasn't the one she'd been reading.

"Oh." John glanced at the letters on the counter. "I didn't have a chance to speak to you on Sunday after church—and then you didn't show up for the singing. I expected to give you a ride home."

She'd avoided him during the meal after church. Stalling, she shoved the letters into her apron pocket. Then she tried to make a joke. "Me and my scooter, huh?"

He didn't smile. "I would have asked at church to give you a ride to the singing if I'd had a chance."

"Sorry." She clearly was not following the usual protocol of Amish courting. "I was feeling a little tired Sunday." She put her hand in her pocket. It brushed against the stamp on the bigger envelope, the one from Menno. He'd chosen a stamp with swans on purpose.

"How about next week?" John asked. "I'll pick you up at five. Perhaps Mark and Evelyn will want to go with us."

"I'd like that," Lois replied, feeling a stab of guilt. Would she?

"I was also wondering if you'd like to come to my house for supper on Saturday. We're having a family gathering—my siblings and their families."

Lois's smile froze. What did his inviting her to a family meal mean? And how could she get out of it—she had nothing planned for Saturday evening. She never did. She squeaked, "Will Mark and Evelyn be there?"

"*Nee*," John answered. "Evelyn has an event at her parents' house after she gets off work. Mark is going with her. But my sisters-in-law are all friendly."

"All right," Lois answered. "I can scooter over. What time?"

"Six."

"I may be a little bit late, but I'll come."

John grinned. "Denki."

After he left, Lois let out a groan. Was she leading him

on? Surely she could develop romantic feelings for John, right? If she had feelings for Menno, someone she'd never met, couldn't she still develop feelings for John? Or maybe it didn't work that way.

Amy was right. She needed to meet Menno in person. Now that he'd suggested it, it could happen.

After work, Lois, conveying Jane, relaxed as she wrote Menno. She felt a measure of peace. A hint of happiness. Jane was a more optimistic and joyful version of herself.

In the last paragraph, she wrote, *I'd like to meet you in person too.* She hesitated. She wanted to ask him what he did for a living, but she wouldn't. She'd hate to have to tell him what she did and where she worked. Jah, she wanted to meet him, but it needed to be planned. She couldn't have him walking into the shop and surprising her. Or worse, walking into the shop and asking Evelyn or Moses for "Jane."

Meeting Menno somewhere would mean she'd have to hire a driver unless she suggested a place close by. She'd wait and see what Menno suggested and then figure out what to do next.

Saturday was downright hot, and Lois arrived at the Miller farm sweaty and overheated. A flock of kids were playing volleyball on the front lawn—all grandkids, she knew. Not surprisingly, several were taller than she was.

John called to her from the porch and waved. "Lois!"

She walked her scooter toward him. He met her and took the scooter, leaning it up against the side of the steps. "I'll take you into the kitchen to meet my sisters-in-law." All of his brothers but Mark had moved out of the district.

The women were working in the kitchen, making hamburger patties, cutting tomatoes, and putting together a fruit salad and a pasta salad. After John made the introductions, Lois asked Wanda, who sat at the table slicing onions, how she could help.

Her youngest daughter-in-law, Abbie, said, before Wanda could answer, "Here, take the baby," and shoved a newborn into her arms. Lois cradled the little one as his mama hurried after a toddler, who ran through the living room with a knitting project in her hands.

"Oops," Wanda said. "You'd think I'd learn to put my handiwork away before family suppers."

Chaos ensued with little kids and big kids coming in and out of the house as Lois swayed the baby to sleep. John came in ten minutes later, gave Lois, who still held the sleeping baby, a smile, and swooped up the platter of hamburger patties. "We'll have these done in a jiffy," he said.

Wanda asked Lois how business had been.

"*Gut*," she answered. "Busy."

Wanda patted the chair next to her and said, "Lois, come sit. The babe won't wake up."

Once Lois settled in the chair, Wanda asked, "How's your new boss?"

Lois really needed to come up with an automatic answer to questions about Moses. "*Gut*," she answered but feared she didn't sound very convincing.

"How's Anna Lantz doing?" Wanda asked.

Lois felt her face grow warm. She didn't know. Not once had she asked Moses about his mother. "All right, I think."

"None of us can figure out how bad she is—if it's even necessary she's in that place."

Alarmed, Lois asked, "What place?"

"The care center." Before Lois could respond, Wanda added, "But Moses can hardly keep her in his one-room apartment."

Lois managed to ask, "Have you visited Anna recently?"

Wanda sputtered, "Jah. Well, it's been a couple of years. She seemed fine last time I saw her."

Abbie called out, "Wanda, are we using paper plates?"

"Jah." Wanda turned away from Lois. "They're in the far cupboard."

The women started carrying the food out. Abbie grabbed a stack of paper plates and napkins and put them on the table. "You take those," she said to Lois, "and I'll take the baby. I need to nurse him."

Lois stood and handed over the little one. She grabbed the plates and napkins, happy to escape any more questions about Moses from Wanda. There was definitely more to his story than she knew.

The family gathered around and John's father led them in a silent prayer. After they all dished up, John sat down beside Lois on a blanket, shared with a couple of the older grandkids. More of them gathered around. Clearly John was a favorite. One of the boys came limping to the blanket.

"What happened?" Lois asked.

"I twisted my ankle playing volleyball."

"Did you put ice on it?"

John butted in. "He's fine. Right, Johnny? You can tough it out."

"But should he?" Lois asked.

"I'm fine." Johnny smiled at his uncle and most likely the inspiration for his name.

"Will you play a game with us after we eat?" one of the older boys asked John.

"After we all clean up." John glanced at Lois. "Want to play?"

She shrugged. He already knew she didn't.

The family fell into place once everyone was done eating. The older girls watched the children while the men and boys carried everything in. Then John put all the paper plates in the burn barrel while the women put the food away and washed what few dishes there were.

There was a lot to like about the Miller family. "This is quite a well-run system," Lois said as she dried a serving bowl. Abbie agreed. "Wanda is all about systems. And making it so the women don't do all the work." She smiled at Lois. "Her sons make good husbands."

"With all these boys and no girls, I bet she's extra thankful for her daughters-in-law."

"Jah." Abbie glanced around the kitchen. "There is a daughter. Mae."

"Oh?"

"She lives in upstate New York."

Lois had never heard of Mae. "I had no idea."

"She left years ago. Before your family arrived."

"Why did she leave?"

Abbie glanced over her shoulder.

"Her parents wanted her to marry a man who farmed near Ephrata. A family friend they adored. Pressured her to, in fact. She ended up running away with an Englisch boyfriend."

Lois winced.

"Jah. It took Wanda a long time to get over losing Mae. I think it changed her some."

"How so?" Lois asked.

"Less controlling." Abbie began washing the cutlery. "Although she still pressures people at times."

Lois felt a connection to Mae. She knew what it was like to be pressured to marry someone she didn't love.

Abbie smiled at Lois. "Wanda really wants Mark and John to marry soon. I think she's ready to move out of the big house and turn it over to John and whoever is fortunate enough to join the family."

Sunday's singing was much like the last one she'd attended. Again, Lois felt old and out of place, although she enjoyed being around Evelyn. The young woman was fun and chatty—everything Lois wasn't.

The next Friday afternoon, John, Mark, and Evelyn came into the store at 5:59, just before Lois was ready to turn the sign to Closed.

"We're going out for pizza," John said. "We have a driver waiting. Want to come with us?"

Lois would rather go up to her apartment, make a peanut butter and jelly sandwich, and read a book. But it would be good for her to go out. "Sure." She'd leave the last of the cleaning of the shop until the morning.

John and Lois sat in the back of the van while Mark and Evelyn sat in the middle. The driver dropped them off at a pizzeria in the community of Willow Street. As they climbed out, he said, "I'll be back in an hour and a half."

That seemed longer than necessary to Lois, but she didn't say anything.

"We'll get ice cream after we eat," John said.

As they shared a pitcher of root beer and ate pepperoni pizza, John and Mark talked about what it was like to grow up with so many older brothers. "They hauled us around the farm before we could even walk," Mark said. "Put us on horses. On top of wagons of hay. On the manure pile. Poor Mamm. She said she doesn't know how she managed not to have a heart attack."

"Is it just you boys?" Evelyn asked. "No sisters?"

"Jah," John said.

"Nee," Mark contradicted. "We had a sister. Mae."

Evelyn glanced from Mark to John and then back to Mark.

"Jah, that's right," John said. "But she left when we were tiny. I don't remember her."

"I do," Mark said. "She was nice. Really nice."

"What happened to her?" Evelyn asked.

"She left," Mark answered. "I don't think anyone knows where she's at now."

Lois inhaled sharply. Mark gave her a questioning look. "You don't remember Mae, do you?"

"Nee. But someone told me she lives in upstate New York."

"Someone?" John didn't look happy with her.

Lois's face grew warm. "I don't mean to gossip—I shouldn't have said anything."

Evelyn quickly asked, "Lois, do you have sisters?"

"Nee. Just one brother."

"I didn't know that," John said.

Lois almost said, *He's not a secret,* but caught herself. "He lives in Big Valley. He's a lot older than I am."

"Is he Amish?" John asked.

"Jah," Lois answered.

Evelyn asked, "Why don't you live up there?"

Lois felt a wave of sadness for herself, for Mae, and for Mark that he'd lost a sister he loved. She also felt relieved not everyone knew her business—even though sometimes it felt as if they did. "I did live in Big Valley for a while—until I was eight and then again after my Mamm died. But I came back to Paradise because it's home," she answered.

John put his arm around her and squeezed her shoulder. "Another example of Gott working things out. He always does."

That was true, but John's comment stopped Lois. It made the hard times in life sound easy. Sometimes there was quite a bit of pain before "things" worked out. Sometimes people were stuck in the middle of something for years before it did work out. Or perhaps it never worked out in the way you hoped and you simply moved on, knowing Gott still had a plan.

After they finished their pizza, they walked over to the nearby strip mall for ice cream cones. On the way back to Paradise, John asked if she wanted to go to the Miller farm and sit around the fire pit.

"I'd better not," Lois said. "I have some things to do to get ready for work tomorrow." She wouldn't leave it for the morning.

John seemed disappointed but didn't say anything. The driver dropped Lois off and then turned back up the lane.

She let herself into the shop and headed to the cleaning closet for the vacuum. There had to be something wrong with her when she'd rather clean than spend more time with the Youngie.

The next day when Evelyn came in at eleven, she yawned several times. "Did you have fun last night?" Lois finally asked.

Evelyn started to smile but then it turned into a yawn too. "Jah. A great time." She laughed. "Maybe too good of a time. Mark didn't get me home until after midnight."

At one, Lois scootered to the post office. She had a letter from Menno, but he hadn't replied to her positive response to meeting. Perhaps her letter hadn't arrived before he wrote and sent his to her. He wrote more about a recent trip to the Delaware shore. How she wished she could join him there.

When she scootered back, hot and sweaty, Moses's car was in the parking lot. It was Saturday. The one day Moses usually didn't come to the shop.

When she stepped through the front door, there was a racket toward the back. "What's going on?" she asked Evelyn.

"Moses is doing some rearranging."

Lois hurried around the corner. All the birdhouses were off the birch tree—and it was on its side. "What are you doing?"

"This is a safety hazard." Moses focused on the tree. "It's an accident waiting to happen."

"Customers love the tree."

"It doesn't mean it's safe."

"It's not a danger."

"A child could pull it down."

Lois stared at the blank wall.

Moses said, "I bought shelves to put in its place."

She turned her attention to the birch tree, to the branches, to the crocheted birds attached to the twigs. She put her hands over her face.

178

"Don't be dramatic," Moses said. "It's only a display. Not the end of the world."

Lois turned away from him. Isabelle stood behind her. "Oh, Lois," she said. "I'm so sorry. Your father worked so hard on that display."

15

Moses sat in his office long after the shop closed. He could hear footsteps above. Lois, with Isabelle's help, was probably reassembling the birch tree in her apartment.

How was he to know Lois's father had made the display? And that Lois and her mother had crocheted the collection of birds? Why hadn't Scotty told him? Or Lois herself?

Why hadn't he thought to ask who had made it?

His phone buzzed, but he didn't look at it. Instead he stared at the payroll program on the computer screen.

His phone buzzed again. Then a text dinged. Finally he turned his phone over. The text was from Sara. So were the two missed calls. It was seven. He'd told her he'd be at the café by six for supper.

He closed the payroll program, powered down the computer, and picked up his satchel. He hadn't had a letter from Jane in his Delaware post office box that morning, although he did have one from Teresa and the Flight of Doves. Had Jane been offended he'd asked to meet in person so soon? After an hour at the market he'd decided to return to Paradise.

He'd stopped by the grocery store first, which was buzzing with tourists. He stocked shelves and helped bag groceries. By the time he reached the shop he was hungry and out of sorts. He should have gone to the café for lunch instead of dismantling the birch tree.

As much as Lois got on his nerves, Evelyn was even worse. Lois despised him. Evelyn fawned over him. These days he preferred Lois's hate to Evelyn's weird positivity, or whatever was going on with her.

He left through the back door, locking it behind him. Then he walked around the corner of the building, veering out away from it, glancing up as he did. The light was on in the apartment window. Lois was standing with her back to him, her Kapp off, her hair down. He quickly glanced away. Isabelle's car was gone. Only his remained in the parking lot.

When he reached the café, he went through the front door. Sara was standing at the hostess station, a frown on her face. "You're late."

"Sorry."

"Go get a table. I'll join you in a few minutes."

Moses sat at the far back table. When the waitress, a middle-aged woman named Jennifer, approached with two menus and two glasses of water, she gave him a smile. "Is Sara joining you?"

"Yes." Moses took the menu from her and thanked her for it.

"You two make such a power couple. You're both so tall and golden and handsome." Her face reddened. "Well, Sara isn't. Handsome, I mean. She's beautiful." The woman chuckled nervously. "Anyway, I'll come back once Sara joins you."

Feeling awkward, Moses agreed Sara was attractive. But he didn't feel handsome. He felt out of sorts. And mean.

As Sara sat down across from him, she said, "It's so hard to find good help."

Moses hated that sort of talk. According to Dat, it was up to management to educate employees into the workers the business needed.

Sara pushed her menu to the edge of the table. "I take it you didn't have a good day either."

"It was okay."

"Still worried about the Paradise Amish Market?"

"I still don't have the permits." Moses pretended to look at the menu.

"That's a bummer."

"The contractor thinks they'll come through by next week."

Jennifer returned. Sara ordered a house salad with chicken, and Moses ordered a cheeseburger. After Jennifer left, Sara asked, "Can you pick me up for church tomorrow?"

"I'm not sure I'm going."

"What?"

"I need to spend some time with Mamm."

"Okay . . ." Her voice trailed off. But then she said, "What's up?"

He shrugged.

"Look, I'm working long hours in *your* café. And you come in here acting all put out. As if you're doing me a favor."

She wasn't wrong.

She leaned forward. "I'm doing this to help you." Her voice was firm but low.

He sighed. "I realize that." He reached across the table and took her hand. "And I'm grateful."

She squeezed his hand. "We're both working too hard. You're going to have to hire another manager for the café sooner or later. Why not sooner?"

Thankfully Jennifer returned with their food, but Moses couldn't shake how he felt. Did Sara believe their relationship was transactional? She expected they'd get married. Was that why she was managing the café? She believed they both wanted the same thing.

He couldn't blame her. But he didn't think he felt as sure of their future as she did. He was at fault. He felt his stomach tighten. Was he leading her on?

"I don't want you to work for me if it's not what you want," he said.

"But I do." She squeezed his hand again. "For now."

On Sunday he spent the morning with his Mamm. He bluntly asked if he was adopted. With a solemn expression on her face, she responded with a question. "When can I go home?"

That broke his heart a little more, and he sat in silence with her for the next hour watching the birds but thinking about his adoption mystery. Finally, he stood and started pacing, until Mamm said, "Paul, stop fretting and come sit beside me." Moses obeyed his mother, his thoughts shifting to what Paul might have fretted about. He'd never know.

Tuesday morning, Casey stopped by Paradise Found to

talk about the Amish market. Moses hoped spending time with Casey would distract him from his worries. He motioned toward the back door. "I'll show you what my plans are."

Once they were outside, Moses stepped off the dimensions of the building and then the outside area. "Hopefully the excavating will be done soon. The building should go up pretty quickly once we can get started. I'm thinking a total of forty-five vendors, once we're in full swing."

The two walked the property.

"How are things going with you and Sara?" Casey leaned on his cane near where the concrete pad would be. "Any wedding plans yet?"

Moses took off his hat and raked his fingers through his hair. "No."

"Don't you think if the two of you were going to marry you would have by now? How long have you been courting this last time?"

"Six months."

"And before that?"

"We weren't courting."

Casey's eyebrows shot up. "She thought you were."

"Well, we did spend time together, starting after she joined the Mennonites too. But it was as friends. Until it wasn't." He'd finally decided Sara seemed like the most obvious woman for him to court. Plus, by then she seemed to be his only support besides Casey.

He pulled his hat back on his head.

He cared for Sara, he truly did. But did he love her?

Casey asked, "Is there someone else?"

"No. Well, kind of." He told Casey about Jane. "I think

about her all the time. Live for her letters." Moses's anxiety rose as he spoke. "One didn't come this week, although the circle letter did arrive." Teresa had written about how birds are mindful and present, always focused on the task at hand because they live by their values. It seemed like a little bit of a stretch, but Moses agreed all of those were good qualities for people to have too. "I asked Jane if we could meet in person—perhaps I scared her away."

"Write to her again." Casey resumed walking, slowly. "Maybe your letter to her was lost or delayed. Or hers has been delayed. But you need to meet her—you need to know who she is. What's her last name?"

"Weaver. Do you know a Jane Weaver around here? Her return address is a Paradise post office box."

"That's odd. I don't know any Jane Weavers."

Moses replied, "Maybe she's not who she says she is. But why would someone join an Amish circle letter as someone they're not?"

Casey shrugged. "Amish or Mennonite?"

"Amish—I assume."

"Does she assume you're Amish too?"

"Maybe." Moses hadn't thought about that.

"She doesn't know you're a Menno."

Moses laughed. "Actually, that's the name I've been using. I didn't want the circle letter members to know who I am."

Casey slapped his forehead with the heel of his hand and mimicked Moses, "Why would someone join an Amish circle letter as someone they're not?"

Moses grimaced. "I regret that now. But I didn't want members of the circle letter coming into the grocery store looking for me. Or complaining about the café or the shop.

You know how it goes." His phone dinged. He slipped it out of his pocket. Sara.

I need you at the restaurant. Call me.

He'd wait until he was back in the office.

As they headed back to the shop, Casey tripped on the uneven ground but steadied himself before he fell. Moses had forced himself not to grab for Casey. "Are you doing all right?"

"I'm fine," he said. "Just a normal stumble—it had nothing to do with my leg."

Moses suppressed a groan. He'd never stop feeling responsible for Casey's injury. He'd never stop feeling responsible for so many things.

Another incoming text stopped him. It was from the contractor.

I've had another delay with the permits. I'll let you know as soon as they come through.

Moses shoved his phone back into his pocket, but then it dinged again.

Sara.

The kitchen sink is clogged. I went ahead and called a plumber since you didn't get back to me, but he won't be able to come by until this afternoon. Get over here as soon as you can.

Moses clenched his phone.

Casey asked, "Is everything all right?"

Overwhelmed, Moses managed to mutter, "Yes." It wouldn't help to complain to Casey about his woes.

As they neared the shop, a delivery truck pulled away. Moses couldn't think of any deliveries scheduled for the day. What had Lois ordered?

Casey said, "I'm going to go into the shop and tell Lois hello."

"So am I." Moses took off at a faster pace. He marched in through the back door and down the hall into the shop. Lois was leaning over a box, cutting through the tape.

"What arrived?"

"Guder Mariye to you too." She opened the box and pulled out a birdhouse.

Moses took a step back. "I told you not to order any more bird stuff."

"I—"

"That's insubordination."

Casey caught up and stepped to Moses's side.

Lois said, "I—" again.

"You're fired."

"What?"

"You can't do that," Casey said.

"Of course I can." Moses pointed to the door. "And I am. As of now."

Lois didn't protest. She simply turned on her heels and walked out the front door. Moses assumed she climbed the stairs to her apartment, but he couldn't hear her. There was no stomping. No slamming the apartment door.

Moses felt sick. He'd gone against his Dat's business advice to always keep a good sense of humor, to never burn any bridges, and to always be kind. He'd failed miserably.

"Wow." Casey took a few steps toward the front door. "Did you actually just do that?"

"It's been coming for weeks," Moses said.

He went to the box. There were four more birdhouses inside, but no invoice. He stepped to the counter. The invoice was next to the register. The address on the paperwork was a business in Ohio, Amish Birding. The date on the invoice was May 1, right after Moses took over the shop.

He picked up the invoice, folded it, and then turned toward Casey. "I'm going to need help today."

Casey shook his head. "I'm not sticking around here."

"Please?" Moses didn't want to beg, but he had too much work to do not to have help.

"Do you hate your life, Moses? Because you just fired Lois Yoder, a woman you used to care about. A woman you loved. A woman who knows this shop better than anyone."

"It was never going to work out long-term. She wasn't happy working for me." Moses ran his hand through his hair. "I really do need your help."

"Not today." Casey gave him a wave and headed to the front door.

Moses left a message on Evelyn's machine but wasn't sure if it was her grandmother's number or her parents'. Was she close by or on the other side of the county?

Then he called Sara at the café. First he gave her the number of a plumber he'd used for emergencies at the grocery store who would make the café a priority. Then he told her what happened with Lois. Sara asked, "Does that mean she's moving? We could really use the apartment." *We.* Sara expected a proposal and soon. And why wouldn't she? She sounded a little too gleeful about him firing Lois, which bothered Moses.

But he found his own reaction puzzling—he was the one who'd fired Lois. It was his fault. That bothered him even more.

He wouldn't kick Lois out of the apartment right away. He'd give her a few weeks to find a new place. Maybe she could move in with Amy and Bennie. He winced. What were they going to think of him?

Car doors slammed outside the shop. The front door opened. An Englisch couple entered. Sara arrived as Moses rang up a big purchase. "We're from Philly," the woman said as he handed her the receipt. "We come here a couple times a year—or more. Has the business sold?"

"Yes, ma'am," Moses said. "I bought it just over a month ago."

"You took down the birch tree with the birds and bird feeders."

"Yes." Moses added, "It was a liability."

"And the nice young woman isn't here. Lisa?"

"Lois."

"Yes, Lois. A real sweetheart. I hope she's still working here."

"No," Moses said. "I'm afraid she's not."

The woman's eyes narrowed. "Did you get rid of her too?"

"I no longer needed her."

The woman pointed at the cash register. "You just charged me twice for the birdhouse. I think you do."

Sara stepped to the register, which was similar to the one at the café, with a smile on her face. "I'll fix it."

Moses backed away and shuffled down the hall to his office. What would local customers think of him for firing Lois? They'd all know soon enough.

He'd stick it out until midafternoon, but then he'd close the shop and head to Delaware. Surely he'd have a letter from Jane by now.

Jah, he knew he was attempting to escape how badly he'd handled the situation with Lois. He hadn't followed Teresa's advice in the Flight of Doves letter to be mindful and present and aware of his values. It was shameful, really. He'd always prided—something he shouldn't do, he knew—himself on being the best personnel manager he could be, but he'd failed miserably with Lois. He'd fired her for an order Scotty had approved. And she hadn't protested—she hadn't even tried to defend herself.

If she had, would he have listened?

16

Lois sat on her bed, numbly staring at the birch tree. Without the birdhouses on the branches, it definitely needed more birds. She took out a skein of yellow-green yarn from her sewing basket, along with a crochet hook. Mamm and she had crocheted the birds at the same time Dat had put the birch tree together, a few months before he died. She climbed back into the center of her bed, leaned against the pillows, and began crocheting.

She'd never been fired. Then again, the only employer she'd ever had before Moses was Scotty. He'd always raved about her work. The way he'd treated her and talked about her with others had given her confidence. She'd always believed she was a good employee. Until now.

Would Moses evict her from the apartment next? She'd known her days were numbered at the shop. She'd known she needed to start looking for a new job. And yet she hadn't. As miserable as it was to work for Moses, the comfort of the shop kept her there. Now she'd lost that. She kept crocheting.

She'd scooter to Bird-in-Hand to see Mary and ask if The

Country Store might be hiring. If she stayed with Amy and Bennie for a few weeks, until she could find a room to rent, it wouldn't be far to Bird-in-Hand. Much closer than it was from Paradise Found.

Her throat thickened. Paradise was home. She didn't want to live in Bird-in-Hand. But anything was better than going back to Big Valley and the threat of Nathan Hertzler.

She put down her yarn and crochet hook. She needed to talk to Moses about the Youngie wiener roast, which was Friday. She'd hate to have to cancel, and it would be a bad look for him if he forced her to.

Lois placed her crocheting in her sewing basket, put on her safety vest, and pulled her scooter out from behind the building. Sara's small car was in the parking lot, along with Moses's big one. Of course he'd called Sara to come over. That had probably been the plan all along.

She scootered up the lane and then turned onto the highway, facing the traffic as she sped through Paradise and then on up the road toward Bird-in-Hand. When she reached The Country Store, Mary wasn't there. An older woman was working and said Mary had taken a few days off because her sister was visiting. They'd gone birding that day.

"Do you know where?" Lois asked.

"Middle Creek."

That was much too far to scooter.

"Come back next week," the woman said.

Lois fought back tears as she left the shop. She would never beg Moses for her job back. Never. Ever. Ever. She hadn't even ordered the birdhouses—Scotty had, even though the invoice was dated May 1. The order must have been delayed and then sat in a warehouse for weeks.

She should have quit when Moses first bought Paradise Found, which was Paradise Lost now to her. She'd known working for him wouldn't end well.

She was tempted to stop by Amy's, but she didn't want to cry in front of the kinner. Or make her problems Amy's. She had enough problems of her own. First Lois needed to speak with Moses and find out about the apartment.

She'd rather know when he planned to evict her than have him spring it on her. She'd march right into the shop and demand to know exactly what his intentions were. And about the wiener roast. If Moses refused to let her host it, John, Evelyn, Mark, and a lot of other Youngie would be upset.

When she reached the shop, Sara was ringing up a customer, two more were waiting in line, and Moses, looking very uncomfortable, was talking with a fourth customer.

"There she is." The customer next in line pointed at Lois. "I was afraid you'd quit," the woman said. "You're the reason we come here."

Lois glanced at Moses. He had an awkward expression on his face. Did he expect Lois to state she'd been fired? She wouldn't.

Instead she said, "How are you? How are things in York?"

"I can't believe you remember where I'm from." She grinned.

"Oh, I definitely remember you." The woman came in every few months and always bought quite a lot. Gifts for family. Seasonal items. Decorations.

"Now that I know you're here I'll do some more shopping," the woman said. "Anything new I should look at?"

"We have a set of spring kitchen towels with flowers. They're discounted fifteen percent." Lois pointed toward the towel rack.

"I'll go look," the woman said.

The fourth customer stepped over to the candles, so Lois approached Moses. "Do you want to talk in my office?" he asked.

"No. I have two simple questions."

"All right."

"One, when do you plan to evict me? And two, may I still host the Youngie on the property for the wiener roast on Friday?"

Moses sighed. "Yes, on the second. It would be bad for business to say no at this point."

Was PR all he was worried about? She forced herself not to react. "And the first?"

"Give me some time to think about it."

"Do I have a day? A week? A month?"

"Closer to a month," he answered. "You're not going to be out on the street."

Was she supposed to thank him for that? She didn't. "I appreciate the information."

As she turned to go, the woman from York said, "Oh, I hoped you'd check me out. I always enjoy chatting with you."

"I'm sorry." Lois smiled at her. "I always enjoy talking with you too, but I'm not working today."

⁓

That afternoon Lois sat on her bed with a childhood book—*Anne of Green Gables*—propped on a pillow, and she crocheted as she read. She must have fallen asleep because she awoke to knocking and then someone saying, "Lois?"

She crawled out of bed, adjusted her Kapp, and went to the door. She opened it to Isabelle.

Lois motioned for her to come in quickly. She'd rather Moses not know Isabelle was visiting her, but perhaps he knew already.

"What's going on? Why are Moses and Sara working in the shop?"

"Moses fired me."

Isabelle shook her head. "He's a fool. What are you going to do?"

Lois shrugged. What could she do? "How about a glass of iced tea?" Lois asked.

"I'd like that." Isabelle sat down at the table. "*Do* you want your job back?"

Tears sprang into Lois's eyes. Moses had definitely stung her *hohchmoot*, her pride, by firing her. For sure. She took two glasses from the cupboard.

"We need to start a campaign." Isabelle placed both palms on the table. "We'll let everyone in the area know Moses fired you. I'll ask people to boycott the store. I have a friend who is a lawyer. We could talk to him and see if you could sue."

"We don't sue."

"You wouldn't even sue Moses Lantz? He's not Amish."

Lois poured the tea. It was tempting. Not to sue—Moses owned the shop and could fire her if he wanted. But to tell everyone what happened. If she told people at the wiener roast Moses fired her, every family in the area would know by Sunday morning. Moses would get what he deserved.

"Perhaps this is what it will take to get him to sell the shop to me." Isabelle grinned but then it flattened. "Although, I found a shop in Charleston, South Carolina. Any chance you'd want to move there?"

"Is there an Amish community nearby?"

"I don't know," Isabelle said.

195

Lois doubted there was one. "Have you made an offer on the shop there?"

"Not yet."

Lois put the two glasses of tea down on the table.

"So what do you say?" Isabelle asked. "Do we spread the word Moses Lantz is a real—" She laughed. "I have no idea what derogatory word you would use."

Lois smiled. "Jerk? Is that good enough?"

"Sounds succinct," Isabelle answered. "We don't want to go overboard and put the focus on your words instead of his actions."

Lois agreed.

After Isabelle left, Lois sat at the table with her half-full glass of tea and reread the latest letter from Teresa and the Flight of Doves. Menno had contributed a report, writing about a mockingbird he'd recently seen. Mary wrote about several orchard orioles—chestnut males and yellow-green females—landing on the front yard of The Country Store. Teresa wrote about birds being mindful and present and focused on the task at hand.

> *They live by their values, something we would do*
> *well to emulate. Everything they do is for a purpose,*
> *from their singing to nest building to hunting.*

Ouch. Jah, Moses had hurt her, but was she really going to lash out and hurt him back?

On Wednesday, Lois heard Evelyn's voice in the shop. Had she taken over Lois's position? That evening, after Moses left,

Lois let herself in the back door to use the phone. Bishop Stephen's stipulation for the wiener roast each year was that it was well chaperoned. Lois had asked Amy, Bennie, and Wanda and Silas Miller to help, but she needed to confirm with both couples and ask if Amy could take her shopping on Friday afternoon. She called the Miller phone number first and put on her cheeriest voice. "Wanda, this is Lois Yoder. I wanted to confirm that you and Silas can still chaperone the wiener roast on Friday. We'll start gathering at seven. See you then." After she hung up she wondered, If Wanda called the store to say they couldn't chaperone, would Moses tell her? Perhaps Evelyn would.

Next she called Amy and tried to put on a cheery voice—but failed. "It's Lois. I'm calling to make sure you and Bennie can still chaperone the wiener roast. And, um, I'm not working Friday. Any chance you could take me to the store in the afternoon while the older kids nap? We could take the baby—and Ernie too, if needed."

As Lois put the receiver down, her hand shook a little. She dreaded telling Amy that Moses fired her. Would Amy think it was Lois's fault for not being nicer to Moses?

Thursday morning, Lois scootered to the post office, hoping for a letter from Menno. None had arrived. Most weeks she had one by now. Friday morning, she scootered to the post office again. She left, disappointed for the second day in a row.

Friday afternoon, Lois sat on the top step of her apartment staircase waiting for Amy. A buggy turned down the lane. Lois squinted into the bright sunlight. Then she stood, ready to hurry down the stairs. It wasn't Amy. It was John. She quickly stepped into the apartment. Evelyn could tell him Lois had been fired. Or did Evelyn even know? What if Moses had told people she'd quit?

She listened for the front door of the shop to buzz. John had entered. No one else, except for Evelyn, was in the shop. She listened intently for another buzz. It came. Next she listened for the hooves of the horse. There weren't any. Instead there were footsteps coming up the stairs, a knock on the door, and then the hooves of a horse on the pavement.

Lois groaned and then opened the door. "John! What are you doing here?" She stepped out on the landing and pulled the door shut behind her. Then she took a step forward, forcing him down to the top step.

"Evelyn said you haven't been working. Is everything all right?"

"Jah." She peered around him to the parking lot. Amy was sitting in the buggy that had just arrived. "I'm on my way to the store to buy supplies for the wiener roast. I'm looking forward to it."

"So am I," John said. "But now I'm curious about your job. Evelyn says she doesn't know if you quit or Moses fired you."

"Jah, I haven't talked with Evelyn. Perhaps I'll see her at the wiener roast." Lois pointed toward Amy and her buggy. "I need to go." She slipped past him and hurried down the steps, not ready to discuss her work situation with John.

He followed her. "Is everything all right? Because I heard a rumor Moses *did* fire you."

"I can't talk now." She deflated a little more with each step. If only she'd had a letter from Menno to cheer her up. Perhaps he regretted suggesting they meet in person.

John asked, "Do you still have a place to live?"

"Jah." Lois had reached the buggy, and she quickly climbed in. She gave John a wave and a smile. "See you tonight."

Amy was holding Maggie in her arms and passed her to Lois. "What was that all about?"

"Oh, you know John. He's a little persistent."

"Does it have to do with Moses firing you?"

Lois groaned. "Where did you hear that?"

"Mamm heard it from her Englisch neighbor, who heard it from a cousin. I have no idea who the cousin heard it from."

Probably from Isabelle.

"Is it true?" Amy asked.

"Jah." Lois held the baby close, breathing in the sweet scent of the top of her head. "Moses fired me." She told Amy about the order of birdhouses that arrived after Moses told her not to order any more bird paraphernalia. "The order must have been delayed. I didn't place it—Scotty did."

"What did Moses say when you told him?"

"I didn't have a chance to."

"Tell him now."

"And beg for my job back?"

"I'll tell him," Amy said.

"Nee." Lois stared straight ahead. "He obviously doesn't want me working for him." He'd rejected her before. Why wouldn't he reject her now? And it seemed Menno had too.

⁓

The first store had what Lois needed—wieners, buns, and marshmallows—but not the rice cereal on Amy's list. As Amy flicked the reins, she said, "Let's stop at Creekside Market."

"Isn't that Moses's store?" Lois always shopped at the less expensive store they were now leaving.

"He won't be there, right? His SUV was at Paradise Found."

"Oh." Lois hadn't noticed in her rush to leave. Hopefully John hadn't talked with him after she left. "That doesn't mean he didn't drive over to the store in the meantime."

Amy sighed. "I really need rice cereal for the baby. I'm hoping it will help her sleep through the night."

"All right."

Thankfully, Moses's SUV wasn't parked at the market. Amy tied the reins to the post and then dashed into the store, leaving Lois holding the sleeping baby in the buggy. But Maggie soon woke up and began to cry. Lois patted her back, but she continued to fuss, so Lois climbed down from the buggy, headed to the boardwalk around the store, and began walking the baby back and forth under the awning.

A couple of Englisch women passed her and smiled as they walked to the entrance of the store. Then one of the regular customers at Paradise Found saw Lois and asked, "Why aren't you at the shop?"

"I'm not working today," Lois answered, which was true.

"Cute baby," the woman said.

"She's a friend's."

"Aww." The woman kept going.

Lois heard a car door slam and turned toward the parking lot. In the last space was Moses's SUV, and he was headed straight toward her.

Did he see her? She wasn't going to scurry away to avoid him.

"Hallo, Moses," she said over the top of Maggie's head as he approached.

He stopped. "Lois. What are you doing here?"

"Amy's in the store. Maggie got fussy."

"Oh." Then he simply kept walking. He'd been awkward when they were young, but she thought he'd outgrown that. Clearly he hadn't.

A moment later she heard voices around the corner of the building, near the entrance.

"You fired her for nothing."

Lois's face heated. Amy was confronting Moses. Maggie began to fuss again.

"She didn't place that order. Scotty did." Amy's voice grew higher.

"It's not your concern." Lois could barely hear Moses.

Maggie began to cry. Then wail. Lois put her up to her shoulder and began patting her back. Then she headed to the entrance.

Amy stood with her hand on her hip while Moses shrugged.

"Come on, Amy," Lois said. "Maggie's ready to go."

Amy stomped away from Moses, handing Lois her bag. Then she took the baby, who immediately quieted.

Once they were inside the buggy, Amy passed the baby, who was almost back asleep already, to Lois. "What happened to Moses Lantz?"

"I don't know." Lois swayed a little. "But I'm pretty sure I bring out the worst in him. And I'm positive you shouldn't get involved in this, considering how your property is financed. And that you want to sell things at his market."

Amy exhaled and pulled the horse around to the highway. As they entered Paradise, Lois asked if Amy would stop at the post office, even though Lois had already been there earlier that day.

"Expecting a letter from Menno?" Amy asked.

"Hoping for one."

To Lois's relief there was a letter from Menno. And one from her brother, or more likely Deanna. She hadn't answered the last letter—even though she knew they'd keep coming. She put that one in her apron pocket. She wouldn't think about it until after the wiener roast. She couldn't wait until she was home to open Menno's, so she opened it in the post office lobby, hoping no one coming in would get nosy. She read it quickly. It was dated Tuesday, three days before.

Dear Jane,

I was so relieved to get your letter (it seems it took a two-week journey to get to me) and read that you do want to meet sometime. Choose a place that works best for you and let me know where that is.

He wrote a couple of paragraphs about birds and then,

Looking forward to meeting you in person,

Warmly,
Menno

She slipped the letter into her apron pocket. When she climbed back into the buggy, Amy said, "You're smiling."

"Jah. I received a letter from Menno. It was short, but he still wants to meet." She hadn't lost him too, after all.

17

By eight o'clock, Youngie filled the property. It was a much bigger turnout than the year before. Three fire pits burned to roast wieners and marshmallows. Lois had set up two tables in the parking lot for sides, condiments, and drinks. Several of the families in the district had contributed to the event. The attendees parked cars and buggies in the parking lot and tethered horses along the woods.

A girl Lois didn't know, wearing jeans and a sweatshirt, snapped photos on her phone. Lois blanched when the girl directed the phone at her as she stood behind one of the food tables. The girl said, "I heard Moses Lantz fired you."

"Who from?" Lois asked, hoping the girl wasn't filming her.

Wanda stepped to her side. "Everyone knows. What happened?"

"What did happen?" Evelyn was on the other side of the table without Mark. "Moses wouldn't tell me. He said it was private information, and I was afraid to knock on your door and ask."

"I don't think he's been happy with me for a while." Lois shrugged. "I suppose Moses is right. It's private." Isabelle's plan didn't sound as good as it had a few days ago. Lois had the chance to let Isabelle know she didn't agree with it—especially after reading Teresa's letter again about living out one's values—but she hadn't. As wrong as Moses was, it didn't feel right to try to turn the community against him, even more than it seemed it already had. For certain, Moses had been wrong about the order, but perhaps she hadn't been the best employee. There was no denying she'd hoped he'd fail so Isabelle could buy the store. Now Isabelle was hoping to buy a store in South Carolina instead.

Lois had failed. She'd always prided herself in having strong character, but she didn't when it came to Moses. She hadn't wanted his business to succeed. Her hurt had gotten the best of her.

"Well, you're being kind," Wanda said. "I heard he fired you for something you didn't do."

"It may have been more of a misunderstanding. And he did allow me to host tonight, plus stay in the apartment for now." Lois grew more and more uncomfortable with each word. She didn't want to be talking with anyone about Moses, especially not Wanda. It certainly wasn't her place to defend him—nor did she need to try to explain all that had happened between her and Moses over the last seventeen years when she didn't understand it herself. "I need to restock the buns." She darted around the side of the building to the back.

As she opened the door, John came toward her from the grassy area. "Lois," he said. "Come roast marshmallows with me."

She grabbed five bags of buns from the box in the hallway. "I will after I deliver these and make sure we don't need any more. I'll find you."

Ten minutes later she stood by John with a marshmallow on a stick. She tried not to stare at a young man wearing jeans and a western-style shirt. She'd never asked Menno how old he was. He could be eighteen and on his Rumspringa. Or twenty-eight and a member of the church for the last decade. Although if that were so, he'd most likely be married. Amy was right—he could be anybody. And anywhere at this moment. Even here. She'd never know unless someone called him Menno.

"Lois!"

She turned.

Casey limped toward her. "How are you?"

She smiled. "I'm fine." She'd always liked Casey.

"How are you doing, really?" His voice was full of kindness.

"All right."

"What Moses did was horrible. Really uncalled for. I told him so—"

Lois put her finger to her lips. "It doesn't matter."

"I know you're having other problems too. I heard that Bishop Stephen isn't happy with you living by yourself."

Lois swung the bag of marshmallows toward him. "We're not talking about any of that tonight."

Casey grabbed the bag.

She motioned toward the metal roasting sticks. "You need one of those."

He gave her a sympathetic smile. "You don't want to talk about any of it?"

"That's correct. Let's enjoy this evening."

Casey glanced around and then smiled at her. "It's a great turnout."

"Isn't it?"

He nodded, picked up a stick, and then pulled a couple of marshmallows from the bag. Then he stepped to John's side and said, "How have you been?"

"*Gut.*"

"I saw your folks down in the parking lot. They look like they're doing . . ."

Lois pulled her marshmallow off the stick and shoved it in her mouth. Then she put her stick with the others and started over to the next fire pit.

As she chewed on the toasted gooey mess, she felt unsettled. She didn't like Moses. In fact, she detested him. And she had wished him ill will, something the Bible, the Amish church, her parents, and her values all taught against.

It probably didn't matter how she treated him, though. He would have fired her no matter what. He was only looking for an excuse.

Evelyn stood by a couple of girls Lois didn't know. Lois asked, "Where's Mark?"

Evelyn glanced around and then said in a low voice, "He went to New York to find his sister. He found out where she lives from one of the older brothers and got in contact with her. She's married to a Mennonite man and has a family."

"Oh wow."

Someone cleared his throat behind them. Lois turned to find John a step away. "Are you talking about Mark?"

"For sure," Lois answered. "That's great he found your sister."

John shook his head. "It's none of his business. It's better to let all of that be."

Lois glanced at Evelyn, who looked very uncomfortable. Lois turned so she was fully facing John. "Not if she wanted to see him."

John crossed his arms. "He'll just stir up old wounds and hurt Mamm and Dat. Our sister already did that once. They don't deserve it again. We should look toward the future—not the past."

Lois exhaled slowly. Who was she to talk about how to handle family problems when she had a strained relationship with her only sibling? But she didn't believe John's approach was the best. She asked, "Do your parents know where Mark is?"

"Nee. But they will soon enough."

Evelyn deftly changed the subject. "So, Lois, what are your plans now?"

"Will you be going back to Big Valley?" John asked.

Alarmed, she answered, "No." Did he want her to go back to Big Valley?

Someone called her name. Amy was standing in the back door of the shop, waving.

"Oh, look." Lois pointed at Amy. John turned. "Amy needs me." She took off toward the shop. John was usually so . . . positive. He was usually overly positive. Was that why he couldn't cope with a serious topic he feared would bring more conflict to his family? If so, what would he think of the conflict she had with her brother?

～⁓

Lois didn't climb the stairs to her apartment until eleven, after she'd finished cleaning up, tossing the garbage, putting away the tables, and cleaning the restroom. Once she was inside her apartment, she locked the door behind her, kicked off her shoes, and, too keyed up to sleep, made herself a cup of chamomile tea. Then she slipped her letter from Randy from its envelope. It really was from him and not Deanna, a first. He wrote he'd had a letter from her bishop that she wasn't living with Amy and Bennie Dienner as he had believed. Randy was disappointed that she had tricked him.

> *You need to move home now. Nathan is still interested in marrying you even after the way you treated him.*

Lois stuffed the letter back in the envelope. How ironic he thought returning to Big Valley would be a move home. She'd lived in Paradise far longer and with many more happy memories. She'd think about writing Randy back later.

She took out her notebook and wrote *Hallo, Menno* at the top of the page. She thanked him for his letter and wrote she was glad hers arrived. She mentioned meeting at Middle Creek or a place in Paradise Township. *Which would you prefer? Let me know.* Then she added more details about the bevy of swans that she hadn't included in her previous letter. There had been one single swan in the flock that hadn't found a new partner yet. She wrote,

> *As you know, swans mate for life. If a partner dies, the remaining one usually finds a new partner. Occasionally a couple will "divorce," usually after a failed nest.*

Her father had given her that information. He hadn't clarified what constituted a failed nest. A structural failure? Or no cygnets? That was a sad thought.

Lois wiped away a tear, which she knew wasn't for the failed nest of a couple of swans. Jah, the tear was for herself. She'd had a failed relationship with Moses. A horrid, unwanted relationship with Nathan. And now a very tepid relationship with John, if it could even be called one.

She put down her pen. She'd finish her letter to Menno later.

Monday morning she added a paragraph about seeing the red-tailed hawk a few weeks before, wanting to add the sighting of a more recent bird to the letter. She scootered to the post office and mailed the completed letter to Menno. Then she scootered on to the shop in Bird-in-Hand. She reminded herself not to bring up the circle letter with Mary. If she did, she'd have to confess she was masquerading as Jane Weaver.

As she walked into the shop, Mary greeted her with a smile and a big "Hallo!" And then, "I heard you stopped by." She lowered her voice. "And that Moses Lantz fired you."

"Jah." Lois winced. "That news seems to be out and about."

"I also heard you've been very gracious, not wanting to call Moses out for being a jerk."

Lois pursed her lips together at Mary's choice of words.

"People are saying you won't talk about it at all, not wanting anyone to think you're gossiping about him."

Were people making her out to be a saint? She supposed compared to Moses she was—but she wasn't.

Mary kept talking. "I also heard you're looking for a job."

"Jah," Lois answered. "That's why I've stopped by."

"We have a part-time position. Fifteen to twenty hours a week. But it won't start for three weeks."

Lois had a fair amount of money in savings, and if Moses allowed her to stay for a few weeks, then she'd be fine. "I can wait. Do you know of anyone who might have an apartment to rent out or even a room?"

"You can check with Claudia Peachy." Mary took a piece of paper from a drawer behind the counter and wrote down the woman's number.

Lois took her notebook and a pen from her backpack and wrote down Amy's phone number on a corner of paper. "Would you leave me a message at this number if you need to get ahold of me?"

Mary took the piece of paper.

"What day should I start?"

"Tuesday, July 2nd. You'll work Tuesdays and Wednesdays, nine to seven." A customer had approached the counter. Mary said, "I'll see you then."

A smile crept across Lois's face as she left the shop. Things were working out. Gott would take care of her, regardless of Moses Lantz.

⌒

On the way home, Lois scootered onto Meadow Lane, past the marsh, and then past the Harris farm, which still had a For Sale sign up. Then she scootered back to the marsh. Why not ask Menno to meet her there? That way she wouldn't need to hire a driver. She'd wait and see what his response to her letter was.

As she headed back toward the farm, aiming to do the covered bridge loop, a car turned into the driveway. She stopped her scooter. Scotty walked toward the car as it parked. She didn't want him to see her. She'd end up telling him Moses had fired her, if he hadn't already heard. And then what? Would he confront Moses and demand he rehire her?

A man and woman climbed out of the front of the car, and a little girl, probably around ten, climbed out of the back. They all wore jeans and T-shirts. Most likely they were interested in buying the farm.

Her heart ached, but she said a prayer for the farm to sell. She still felt connected to the property with Scotty and Barb living there—but she knew it would be best for it to sell. She waited a few minutes after Scotty and the little family disappeared, hoping they were in the house. Then she scootered by. She hadn't waited long enough. Scotty waved but she pretended she hadn't seen him and kept on going.

Tuesday, Wednesday, and Thursday she helped Amy with the kids and the garden and candle making.

On Thursday, Amy made goat's-milk soap in the afternoon while the kids napped, using the heat method and making plain bars without any decorations. Obviously Moses's market wouldn't open any time soon, but Amy wanted to be prepared when it did. "I hope you won't despise me for wanting to sell at Moses's market even after he fired you," Amy said to Lois as she stirred the pot on the back of her stove.

"Well, if he'll let you be a vendor after you yelled at him, I can't fault you for taking him up on it." Lois concentrated on washing the dinner dishes as Amy worked. "I understand why you need to do it."

"I don't feel good about it—I'm not sure what to do." Amy turned the heat down a little.

"You need the money." Lois put the last of the plates in the rack. "Give it a try and see how it goes."

Amy turned toward Lois as she stirred. "I've been thinking about the two of you, about what happened. You seemed so happy, so right for each other."

"We weren't."

Amy looked so sad. "I should have asked this a long time ago, but did he contact you in Big Valley?"

"Nee. Did he go to your wedding?" It had always pained Lois that she'd missed Amy and Bennie's wedding, but Randy insisted she return to Big Valley with him immediately after Mamm passed away. Lois, at the time, hadn't thought she had any choice but to go.

"No, Moses didn't come to the wedding. He had a lot going on then too," Amy said. "I think more than we knew at the time. Sure, we knew about the wreck and that Casey was in the hospital in traction and Sara had a concussion and all of that. It seemed Moses was unscathed, but I think he had a lot of guilt about the accident. And it seems his Mamm was already having problems, we just didn't know yet."

Lois turned toward Amy. "What do you mean?"

"His Mamm has dementia. Maybe Alzheimer's. It came on early."

"Wanda said she's in a care center. I didn't know that."

Amy scrunched her nose. "I guess everything happened while you were gone."

The mixture began to bubble and Amy turned her attention to it.

Lois asked, "Why did Moses feel guilty about the wreck?"

"He was driving."

"I assumed Casey was—it was his car."

Amy shook her head.

"Oh." Moses must have left his car at the river that night and retrieved it later.

"Don't you remember all of this?" Amy turned toward Lois again.

"Nee. I told you not to tell me anything about Moses."

"I guess I followed your instructions." Amy grimaced. "Moses's Dat died—maybe six months after the accident. And then stuff kind of got out of hand with his Mamm around the time Ernie was born. So, jah, I guess maybe I didn't tell you. When I went up to Big Valley to get you, we had other things to talk about."

Lois didn't respond.

"The night of the accident, there was a party on the Susquehanna River—"

"A week before you got married?"

"Jah," Amy said.

Lois thought of the owl in the sycamore tree, and the full moon shining down on the river as she and Moses walked along the bank. It had started out a perfect night. And then everything turned once Sara arrived. "I was there."

"You never told me that."

"I thought I had." She and Moses had sat on a log by the fire, all their years of schoolyard animosity gone. He had his arm around her and pulled her close. She felt safe. Protected for the first time since Dat had passed away, as if she wouldn't have to find her own way in life after all and take care of her Mamm at the same time. They talked softly, unaware of anyone else around them. He asked to give her a ride home. Before she could respond, Sara showed up. She sat across from Moses and Lois and stared at them. She was wearing a sweater, jeans, and boots. She smiled and then asked, "How long have you two been courting?"

Lois, feeling self-conscious, sat up straight.

Sara chuckled. "Lois, do you know who else Moses has been courting?"

When Lois didn't answer, Sara tapped her chest. "Me."

Moses leaned backward. "Sara, you know that's not true."

Sara pointed at Moses. "You're a two-timer."

Glancing from Sara to Moses, Lois stood and stepped over the log. Moses reached for her hand. She jerked it away.

Lois had always been intimidated by Sara's confidence and beauty. Lois wasn't going to compete with her in front of Moses and everyone else. She headed toward where the cars were parked, hoping Moses would come after her. Soon footsteps followed her. She let out a sigh of relief.

"Lois!" It was Casey. "I'll take you home."

She turned and shook her head. "I'll ask Mark Miller. He lives close by."

She fought back tears the entire ride. Moses hadn't come after her.

Sara hadn't been lying.

Moses had betrayed her. Lois had never felt so rejected in her entire life.

She'd been fighting those memories since she first saw Moses in the shop in late April. Now, as it all came rushing back, she felt like she had riding back to the apartment with Mark Miller.

"Lois?" Amy stood with the wooden spoon in her hand. "Are you listening?"

"Jah. Sorry."

"So anyway, Moses ended up driving Casey's car that

night. Sara was in the back seat and Casey was in the front. Moses took a turn too fast, or something like that, and rolled the car. Casey ended up with a compound fracture in his tibia. Sara had a really bad concussion that took months to heal."

"What about Moses? Was he all right?"

"Perfectly fine."

"Had he been drinking?"

"Nee. They tested him. Not a drop. However, Sara had been."

Lois flinched. That could have explained Sara's behavior, but not Moses's.

Amy said, "Casey said Sara was drunk. Bennie and I always wondered if she distracted Moses while he tried to drive her home."

18

The next Wednesday, Lois received another letter from Menno but it seemed he hadn't received her latest, because he didn't write whether he wanted to meet in the Paradise area or at Middle Creek.

On Thursday, Claudia Peachy finally left a message on Amy and Bennie's machine that she'd be willing to rent Lois a room in Bird-in-Hand. "Stop by Saturday at noon and look at the room."

Saturday morning, Lois scootered back to Amy's and borrowed her buggy. Lois didn't exactly feel comfortable handling Amy's horse. She used to take Dat's buggy to work at Paradise Found occasionally when they still lived on the farm, but it wasn't far and she wasn't on the highway for long. This was definitely a longer drive. But it was hotter and muggier than it had been when she'd scootered before, and she didn't want to arrive dripping sweat.

Once Bennie had the buggy ready, Lois climbed up onto the right side of the bench. Bennie stepped to the open door. "Do you remember how to drive?"

"Jah." Lois flicked the reins as she reached for the door handle. The horse took off, and Bennie laughed as he managed to close the door for her.

Once she reached the highway, Lois had to wait for a string of cars filled with tourists to pass, but finally she was able to make the left turn.

When she reached the address, just off the highway and about a half mile from the Bird-in-Hand gift shop, she tied the reins to the hitching post and then knocked on the door. Claudia opened it immediately. Without saying hello, she said, "You're late."

"Oh." Lois couldn't be more than five minutes late.

"I appreciate punctuality."

Lois said, "I'll remember that."

Claudia ushered Lois into the entryway. "My husband passed away six years ago, and I've been renting rooms to Amish women since then. I have three rooms, all furnished. Only one is vacant. I'll show it to you."

Lois followed her into the living room. It was clean and tidy and sparsely furnished. "I'll show you the second and third floors."

Lois glanced up at the open staircase.

"The room that's open is the attic room. You would have the entire area." Lois followed her up a set of stairs onto a landing. Down the hall were several doors. "I have my sewing room up here too," Claudia said. "And a guest room for when company visits." She started climbing the next set of stairs, which was very narrow.

"I'm afraid the room is a little stuffy today. I failed to open the windows last night to air it out." She opened the door and stepped inside. Lois followed her.

The room was big—and hot. There was a single bed under the gables on one side, and a small desk and chair on the other, where she could write letters to Menno. Under a window was a set of drawers. There were pegs on the far wall to hang clothes.

"You would share the bathroom on the second floor with the other women."

"What do they do for work?" Lois asked.

"One is a receptionist at a cabinet-making business. The other works at the bakery. Their homes are too far away to allow them to live at home and work in Bird-in-Hand, but they are able to go home for the weekends or at least Saturday evening to Sunday evening."

Lois would have nowhere to go. She imagined hiding away in the hot attic room all summer when she wasn't working—her part-time job would allow a lot of time for sweltering. Perhaps Amy and Bennie would let her stay with them on her days off. She could help Amy make more soap and candles.

"Denki for showing me the room," Lois said. "I'll leave a message on your phone by Tuesday with my answer."

"Do you have other options?" Claudia asked.

Lois simply smiled at her. "I'll let you know my decision by Tuesday."

After she returned Amy's horse and buggy, Lois scootered to the post office to check her mail. She had a letter from Teresa and the Flight of Doves, another from her brother, and one from Menno. She put them in her apron pocket and then scootered on to the park and stopped at a picnic table.

A car drove by and a woman in the passenger seat raised her phone. Lois turned her head away. If someone was going to sneak a photo, she'd do her best to only show the side of her face, or better yet the back of her head.

She opened the letter from her brother first. He simply asked why she hadn't replied to his previous letter.

> *You belong here. And, as I wrote before, Nathan is still interested in you as his wife, regardless of your previous behavior.*

Her brother's words—and assumptions—were bad enough, but the thought of Nathan made her want to retch.

She stuffed the letter back in the envelope and into her backpack. Then she opened the letter from Teresa, saving the best—Menno's—for last. Teresa wrote,

> *Spread your wings! First of all, don't be afraid to leave the nest and explore new areas of life, no matter your age.*

She wrote about fledglings going farther and farther from the nest.

> *Embrace change, and follow the lead of our feathered friends and go with the seasons. As Plain people we might not "migrate" at all in our lifetime or maybe only a handful of times, but we too can find joy in the seasons and moving through them. Keep a song of joy, faith, and grace in your heart.*

Sweat trickled down the back of Lois's knee. She certainly had a lot of change to embrace in her upcoming season. Could she do it with joy, faith, and grace?

Teresa finished her letter with *Be brave!* Lois had seen countless brave birds, flapping at a predator or calling for help. One time a murder of crows settled in the cherry trees along the lane and cawed until she finally went outside to see what the matter was. Once the crows saw her, they swooped down beside a dead crow in the grass. Lois got gloves and a bag and picked up the crow. The crows flew after her to the edge of the woods, where she buried the dead one. Once it was in the ground, the other crows flew back to the cherry trees. The crows had asked for help, from a human.

She read through the Flight of Doves reports. Mary had written about rescuing a robin from a neighbor's cat. Menno wrote about seeing a murmuration of European starlings over a farm west of Dover. Lois loved the word *murmuration*, and had seen her share of starlings twisting and turning and swirling and swooping in shape-shifting dark clouds. There was something so mystical about a murmuration that it felt holy. Menno wrote there was such harmony in the murmuration that the sight of it had given him hope.

Lois pressed her hand to her chest. When humans worked in harmony, she felt hopeful too. She felt that way working with Amy. She'd felt that way working with Barb and Scotty and with Mamm and Dat. She never felt that harmony with her brother and his family in Big Valley. And she certainly hadn't felt that way working with Moses. That made her sad because she had felt harmony with him five years ago.

She opened Menno's letter. He wrote,

I'm thankful you want to meet. The Paradise area will work for me. Let me know an exact location, small or large, birding or non, and a day and time.

Then he wrote that he'd been thinking quite a bit about what she'd written about the red-tailed hawk she'd seen flying over the creek. He wrote,

Red-tailed hawks are one of the most common hawks in the area, and in the entire country, but we never tire of seeing them. They're majestic and serve the land, besides being beautiful in their own way. But small birds have just as much beauty and contribute as much as the more powerful raptors.

Lois liked that. Maybe Menno wouldn't mind if she— Jane—was a little brown bird. That gave her pause. Should she explain in her reply that Jane was her middle name? Or wait until she saw him?

She took out her notebook and wrote him back, suggesting they meet at the marsh on Meadow Lane, just off the highway in Paradise, on Monday, July 8, at one p.m., which was two weeks away—plenty of time for him to receive her letter and respond. She included the address of the farm and wrote that the marsh was right before it, along with other detailed directions. She stamped the envelope and dropped it through the slot. She'd write her report for the Flight of Doves by Monday.

She wasn't sure what she'd do about her brother, but

she should respond soon—before he wrote Bishop Stephen that she hadn't replied to his letters. The problem was, she couldn't think of anything she could write to Randy that would change his mind.

She put Menno's letter back in the envelope and into her apron pocket. By Tuesday she needed to have an answer for Claudia. The next Tuesday she'd start at The Country Store in Bird-in-Hand.

She felt uneasy about moving. She loved Paradise. She would be part of a different Amish district in Bird-in-Hand. She'd be farther from Amy. Farther from the farm on Meadow Lane and the marsh and the covered bridge and the park.

As she scootered, the hot wind whipped against her skin and tangled her dress between her legs. Why did Moses have to buy Paradise Found? Her life was simple before then. Nee. That wasn't true—Bishop Stephen had already wanted her to move back to Big Valley.

Perhaps the bishop of the new district would feel better about her living with Claudia and the other single women. But after having her own home for the last three years, would she adjust to living in a house full of strangers?

Why couldn't she be trusting like the birds in the book of Matthew? *Behold the fowls of the air: for they sow not, neither do they reap, nor gather into barns; yet your heavenly Father feedeth them.* God would take care of her. She needed to embrace this coming change. The fact that she would soon meet Menno at least gave her some hope—and a hint of harmony. Enough to make her smile as the hot wind stung her face.

As she reached the Miller farm, John was walking the fence line along the highway. She waved. He tipped his hat back, and then waved back. "Lois!" he called out. "How are you?"

"*Gut!*" She came to a stop on the highway across the fence from him.

"What have you been doing to keep busy?"

"Helping Amy. Finding another job."

"Have you found one?"

Tears threatened as she said, "Jah. In Bird-in-Hand. I'm just trying to figure out a living situation."

"How can I help?"

She shook her head. "I'm fine, really."

"Should I pick you up at your apartment tomorrow for the singing?"

"Nee. I have plans with Amy and her family tomorrow evening."

He looked hurt. Could he tell she was lying? She didn't have plans with Amy. She just couldn't bear another singing, and she couldn't seem to force herself to be interested in John.

"Is Mark back from New York?"

"Jah." John frowned.

"How is he?"

"He says he's doing fine, but he's moody. He broke up with Evelyn."

Lois gasped.

"Jah." John sighed.

"Why?"

"Mark is talking about going Mennonite now. He says Mae and her husband and kids have a good church and home. One of the kids was depressed and went to counseling. Things like that impressed him." John shook his head. "He's breaking Mamm's heart. I knew he shouldn't have gone."

Lois had been the one who told Mark where Mae was. Perhaps John was angry with her about that. "Isn't it a relief to know Mae is doing well, though?" she asked.

John took his hat off. "Nee. It's confusing, actually."

"How?"

"God's favor brings blessings. And yet she left—and it still seems she's been blessed with a good husband and a house full of children."

"You don't think God favors those who leave?"

"Not in the long run. Mae will still pay the price. Moses will pay the price someday too."

Lois's eyebrows shot up. How quickly John had shifted to Moses. And John's idea of a *price* was something she hadn't heard phrased like that before.

"Are you sure you can't go to the singing tomorrow?" John's voice sounded hurt.

"Not tomorrow." She rolled her scooter ahead a few inches. "I should let you get back to work."

The next day was a non-church day, and all Lois wanted to do was curl up in her bed and not have to face thoughts of a job or where to live or John or Moses. Or even Menno.

That was exactly what she did.

Then on Monday, in the midmorning after she'd done her wash, she scootered down to the post office to mail her report to Teresa. She hadn't managed to write Randy back even though she knew she should. She found the thought of communicating with him benumbing.

She'd rather live and work in Bird-in-Hand than move

back to Big Valley. She'd rather marry John than move back to Big Valley. John would be much better than Nathan. But she didn't love John—so she couldn't marry him. That went against her values. That wouldn't be fair to herself or to him.

On the way back, storm clouds scudded across the horizon. The air grew heavier. Lois swiped her left hand across her forehead.

The raindrops started as she reached Paradise Found. As she started toward the stairs, she heard a commotion in the shop. Someone was yelling. Then Evelyn stormed out the front door shouting, "I quit."

Lois froze. Evelyn turned toward the staircase and burst into tears.

"Come up to my apartment." Lois leaned the scooter up against the staircase and grabbed Evelyn's hand.

The two started up the stairs. The front door of the shop opened and then closed. The warm rain began coming down in sheets, and thunder boomed in the distance. By the time Lois had the front door unlocked, both she and Evelyn were soaked.

Once they were inside, Lois directed Evelyn to the bathroom to towel her hair. "I have a dress you can wear." Lois stepped into her bedroom.

"It won't fit," Evelyn answered.

"Put on my robe."

Lois changed her dress in her room, and when she came out Evelyn sat at the table in Lois's robe. The morning's laundry hung on the clothesline Lois strung across the apartment on washing day, and on the birch tree. She quickly closed the windows she'd left open to dry the clothes. Evelyn had hung her dress on the end of the line. "How about some tea?" Lois asked.

"I'd like that." She glanced around. "You don't have a phone in here, do you?"

"Nee. Who do you need to call?"

"Someone to come get me."

Lois wondered who that someone was as she filled the tea kettle. "What happened down there?" She started the propane burner and put the kettle on it.

"Moses has been impossible to work for. He keeps expecting me to know things I've never been told about, such as inventory and ordering. He gets upset if I'm a few minutes late." Evelyn wrapped her arms around her middle. "I never wanted a full-time job—just a part-time one to give me an excuse to live in Paradise Township."

"What are you going to do now?"

"I don't know," she wailed. "Did you know Mark broke up with me?"

Lois nodded. "I'm sorry."

A knock fell on the door. And then another one. Lois gave Evelyn a puzzled look. Lightning flashed over the woods.

Whoever was at the door knocked again. "Lois, it's me! Moses. I need to speak with you."

Lois stared at the door.

His voice lowered and grew louder at the same time. "Please?"

"Talk with him," Evelyn said. "He probably wants to offer you your job back. If you take it, could you ask him to let me work part-time again?"

Lois slowly nodded as she started toward the door. That probably wasn't what Moses wanted to talk to her about.

She opened the door.

Moses stood with his hat in his hands, his shirt and pants

soaked. "The birdhouses were ordered before I bought the shop. I saw the invoice after I fired you." The rain continued to pelt him on the landing.

She wasn't going to ask him in. "Scotty ordered them."

"I can see why. They've sold out." Moses held his hat to the side of his head, trying to protect his face from the rain. It wasn't working. "I'm sorry I fired you—that was wrong of me." He lowered his head.

Lois met his brown eyes. Was that sorrow she saw?

"I know the chance of this is low, but would you consider taking your position back?"

Lois glanced back at Evelyn and then took a step closer to Moses. "Would you hire Evelyn back for her part-time job?"

"Jah. Absolutely. I need to apologize to her too."

"You can do that later." Lois held his gaze. "I need a contract for the job and the apartment."

"How about six months?"

"A year."

"All right." He exhaled as if in relief. "Can you start now?"

"Is Sara in the shop?"

"No. She's at the café."

"I'll be down in a half hour to sign my contracts. I'll work the rest of the day and then my regular schedule next week. Evelyn will come in on Saturdays and Mondays."

"And Fridays, if she agrees," Moses said. "I expect business to pick up once our regulars know you're back. Would you help spread the word?"

"Maybe." Lois stepped back and gripped the doorknob. "Bye."

19

Once Lois signed her contracts, Moses retreated to his office with a sigh of relief. He felt like a fool, but Lois was back. His feelings were irrelevant.

Everything in the store had fallen apart in the last two and a half weeks. No one knew Lois's method of inventory. No one knew when the deliveries were arriving or what needed to be ordered. Finally, Moses found Lois's notes—thorough but hard to read—in the bottom drawer of the counter along with the file of invoices, but he wasn't sure what orders to copy or what to change.

And he'd learned just how many birdhouses and feeders sold in the store and just how short they were on those items, due to his moratorium on ordering more. He also learned how many customers adored Lois, and how many local customers were loyal enough to her not to come into the shop at all once he'd fired her.

Sara wouldn't be happy to hear he'd given Lois her job back, nor that he'd given her a contract for the job and the apartment. Sara wanted both. But Sara was stretched tight with the café to manage, and she wasn't right for the shop position. Only Lois seemed to be.

On Tuesday morning, Moses spent a couple of hours in the office at the shop. Everything seemed to be going smoothly. He hadn't had a letter from Jane at the Delaware mailbox on Saturday, but perhaps one had arrived now. With Lois back in the shop and Sara at the café and things going smoothly at the grocery store, he could drive to Byler's Corner.

As he left Lancaster County, a raven sat on a fence post, watching him go. He'd been in denial about why he felt unsettled. Sure, there were several reasons, but there was one that he needed to deal with as soon as possible. And that was Sara. Five years ago, he hadn't been interested in her despite her interest in him. But he'd been too timid to be firm with her. He'd hoped her feelings for him would go away. It was hard to believe now, but he'd been head over heels for Lois. Then, that night at the river, Sara had arrived acting as if she owned him, which sent Lois running. He knew it had been a risk for Lois to trust him—and he'd completely failed her by not making things clear with Sara at that moment. If he'd only figured out earlier in the evening that Sara had been drinking, perhaps he would have stood up to her.

After the accident, he was racked with guilt over Casey's and Sara's injuries. Neither had their seatbelts on and both had been thrown out of the car. He was also shaken by his father's anger with him. And haunted by what-ifs. Mainly, what if they'd both been killed? But also, what if Lois hadn't gotten a ride home with Mark Miller? What if he'd taken her home? What if he'd killed her?

He'd wondered what Lois thought of him—and yet he didn't contact her. He didn't even know she'd moved for several months. For the last five years, he thought of her when he drove by Paradise Found, about when she and her Mamm lived in the apartment. To be honest, he thought about her every day—thought about her being in Big Valley, most likely married with children. Not once did he think she'd returned to Paradise Township. He thought she'd made Big Valley her permanent home.

Had Lois been part of the reason he'd wanted to buy Paradise Found in the first place? The memory of her working there in the past?

His Dat's death was traumatic. And then Moses had the weighty responsibility of caring for his Mamm and sorting out his father's businesses and selling the farms to ensure he had enough money to care for her long term. Well, and to be honest, he'd never been interested in farming or even managing farms.

Once he decided not to join the Amish and join the Mennonites instead, Sara joined the Mennonites too—but it wasn't until they started courting that she confessed he'd inspired her to do so.

When the café in Paradise went on the market, Sara arranged for Moses to speak with her uncle. She was delighted he was interested in buying a restaurant and said she'd help him with the café, even work there. She'd been wanting to get back to Paradise. She strongly encouraged him to buy it, even when he began to have doubts. She convinced him. That was his first mistake. Buying a business on someone else's urging.

Casey was right. If marrying Sara was the right thing to do, he would have already.

He feared he never would have had a serious relationship

with her if he hadn't almost killed her, which wasn't a reason to marry someone. Being alone certainly wasn't reason enough to marry someone he didn't love either.

When he reached Byler's Corner, he pulled up in front of the mailbox. Down the block was the vacant market space. Come Friday, it would overflow with life. That's what he wanted in Paradise too.

He unlocked his mailbox and pulled out a stack of envelopes. Bills and payments. And then a letter from Jane.

Had she written about a place to meet? He was doing the same thing he'd done five years ago when he knew Sara was interested in him—although this time he wasn't in love with Lois. He was interested in Jane. And even if Jane didn't turn out to be the right woman for him, Sara deserved better than being in a relationship with someone who could so easily fall for someone else, someone he hadn't even met.

He needed to be honest with Sara before he met Jane. He couldn't make the same mistake he'd made five years ago again.

He drove straight to the café. Sara's car was in the parking lot.

When he entered through the front door, he saw her sitting at the back table. She noticed him, waved, and motioned him over. When he reached her, she said, "I'm taking my break." She held up a cup of tea.

"Of course." He sat down.

"Do you want a cup of coffee?"

"No, thank you." He put his hat on the chair beside him.

"You look serious." She flashed a smile. "You're not firing me, are you?"

"No," he said. "But I have something important I need to talk about."

She cocked her head. "You're breaking up with me." She said it as a fact, not a question.

"Jah."

"I knew it. You've been acting so weird, worse than usual." She spoke rapidly. "It's someone else, right? It's Lois. I knew it. I heard you hired her back."

"It's not Lois."

"Are you sure?"

"Absolutely. I care about you. I appreciate you. But I'm not in love with you. And I'm definitely not in love with Lois." Moses took a deep breath. "I have been corresponding with someone from the birding circle letter. I haven't met her yet, but I have feelings for her."

Sara laughed with contempt. He couldn't blame her.

"Good grief," she said. "You're dumping me for someone you've never met?"

"No. I'm not continuing our relationship because I'm not being fair to you. I need to be honest."

Sara leaned toward him. "We're good for each other. We have businesses to run together. We know we can build a good life. The rest doesn't matter."

Moses saw Sara for a moment as if for the first time. "You don't love me either?"

"I decided years ago that you were the right man for me. And then I waited until you were ready."

"I see."

"I overlooked your awkwardness as a teenager and a young man. I saw the man you would become. I helped you become that man."

"But you don't love me?"

"Of course I love you—because I choose to love you. I want to be connected to you. I want to be with you."

He couldn't get past the fact that she wasn't in love with him. It hurt his pride, and yet he hadn't been in love with her either. Not only was he prideful, but he was hypocritical too.

"Well." He stood. "Thank you for listening to me."

"You can't just leave."

He glanced around the dining room. People quickly glanced away.

Sara looked up at him, her hazel eyes cold. "You need some space is all—you'll figure out this fantasy girl isn't who you think she is, and you'll return to me. And that's fine. I'll take you back."

Moses smiled faintly but barely felt it. It stayed on his lips without reaching his heart. Or soul. "I'm sorry, Sara. I truly am. I hope you can forgive me."

"Of course I can forgive you—this isn't the end. You'll see. I'm giving you space for what—a month? Two months? Three?"

He shook his head.

"Three it is. We'll figure things out then."

Moses walked away. He expected her to follow him out the front door, but she didn't. On the short drive to the shop he found himself thinking about Lois. If he hadn't rolled Casey's car, would he have found her the next day and explained he and Sara weren't dating? If he hadn't found her the next day, would he have followed her to Big Valley? He guessed so.

He'd been stupidly ornery to her when they were little because he hadn't known how to be her friend even though he wanted to. Five years ago, when he'd realized how much he cared for her, he'd ruined that too. And then that day he'd seen her in Paradise Found, he'd reacted like a fool instead of showing how happy he was to see her again.

He *was* a fool.

When he reached the shop, he parked in the back and went straight to his office, intent on avoiding Lois. Then he firmly closed the door, sat down at the desk, and took out the letter from Jane.

Dear Menno.

It was the first time she'd addressed him—well, Menno—as *Dear*.

> *Thank you for your last letter and for asking me to choose a place to meet. Would the marsh on Meadow Lane in Paradise Township work for you? There's a willow tree in the middle and several paths around the area. I've seen egrets, marsh wrens, bittern, snipes, a great blue heron, and many other birds on the property. Monday, July 8, at one p.m. would work for me. Let me know as soon as possible if that doesn't work for you.*

She added a nearby address and detailed directions, but—of course—he knew exactly where it was.

Then she wrote,

> *I stood on the side of the road and watched the sunset last night as it turned orange and then pink over the neighbor's farm. What would it be like to head west—and keep on going? I've never seen the ocean, neither the Pacific nor the Atlantic. I've never left the*

state of PA. I've never seen a bird that's not native to
PA or migrating through, unless it's an accidental.
When I was younger, I dreamed of going to Costa
Rica, where the ruby-throated hummingbirds winter.
My dream seemed doable as a child. I know better
now, but I'm not sad about it. I had the dream. It
brought me immense joy. That is enough.

Warmly,
Jane

Moses read her words again, feeling sad at her lost dream, even though she said it brought her joy. He took out his notebook and an envelope from his satchel and printed, from memory, Jane's address on the envelope. Then he wrote on the notebook paper.

Dear Jane,
Thank you for your letter. Monday, July 8, at 1 p.m. at
the marsh on Meadow Lane works perfectly for me.
I look forward to seeing you then.
In regard to your desire to travel, I haven't been far
either. Thankfully, Pennsylvania is a big state with a lot
to see, but I can understand your dream. I've longed to
go birding in other states, besides Delaware, too. Perhaps
even other countries. It all depends on what might fit my
time and budget, meaning what the Lord allows. I hope
you'll keep dreaming too. You never know what the Lord
might provide.

He sensed Jane had painful losses in her life too—and that money wasn't plentiful. He appreciated her openness in sharing about her dream and a glimpse into her situation.

He wrote a paragraph about being in charge of the hummingbird feeder on his family's farm when he was a boy and how much the birds liked his mother's salvia.

> *The hummingbirds against the purple salvia was a beautiful combination. I often think of the image of the two when I remember my childhood. No doubt you have many similar images.*

He signed the letter, *Warmly, Menno.*

He decided to drive into Lancaster to mail the letter. He didn't have time to drive back to Delaware, and he needed to mail it before Saturday.

As he put the letter in the envelope, a knock fell on the door. "Moses?"

He flipped the envelope over. "Come in."

The door opened and Lois appeared. Her blue eyes seemed larger and brighter than usual. He felt a pain in his chest as she said, "We only have three birdhouses left. I can place a phone order and have more by the end of the week."

"All right."

"How many should I order?"

"How many have we sold in the last month?"

"Fourteen."

"How about twenty?"

"Sounds good." She took a step backward.

"I've been thinking," Moses said.

She stopped. "Jah?"

"Should we reinstall the birch tree? Maybe add some wire or something to make it more secure?"

She exhaled rather loudly. "Why don't we both give it more thought and talk about it later."

"All right." He stared at the door as she pulled it shut. Lois was even prettier than she was five years ago. Perhaps as she'd grown more independent, she'd grown more attractive. She was a woman now—a strong woman. And beautiful.

He turned his attention back to the envelope, sealed it, stamped it, and then put it in his satchel.

As he drove to Lancaster a wave of hope swept through him. But then his phone dinged and a text message from Sara popped up on the SUV's navigation screen. He didn't open it.

He took Highway 30 and then turned left toward the post office when he reached downtown. When he parked he opened the text from Sara.

How is your day going?

Without replying, he climbed out of his SUV, stepped into the lobby, and dropped the letter through the slot with a flourish. He'd soon know if Jane was as incredible as she seemed. Hopefully Sara would give up on him sooner rather than later.

On Friday Moses arrived at Paradise Found to find Lois unboxing birdhouses. "Guder Mariye," he said.

"Hallo." She held up one of the birdhouses, which was a replica of an Amish house with a horse and buggy in front of it. "I think these are going to be big sellers."

He stepped closer. The house looked like the one he grew up in. "Who made these?"

"Casey," Lois answered. "He's really improved his craftsmanship."

"I want one." Moses would hang it up outside Mamm's window. Perhaps it would help her remember.

Lois handed him the birdhouse. "Take this one."

"I need to pay for it," Moses said.

Lois stepped to the register and rang up the sale. Moses handed her his debit card. After she handed him the receipt, he picked up the birdhouse. "Denki. Call my cell if anything comes up."

Instead of going back to his office, he headed to the parking lot and then to the Green Hills Care Center.

Every time he walked down the hall to Mamm's room, he noted there were no other Plain people in the center. But other Amish families had siblings, aunts, uncles, and cousins. Other families had women who could help older members. He and Mamm were a family of two, not of fifty or a hundred or even two hundred as some of the three- and four-generation families in the area were.

He knocked on Mamm's door, which was half open. No one answered. He pushed the door open. Mamm was sitting at the window watching a cardinal peck the feed in the acrylic bird feeder he'd hung a couple of months ago.

"Hallo, Mamm." He held up the birdhouse. "I've brought you something."

She turned toward him with a smile on her face, then clapped when she saw what he held in his hand.

"Casey made it."

Mamm stood and took a step toward him. He held out his free hand, and she grasped it.

"It looks like our house, doesn't it?"

"Jah." She squeezed his hand.

"I'll put it on your dresser where you can see it." He

positioned it in the middle. Perhaps she'd enjoy having it in her room.

She shuffled closer and touched the horse and the buggy. Then she ran her hand over the roof of the house. "Our house," she said.

"Jah. Casey must have used it as his pattern." He took her free hand in his. "Do you remember when we used to go birding?"

"Jah."

"Dat would work on Saturdays and before he needed me as much, we'd take the buggy and go birding. Or sometimes hire a driver. A few times Dat came with us."

"Jah," she said again. And then, "Paul died in a buggy accident."

"Paul?"

"Nee." She shook her head. "It was a car accident. You were with him."

"He was injured in an accident?"

"Jah," she said. "He died later."

"Was my mother—" Moses hesitated. "Was Paul's wife with us?"

"Nee," she said. "She was gone. He didn't want her to find you."

"Oh." That wasn't the story Moses had imagined. But perhaps Mamm was talking about a dream she'd had or a distorted memory. Or something that had happened to someone else. How could he know what was a legitimate memory and what wasn't?

"Mamm." He squeezed both of her hands. "Would you like to go birding today? Right now?"

She broke out into a smile. "Jah."

It took a while to get her ready to go and out to his SUV. On a whim, he decided to go to the marsh on Meadow Lane. It was only a short distance away, and Mamm might not do well being away from the care center for long.

As they rounded the curve of the lane before the marsh, Mamm said, "That's Lois's house ahead. Beth and Randall's farm."

"It was," Moses said. "It's not anymore."

He slowed and pulled over under the willow tree. He took his mother's walker out of the back first. He figured she could sit under the willow tree and look through his binoculars. Hopefully something would turn up.

Maybe Jane would. She might live close by. Of course, she wouldn't recognize him if she did. Every time a buggy passed by Moses glanced at the driver. Most were men, but one was a woman in her twenties he didn't recognize. But then the head of a little boy popped up in the back.

Jane was right—there were marsh wrens and an egret in the middle of the marsh. Mamm could see the egret. Then a blue heron swooped down.

"Awww," Mamm said.

"Awww," Moses repeated.

After thirty minutes, he said, "I need to get you back to the care center."

"He loved you," Mamm said. "Paul did. He told us not to tell. He said it would be best."

Moses's head jerked backward in surprise. "Not to tell me I was adopted?"

"Jah," she said. "Faith's brother was tall. I'm sorry."

Moses wasn't sure how to respond. Finally, he asked, "What was Faith's maiden name?"

"Byler."

"Byler? As in Byler's Corner?"

"Jah."

"Why didn't I ever know that?" It was one property in Dat's portfolio Moses hadn't sold.

His mother answered, "We loved you."

"I know." He bent down and put his arm around her. "I've always known you loved me."

Mamm looked up at him. "Take me home."

Moses knew she didn't mean the Green Hills Care Center when she said the word *home*, but it was the only place he could take her.

On the way back, he thought about his Dat coming to the hospital the night Moses rolled Casey's car. It was the only time his father had ever been angry with him. And he'd been livid.

20

On Saturday, the store buzzed with customers. Lois was sure it was their busiest day ever, and she was very grateful for Evelyn's help. And that Moses was away—to wherever he went on Saturdays.

In the early afternoon, the register ran low on change. Lois headed into the office to buy money out of the bank bag in the safe. As she counted out the money on the desk, she bumped the chair, which bumped the desk, which must have made the mouse move. The computer screen came to life. Lois turned toward it.

An article was on the screen. She stepped closer. *Father Dies in Accident—Son Survives.* The date was October 21, 2000.

She read it quickly. A twenty-four-year-old Mennonite man named Paul Schwartz had been driving a car with his infant son in the back seat near Gap. The car rolled three times. The unnamed baby, who was nineteen months old, was in a safety seat and survived with only a few scrapes and bruises. Paul Schwartz died at the hospital a day later.

Speed seemed to be a factor, but no drugs or alcohol was involved. The baby's mother had not been located. Her name was Faith Byler Schwartz, and if anyone had information on her whereabouts they were asked to contact the Lancaster County sheriff.

Lois's stomach dropped. Who was the unnamed baby? What happened to the mother? If the mother wasn't found, who took the baby?

And why did Moses have the article open on his computer?

"Lois?" The door pushed open. "I need the change." Evelyn stood in the doorway.

"I'll be right there." Lois quickly turned away from the computer, hoping Evelyn hadn't read the title of the article. She recorded the exchange and put the large bills into the bag, which she placed in the safe. Then she locked the safe and scooped up the equivalent in ones, fives, tens, and coins.

The rest of the afternoon sped by with customer after customer. Lois gave Evelyn a half-hour break, but she didn't take one at all. Just before closing time Isabelle came in. "I heard you'd been rehired. Are you sure it's what you want?"

Lois glanced around, hoping the three customers in the shop hadn't heard Isabelle. "Jah. It's what I want. What have you decided about the shop in Charleston?"

"I haven't," she said. "But I heard Moses doesn't have the permits for the market yet. Should we put more pressure on him?" She winked at Lois.

"No. In fact, could you let people know I'm working here again? Business is good—but I don't want people *not* to come in because they think Moses treated me badly. He's corrected that."

Isabelle gave her a disbelieving smile. "Don't sell yourself short. Moses deserves for business to be slow."

"Jah, he's made some mistakes. But haven't we all?" Lois certainly had. "I'd like to give him another chance."

"All right." Isabelle smiled faintly. "I'll let people know you're back." She left without buying anything, something she seldom did.

At closing time, Lois sent Evelyn home and then she began to tidy up. She couldn't stop thinking about the article on Moses's computer screen. She was tempted to ask Moses about it. But then he would think she'd been snooping, which she had been.

The next day at church, the preacher taught on Matthew 22:36–40 and Isaiah 41:10. *Love your neighbor as yourself* and *Do not fear*. "Everything we do is motivated by either love or fear," he said. "We must decide which will motivate us before a trying situation arises. Will we be motivated to love our neighbors or fear them?"

Lois thought about Moses. How much of her reaction to him had been out of fear? He'd hurt her in the past— she feared he'd hurt her again. Her motivation toward her brother was fear too. He wanted her to marry someone she didn't love, who wouldn't treat her well. How could she, even when she had reason to fear, flip her response to love?

She would, Gott willing, meet Menno in a week. Just the thought of it made her feel more loving. Yesterday, she'd reacted with compassion—with love—to the article on Moses's computer. Was that because Menno helped her feel more loving? And she'd discouraged Isabelle from hurting Moses's business more.

She prayed she could keep responding in love. But was

there more she needed to do about Moses? Perhaps apologize for the things she'd said when they were children? She frowned. Nee. Surely Moses didn't remember any of that.

What could she do about her brother? Write him a letter and tell him why she couldn't return to Big Valley and why she'd never marry Nathan?

And how could she be loving toward John even though she was certain she didn't want to marry him either? *Tell him*, the still, small voice whispered. *Before you meet Menno.*

Who was the voice? Her own conscience? Gott? Her imagination? It didn't matter. She knew what she needed to do.

After the service and dinner, Lois stopped by Amy and Bennie's. She rocked Maggie to sleep while Amy put the two middle children down for a nap. Ernie looked at books in the living room, and Bennie went out to check on the cows.

John hadn't come by during the week to ask her to a singing or a volleyball game or whatever it was that was going on. It felt awkward to stop by the Miller farm to tell him she wasn't interested in him when perhaps he was no longer interested in her. Perhaps he never had been. Perhaps he now saw her as the quirky old maid and bird lady she was.

When Amy came back downstairs, Lois stood and slipped Maggie into her friend's arms. "I should get going," she said. "But first I wanted to tell you something. Our sermon today was about being motivated by love instead of fear. I want you to know your friendship helps motivate me to act in love."

"Denki." Amy cradled the baby in one arm and wrapped her other arm around Lois. "I feel the same way."

But Lois knew it wasn't the same. Amy had all sorts of support. All Lois had was Amy.

As Lois scootered home, she thought about how Mamm and Dat would never have tried to force her to marry someone like Nathan. Never. Ever. Tears threatened. One slipped down her cheek. The hot wind stung its pathway. She swiped at her face with one hand as she gripped the scooter handle tightly with the other.

But as much as she needed support, she couldn't manufacture a relationship with John Miller to receive it. Jah, she would have in-laws, thirty-plus and counting. But she wouldn't have love.

As she neared the Miller farm, she started down their lane to see if John was home.

As she rounded the curve, she saw John at the volleyball net, gently lobbing the ball across. She expected a nephew to be on the other side—but it was a young woman.

Evelyn.

She bumped the ball back to John and then broke out in laughter. He slowly set it up and hit it back over the net. It was just the two of them playing.

Lois stopped her scooter.

Now Evelyn was serving. She missed. John came up to the net and then ducked under it and stepped behind her, placing his arms on hers, showing her how to serve correctly.

Something was going on between John and Evelyn. Lois smiled and turned her scooter around and headed back out to the highway. When she reached it, she glanced to the left and then to the right.

It wouldn't hurt to go by the marsh and go birding for a few minutes.

246

She turned a block early. There was a trail that crossed the run and the train tracks that led to the back of the marshy area from the side street.

She usually left her scooter in the bike rack at the care center, which was across the street from the trail. She slowed as she approached it. Why was Moses's car in the parking lot?

"Oh," she said aloud. Lois hadn't realized Anna—Moses's mother—was in *this* care center, so close by. Why hadn't Amy told her? "Oh," she said again. Lois had instructed Amy not to talk about Moses or anything to do with him.

She parked her scooter, took off her safety vest and put it in her backpack, and then stared at the double doors of the center. She'd always liked Anna. She glanced at the trail.

It wouldn't hurt to stop in and see Anna and Moses. Perhaps Moses would be all right with her visiting Anna from time to time.

A woman was sitting at the counter in the lobby. Lois said, "Hello. I'm here to visit Anna Lantz."

The woman nodded to a piece of paper on the counter. "Sign in."

After Lois did so, the woman handed her a badge that read Visitor. "Put this on your dress."

Lois took it, squeezed the clip, and attached it to the strap of her white apron. "Thank you." She'd never been in a care center before, but she guessed it was similar to a hospital.

"Anna is in room 134." She pointed to the hallway on the left.

Lois strolled down the shiny linoleum floor, her shoes squeaking a little as they hit the floor. The smell of the disinfectant reminded her of the hospital. The ambulance had taken Dat there after the workhorses spooked and he'd been thrown while cutting hay. A farmhand ran to the neighbors and called 9-1-1. Mamm rode in the front of the ambulance, and Scotty and Barb came to the shop to get Lois. She didn't know her father was dead until she saw her mother in the waiting room. Mamm hadn't been the same after that day— it was as if Lois had lost them both at once.

She passed room 130. Then 132. The door was wide open to room 134. She didn't want to knock and wake Anna if she was asleep.

Lois stepped a few inches into the room. Moses and Anna were sitting in two chairs in front of a large window. The acrylic bird feeder Moses bought at the shop hung on the outside of the window. Several sparrows bopped around in it, pecking at the seed. The Amish birdhouse Casey built sat on the dresser.

Anna had her head resting on Moses's shoulder, and he had his head resting on his Mamm's, on her perfectly starched and bleached Kapp. His golden hair curled a little at his collar. His shoulders appeared even broader than usual next to Anna's narrow frame. It was clear, whatever Moses's reasons for putting his Mamm in the care center, that he loved her and cared for her. And she deeply loved him too. Lois wouldn't interrupt the two. She'd come back and visit Anna some other time.

The next week passed in a blur of busy days at the shop. Tourist season was as good as it had ever been, and Lois found herself in motion all day long. Finally, on Saturday, she managed to have a half hour to scooter to the post office. She had a short note from Menno saying how much he looked forward to meeting her.

After she awoke Monday morning, Lois sat in the middle of her bed with her legs crossed under her nightgown, staring at the birch tree that she'd completely filled with the birds she'd crocheted—doves, snowy owlets, northern cardinals, and painted and indigo buntings.

Anxiety filled her over meeting Menno. What if he wasn't what she expected? She closed her eyes, bowed her head, and prayed that Gott would guide her. And give her wisdom. And help her to be accepting of whatever happened.

After she showered and dressed she started her chores, washing her laundry in the bathtub first and then wringing everything out. She hung her underwear in her bathroom and then hung her dresses and aprons on the clothesline she'd strung across her living room. Then she opened the windows to get a breeze blowing through the apartment. Next she scrubbed her kitchen and then swept the floors. After she finished, she wrote a paragraph for the circle letter about the owl she'd seen at the edge of the woods the night before and then how, soon after, lightning bugs had lit up the woods. She'd hurried out through the field and then ran with the lightning bugs. That was something she would have saved to write to Menno, if she were writing to Menno today. But she was going to see him.

She ate half a peanut butter and grape jelly sandwich for lunch and then stopped in at the shop. Evelyn was standing at the counter looking through a flyer.

She glanced up. "Lois. What are you doing here?"

"I thought I'd stop in and say hello."

Evelyn's face reddened.

"How are you?" Lois asked.

"*Gut.*" Evelyn wrapped her arms around herself.

"How was your Sabbath?"

"Just fine." Evelyn's face grew redder. No doubt she and John had spent more time together.

Lois was tempted to ask how John was doing, but she held no ill will toward Evelyn—nor John.

"I'm going into town," Lois said. "See you later."

"Later," Evelyn echoed.

It was another humid summer day, and Lois grew sticky as she scootered down the highway, hugging the side of the road when a car or truck or buggy passed. A pickup truck flew by, honking at her. A man waved his baseball cap out the window. She kept her expression blank and stared straight ahead.

When she reached Meadow Lane, she slowed some but took the turn as quickly as she could, breathing in a big gulp of hot air. She was arriving early, as she'd planned. She much preferred to be at the marsh before Menno.

The willow tree hung heavy with leaves. She leaned her scooter against its trunk. There were more pussy willows on this side of the marsh than where she'd been the day before, on the care center side. A dragonfly floated by. She stepped to the willow tree and made her way around to the far side. She sat down on a root and drew her knees to her chest.

The marshy soil smelled slightly like rotten eggs from the decaying wetland matter, but she didn't find it bothersome. She couldn't estimate how many times she'd played in the marsh as a child, chasing monarch butterflies and peeking around the willow at birds, afraid she might scare them off. She'd caught toads in jars and taken them home only to be sent back by Mamm to release them.

She heard a car door slam and stepped to the edge of the

tree. She couldn't see a vehicle. Perhaps someone had stopped at the farm to look at the property.

Instead of going to the far side of the willow, she leaned against it with a view of the road. Menno would arrive by car—he couldn't drive a horse and buggy from Delaware.

Lois looked up into the tree. As a child, she'd spotted all manner of nests in the marsh—ground nests, platform nests, cup nests, pendulous nests, cavity nests. One of her favorite activities in late fall and winter was to search for nests once hidden in the spring and summer by foliage but now vacated and bare. It was like looking into a house with no walls.

A bird twittered. Lois turned toward it. Overhead on a branch, against the green of the willow leaves, was a cup nest with three fledgling song sparrows in it. She watched them for a few minutes, committing the scene to memory.

She glanced at her father's pocket watch. *1:10.* Menno was late.

Time dragged by. *1:24.* Still no Menno. But perhaps traffic coming from Delaware had been slow. *1:29.* Her stomach twisted in a knot. Maybe his driver had a flat tire. Or car problems. *2:10.* She sat down on the root and drew her knees back to her chest. He wasn't coming. Still, she stayed until *2:25.*

She slipped the watch back into her apron pocket. A lump formed in her throat. She tried to swallow it away, but it only grew larger. She knew this feeling. It was the same way she'd felt when Moses rejected her. It wasn't anger—that hadn't come until she'd seen him again in April.

It was complete sadness. This time caused by Menno.

Perhaps Amy was right. Maybe Menno didn't exist. Lois had been duped. Fooled. Humiliated.

She pulled her scooter out from under the willow and climbed on. She started off at a slow pace, heavy with rejection, heading toward the covered bridge.

As she reached the driveway to the farm, she turned her head toward the house. A Plain man was standing next to a black SUV. Her heart lurched. Perhaps Menno's driver had stopped to ask for directions.

Then her heart fell. It was Moses. She was tempted to pretend she hadn't seen him, but then he called out her name.

She turned into the driveway. "Hallo."

He waved.

She asked, "What are you doing here?"

"Scotty hasn't had many bites on the farm. I'm trying to figure out if I should make an offer or not."

Most likely a low one.

Lois gave him another wave and scootered away. Menno had played her. Now Moses was going to buy the property that used to be *her* home. A day she'd expected to be joyful had shattered her heart.

She couldn't stop the tears as she scootered along the covered bridge, the thud of her foot against the planks reverberating. She continued on to the highway. A few minutes later when Moses passed her and waved, she didn't wave back. Instead she stared straight ahead, tears still streaming down her face.

21

When Moses arrived at Paradise Found, he entered through the back door, went straight to his office, and closed the door. Then he sat down at his desk and put his head in his hands and let out a single sob.

Lois was Jane. He'd lost Lois five years ago. Now he'd lost Jane too. He'd never have a relationship with either.

His heart hurt. For himself. And also for Lois. She'd looked so sad when she scootered by the farmhouse—her old farmhouse, and when he passed her on the highway too. Menno had stood her up.

No. *He'd* stood her up.

But what could he do when he saw her leaning against the willow tree? At least he'd had the foresight to park in the farm driveway instead of driving right up to the marsh. He didn't want Jane to know right away that he owned and drove a vehicle. That was another thing he hadn't made clear—that he was Mennonite. Most likely Jane—Lois—had assumed he was Amish.

He'd seen Lois leaning against the tree, staring up into

the branches. He'd frozen for a moment and then quietly retreated.

At first he wasn't sure if Lois was Jane, but then he walked to the border of the farm, where he could see her but she couldn't see him. She was obviously waiting for someone and glanced at a watch several times.

Lois never talked about birding, but she'd filled Paradise Found with bird-themed merchandise. Feeders, birdhouses, hummingbird feeders, towels and cloth napkins and table-cloths covered with birds. Bird greeting cards. Bird books. Bird bookmarks.

And yet, Lois and Jane were nothing alike. Lois was cold and unrelenting. Jane was kind and caring. They couldn't be more different—and yet they were the same person.

He stared at his blank computer screen. Jane had a Paradise post office box. Lois would scooter into town to run "an errand"—most likely to check her post office box.

How had he missed it?

Lois had missed that he was Menno too. She hadn't figured it out, and he didn't want her to. That would only cause her more pain than she'd already gone through. And he wanted to protect her from that.

He heard footsteps upstairs. Lois had returned. A few more times in the next ten minutes he heard footsteps and then nothing. Only silence.

A half hour later, he heard a man's voice in the shop. John Miller. Had he come to see Lois? Moses could no longer see the two as a couple—Lois was much too smart for John.

Evelyn giggled. Moses groaned. John Miller had come to see Evelyn, not Lois.

The next morning, Moses worked in the grocery store for a couple of hours and then stopped by the café at Sara's urging. She had been acting as if nothing had changed in their relationship, texting a couple of times a day and asking him to stop by the café for minor issues. He'd reminded her that they were no longer courting. She'd simply smiled and said, "We'll see. We broke up before and got back together." Apparently she'd rewritten their story to include that they'd been courting five years ago—even though they hadn't been. His inclination was to avoid her. But he needed to make sure things were running smoothly at the café.

They weren't.

One of the kitchen workers hadn't shown up for work and hadn't responded to Sara's phone call. Sara and the waiters were trying to make do.

"I'll pitch in." Moses rolled up his sleeves. An hour later the worker hurried in, saying he hadn't heard his alarm and apologizing profusely.

Moses dried his hands on his apron as Sara asked, "Do you have time to talk?"

"About the café?"

Sara smiled. "No. About us."

He shook his head. "There's nothing to talk about."

She put her hand to the back of her neck. "You'll change your mind. I promise."

She was relentless—but at some point she needed to accept that their relationship was over. Finding out Jane was Lois made him even more sure he'd done the right thing to end things with Sara. As sad as he felt, he was convinced he'd just stepped back from a cliff. And for that, he felt very grateful to Jane.

To Lois.

When Moses reached Paradise Found, he parked in the lot and then walked in through the front door. No more sneaking in the back and avoiding Lois.

She always stepped into the center of the store, where she could greet a customer when the door buzzed. But this time she didn't. She stood at the counter staring off into space.

Moses took a couple of steps toward her. "Hallo, Lois."

Her eyes darted to him as if in surprise. "Oh. Moses."

"How are things this morning?"

She shrugged. "Fairly busy. It's the first time the shop has been quiet."

"Are you doing all right?"

"Jah." She gave him a half-hearted smile. "I'm fine."

His heart skipped a beat. He didn't believe her.

An hour later his phone rang, distracting Moses from staring at his computer screen. J&R Contractors.

He waited a long moment and then hit Accept. "Hello, this is Moses Lantz."

"Jeremy here. Good news! I just picked up your permits. We can start tomorrow."

"All right." Moses had waited so long to hear the news that it now seemed anticlimactic. Honestly, it seemed like one more loss for Lois. He knew how much she liked the field and the birds it attracted. "Do you need anything from me?"

"No. Just be prepared for us to arrive in the morning. Eight sharp."

"Thank you," Moses said.

He stared at the screen for another few minutes, thinking about Jane. *Lois.* There was no reason he couldn't keep writing to Jane. He'd make up an excuse for not meeting her. Then he could write for a few more weeks and then gradually stop writing. He took his notebook from his satchel and began writing.

> *Dear Jane,*
>   *Please forgive me . . .*

After he finished the letter, he focused on his work. Payroll. Ordering. Schedules. The light in the room faded some. It was six fifteen. He hadn't told Lois about the construction starting the next day. He bolted into the shop. She'd already left. All the lights were off and the front door was locked.

He hurried through the shop and out the back of the building. He glanced up at the windows to the apartment. There weren't any lights on, but it was hours until dusk. There was no reason for Lois to have lit a lamp.

A figure stepped in front of the window. Moses darted back into the rear of the building. The last thing he wanted was for Lois to think he was spying on her. He was a lot of things but hopefully not a creep.

On his way to the warehouse and his hovel behind it, he was tempted to mail his letter from the Paradise post office but decided against it. He'd mail it from Byler's Corner on Saturday. Lois—*Jane*—would hear from him—*Menno*—soon enough.

The next morning, Moses paced back and forth behind the store. Should he knock on Lois's door and tell her construction was starting? Or let her figure it out herself?

"What is happening?" Lois came flying around the corner of the building. She wore one of her green dresses and her hair was in a bun, but she wasn't wearing her apron or Kapp. "Moses!" She pointed at him. "Why didn't you tell me construction was starting?"

"I just found out yesterday, and when I remembered to say something you'd already closed up for the day."

"Were you too afraid to knock on my door and let me know?"

Jah, actually I was. He didn't say that. "I'm sorry. I should have warned you."

"What about the red-tailed hawks nesting in the pine tree?"

"Have you seen them?"

"No. But they still might come back. And there are sparrows in the maple trees on the edge of the woods. Can't you wait until September, when the last of their broods leave the nest?"

"The contractor won't be doing anything to the woods, just the field."

"They'll still be disturbed."

"I'm sorry," Moses said. "I know how much this field means to you."

She stared at him for a long moment, her eyes burning a hole through his heart, and then spun around. She stomped back up the stairs.

He wished he could tell her he needed to make a profit to pay for his Mamm's care and therapy. He didn't know how long he'd need to budget for, and it was expensive. Extremely so. The doctor said her physical health was good enough that she could live for another decade or two.

Moses spent the day between the office and the field, addressing questions about the property line, the plans to enlarge the septic system, and the need to adjust the location of the restrooms.

As he walked back to the shop his phone rang. *Casey.* Or at least the phone number of his family farm. It could be Walter.

"Hallo," Moses said.

"Casey here. Want to go with me to the park this evening? There's a volleyball tournament and a pie social."

Moses hesitated. Did he want to go to an Amish event? On the other hand, did he want to sit at his desk in his studio apartment by himself on a beautiful summer evening? "Sure," he said. "Want to grab a bite to eat at the café first?"

"Sounds good," Casey said. "But we should get sandwiches to go. People are meeting with picnic suppers at six."

"All right," Moses said. "I'll pick you up at five forty-five." After he ended the call, he wondered if Lois was going. She didn't get off until six—she'd be late. He needed to ask her.

As he walked into the shop, Isabelle was standing at the counter buying a candle and talking with Lois. He doubted he wanted to overhear what she was saying, but he couldn't help it. "Such a shame," Isabelle said. "It really is a lovely area. Of course, a month ago, I would have been happy to have the market going up, hoping Moses would sell me the shop."

"Have you decided about Charleston?" Lois asked.

"Yes. I've decided to go ahead and buy it. I feel bad leaving you. And Scotty and Barbara will be leaving soon too. You won't have much support left."

Either Lois didn't say anything or her reply was too low for

Moses to hear. He doubted Lois was offended by Isabelle's comment, but he was. Lois had Amy. And her church. And she had him, although he knew she didn't consider him an asset. He'd been nothing but an—opposite of that.

"Well, I'd better be on my way," Isabelle said. "I think I'll order some of these candles for my new shop."

Moses waited for the door to buzz and then waited another long moment. Then he stepped out into the shop.

Lois was staring off into space again. "Lois?"

She startled and then dropped the bird saltshaker she'd been holding. It shattered on the counter.

"Sorry." Moses turned toward the hall. "I'll get the broom and dustpan." When he came back, Lois was still staring at the broken ceramic pieces.

The door buzzed and a couple of tourists stepped into the shop.

"I'll clean this up," Moses said.

Lois slipped around the end of the counter, and he swept the pieces into the dustpan and then stepped behind the counter to see if there were any broken pieces on that side. He swept up what he could see and headed back to the cleaning closet, dumped the dustpan's contents in the garbage, and then grabbed the vacuum.

When he returned the tourists had left. Lois grabbed the vacuum out of his hand. "I'll do it."

"Are you going to the park this evening?" Before she could answer, he rushed ahead. "Because if you are, I can close and you can leave early."

She held the vacuum against her chest. "Why are you being nice to me?"

His face warmed. "I—"

"I'm planning on going to the park, but I don't need to leave early. Amy said she'd share their picnic with me."

"All right." He wouldn't press it. "I'll see you there. I'm going with Casey."

Her mouth shifted to the side. He thought she was going to smile—but she didn't. Instead she plugged in the vacuum.

When Lois arrived at the park at six thirty on her scooter, he smiled her way, trying to get her attention. But as she headed for the table where Amy and Bennie sat with their children, Lois turned her back on Moses and ignored him.

22

A week later, Lois stood at the window of Paradise Found and held her hands over her ears as the concrete truck's mixer spun in the parking lot. First it had been the excavators. Then the pounding to build the foundation frame. Now the concrete company had arrived. What havoc Moses had wreaked. He'd created as much chaos in her outer world now—and the world of her feathered friends—as he had in her inner world five years earlier. Her anger toward Moses nearly matched her sadness about Menno.

She ground her teeth. There was no way all the birds would stay in the woods. They probably believed a gigantic woodpecker had moved into the field. She was trying to accept that the property was changing and there was nothing she could do, and jah, the new market would help Amy and her family and others in the community, but the loss of the birds weighed heavily on her.

Why did Scotty have to sell the shop and land? Why did Moses have to buy it?

At noon, Moses came into the shop and told her to take a lunch break. "I insist," he said. "I'll take care of things here."

She scootered to the post office. She was happy to get away from the sound of the concrete truck.

She had two letters. One from Randy and one from Menno. She read the one from Randy first. It was an exact copy of the one he'd sent before, except he'd added, *You're being very disrespectful not to reply to my letters.* She hadn't written him back, but she hadn't meant to be disrespectful. She simply had no idea how to answer him.

Then she read Menno's. It was postmarked Saturday.

Please forgive me for not meeting you. I had an unforeseen emergency and no way to contact you. I hope you can see past my letting you down and continue with our correspondence.

Lois put the letter back in the envelope and slipped both letters into her apron pocket. She needed to go to Delaware and look for Menno. She wouldn't write him again until she had evidence he actually existed.

When she returned to the shop, Moses was ringing up a sale for an Englisch woman. When the customer left, Lois asked, "Would it be all right if I take Friday off?"

A puzzled expression passed over Moses's face.

Lois pulled Randy's letter from her pocket. "I've had a letter from my brother in Big Valley."

"Is everything all right?"

"I think so."

"Sure. If Evelyn is okay working by herself."

"Denki." She felt bad about her deception, but she wasn't

going to tell Moses what she was up to. She called Evelyn's grandmother's phone and left a message. Then when she heard the back door close, she called Dave, the driver her family had often hired from the time they first arrived in Lancaster County.

He had a cancellation that day and said he could take Lois. Just before six, Evelyn called back and said she was fine working by herself.

"I'll be gone before you arrive," Lois said. "But I should be back by midafternoon. I'll help close."

"All right," Evelyn said. "I'll see you then."

Lois hung up the phone feeling better than she had since the day Menno hadn't shown. He hadn't come to see her—but that didn't mean she couldn't go find him.

⁓

Friday morning, Dave arrived at seven thirty, before Moses or the builders arrived. Lois climbed in the back, not feeling comfortable enough to sit up front even though she'd known Dave for years. He'd been the one who drove Mamm and her to the funeral home after Dat passed. He was the one who drove her to Big Valley five years ago. He was the one who drove Amy to Big Valley to collect her. He was a kind older man and happy to see her.

Lois had checked the distance on her atlas the evening before. The trip was eighty miles. The first section was through the Pennsylvania countryside and across the border into Delaware. Lois marked the moment with a smile—her first trip outside of Pennsylvania. The next section was through the southern suburbs of Wilmington. The last third of the trip was through farm country.

When they reached Byler's Corner, a market came into view.

"I've heard about an Amish market over here," Dave said. "But I've never been."

"Jah . . ." Lois nearly pressed her face to the window. It appeared to be a big market.

"I'm not quite sure where this address is," Dave said. "But it's right around here somewhere." He slowed. "Oops, I missed it. I'll drive past the market and then come around again."

On the way back, Lois looked for the street address too.

"It should be right here, on the right." Dave stopped the car.

There was a building and to the side of it a shed. "I'll get out," Lois said, "and see if I can find it."

"I'll park a block down on the righthand side. Take your time."

"Thank you." Lois climbed out and pulled her last letter from Menno from her pocket. She reread the address, then turned toward the store across the street. That address almost matched Menno's, but it was odd numbered. She headed to the market building. Was that what Moses had in mind for the Paradise Amish Market? The thought left her unsettled for a moment. She went into the building, but there wasn't an office or mailboxes. Just a lot of booths with people, many of them Amish, selling baked goods, vegetables, quilts, garden benches, honey, and so much more.

She went out the side door toward the shed. In front of it was a locked mailbox with a keyhole. When she reached it, she saw the address on the side. It matched Menno's.

She knocked on the shed. No one responded. She tried the doorknob. It was locked.

She turned on her heels and returned to the building, asking vendor after vendor if they knew Menno Stoltzfus. None of them did. She wouldn't bother asking anyone in the outdoor booths.

There was no doubt about it. She'd been tricked. Who-ever Menno was, he wasn't trustworthy. Amy was probably right—most likely he didn't even exist. Someone was using the mailbox for the circle letters. And her letters. No, *Jane's* letters.

She continued down the street to where Dave had parked. When she climbed into the back seat, he simply inquired, "Where to now?" She appreciated that he didn't ask whether she'd found who she was looking for.

She hesitated a moment.

"Lois?"

"Have you ever been to the Delaware shore?"

"A long time ago."

"Would you mind going again?"

"Not at all," he answered as he pulled back onto the road.

Lois waded in the Atlantic Ocean as killdeers scurried over the sand, darting back and forth at her feet. The screams of gulls filled the air, and in the distance pelicans flew above the waves.

She fantasized that Menno would show up, somehow knowing she'd been looking for him at the market, some-how knowing to follow her to the Delaware Seashore State Park. She chuckled wryly at how ridiculous she was. "Give it up," she said out loud. "Menno is a figment of your imagination."

She picked up a rock and held it in her hand. Then she threw it into the ocean—it didn't go very far—and said, "Goodbye, Menno!" as it plunked into the water. A bigger wave came rolling in toward her, and although she started backing up it still lapped the bottom of her dress.

She thought of her parents at the Maryland shore as newlyweds nearly forty-five years ago. If only they had come to the seashore again before they'd died. If only her family hadn't always been scrambling to make ends meet after they left Big Valley.

She turned toward the trail that led to the parking lot. Dave was standing at the top of the hill as if guarding her. She waved, then turned back to the killdeers and the Atlantic to whisper goodbye.

When she arrived back at Paradise Found, Amy was pulling her buggy around as if leaving. Lois quickly handed Dave a check for the agreed-upon payment and thanked him. Then she grabbed her bag and scrambled out of the back seat of the car and called out to Amy, "Wait!"

Amy pulled back on the reins. "There you are. Evelyn said you took the day off to go to Big Valley. I was worried."

"I'll explain." Lois hurried around to the other side of the buggy and climbed up. As she sat down, she said, "I didn't say I went to Big Valley, although I implied it. Moses must have told Evelyn. I went to Delaware."

"After Menno?"

"Jah." Lois slumped against the back of the seat. "No surprise, I didn't find him."

"I'm sorry." Amy shot her a sympathetic smile.

"You were right—he *is* like one of those online people."
Lois explained about the locked mailbox. "Basically, I fell
for a fake person."

"I wish I hadn't been right," Amy replied.

"Jah, me too." Lois took her peanut butter sandwich from
her backpack. She and Dave had stopped for lunch at a road-
side cafe on the way home. "Want half?"

Amy laughed. "Sure. Just like when we were in school."
Back then they shared all their food, picnic-style.

"I have apple slices and cookies too." She'd given a plate
of cookies to Dave. "Peanut butter."

"Of course you do." Amy took the half sandwich. "Now
what?"

"I had another letter from Randy. He said Nathan is still
willing to marry me."

Amy groaned. "You're not thinking about going back to
Big Valley, are you?"

"I might if it wasn't for Nathan."

"And the fact your brother wants to marry you off."

Lois held her sandwich in midair and sighed. "My life, as
it is, in Paradise Township isn't sustainable."

"But it is. You have a job. An apartment."

"And a bishop who doesn't want me living alone and a
boss who wants the apartment and who barely tolerates me."
Though Moses had been nicer lately.

"Do you regret not seriously pursuing John?"

Lois hesitated for a moment and then said, "No."

"You don't sound very convincing."

Tears stung her eyes but not over John. "He wasn't right
for me, and he's too nice for me to pursue just to use him
so I can stay here."

Evelyn opened the front door of the shop. "Lois! Can you come in? I have a question."

"I'd better go." Lois took a bite of the sandwich and gathered up her bag. "Denki for listening."

"Any time," Amy said.

Lois blew a kiss to her friend, jumped down, and hurried into the shop.

On Monday afternoon, she scootered to the pond and then made her way along the run to have something current to write to the circle letter. A ruby-throated hummingbird buzzed by, and then a fledgling bluebird hopped along on the other side of the run. As she turned to go, a male goldfinch pecked at a dried purple coneflower a few feet away. Lois froze and watched it for a few minutes, committing the image to memory.

When she reached her scooter, she waited as an Amtrak train flew by. Then she continued on to find the Strasburg Rail Road train had stopped at the Paradise station. From there she scootered to the post office. She had a circle letter from Teresa and a letter from Menno. Why had she been so trusting? She felt the same way she had after Moses dumped her, before she arrived home and found Mamm unresponsive in the apartment. All by herself. Lois shouldn't have gone to the river that night.

She took a giant step to the garbage can and dropped Menno's letter inside. She wasn't ready to return to her apartment and listen to the construction racket outside her window. She'd make one more stop.

When she arrived at the care center, she scanned the parking lot. No sight of Moses's SUV. No doubt he was at the shop, conspiring with the builders.

She parked her scooter and headed inside. This time she knew the drill. She signed in, took a visitor badge, and turned left toward room 134.

When she arrived the door was half open. She knocked.

"Come in, dear," a sweet voice said. *Anna.*

Lois pushed the door all the way open. Anna sat in front of the window, an empty chair beside her. "Hallo, Anna. It's me—".

"I know." Anna smiled and patted the chair beside her. "Lois, come sit." She turned back to the window. "Let's watch the birds together."

23

Two weeks passed by quickly with the construction going on behind the shop. It was everything Moses had dreamed of—soon he'd have a tourist destination in Lancaster County. Something he'd wanted since he first saw the market in Delaware.

He guessed he'd been in denial, but he hadn't asked Joey about the Byler family yet. He hadn't done more research on Paul and Faith. He hadn't asked his mother for any more information. He hadn't requested a copy of his birth certificate, which he couldn't locate in the important papers he had in the lockbox in his apartment.

No, he'd been doing his best to not think about any of it. Or about Sara, except to talk to her about the café. Or about Jane. He hadn't received a reply to any of his—*Menno's*—letters that he'd written after July 8.

He'd been putting all his energy into the Paradise Amish Market. Things were going well, finally, as far as his businesses were concerned. The grocery store was having the best summer yet. Business at the café was doing better. It seemed Sara had been putting more effort into managing it. And Paradise Found's profits were higher than last year, even with paying more wages with Evelyn working part-time.

But two things weren't going well. The first was Sara. She still seemed convinced that they'd pick their relationship back up in three months—two months now—even though he'd made it clear he wasn't interested. She continued to claim they'd "gotten back together" before.

The other thing that wasn't going well was Lois. She was so kind and open with customers, genuinely wanting to help them, providing tidbits of information about Lancaster County and special events and answering their questions about the Amish. She worked hard to make sales in a helpful, not pushy way. But she still barely tolerated him.

After he finished up at his office, he drove over to Casey's parents' farm to talk with Casey. The builders believed they'd be done by the last week of August. Moses planned to open the market the Friday before Labor Day. He wouldn't start to see a profit from the market until the next year, since the summer season was the most profitable, but he was sure his investment would pay off.

He turned down the lane without looking across the road to where he'd grown up. He parked by the workshop. The door was open. Casey often worked after supper for a couple of hours.

Moses knocked on the doorframe and said, "Hallo."

Casey looked up from the birdhouse on his bench. It was identical to the one Moses had bought for Mamm. He gave Moses his wide smile. "Hallo."

After they chatted about the hot weather and the thunderstorm that was brewing, Moses said he wanted to give

Casey an update about the market. "Have you decided about whether you'd like to manage it or not?"

"You think I can manage it and sell my things?"

"Jah," Moses said. "You can do the market business part during the week. It will take several hours, but you'll be saving time not having to commute to Delaware."

Casey nodded. "That's what I figured too. And I'd have a guaranteed spot inside before Christmas?"

"Jah. You can be inside or outside for the few weeks we have it open this fall. And then inside for sure through the winter. You can decide if you want to move outside by the time the weather warms again."

"All right." He placed both hands on the workbench. "I'd like to take the job."

On his way home, Moses decided to swing by the care center to visit Mamm before she went to bed. As he parked his SUV, Lois came out the front door. She hopped on her scooter and sped away, with her reflective vest on, before he could call out to her. When he signed in at the counter, he scanned the visitors' sheet. Lois had signed in at 3:14 to visit his Mamm. She'd stayed for over four hours. His heart lurched.

When he reached Mamm's room, she was already in bed asleep. It seemed Lois had helped get her ready for bed. Most likely she'd tucked her in. Moses kissed Mamm's forehead. He had a funny feeling that Lois had probably done the same just minutes before.

That evening, Moses sat at his desk in his apartment and stared for a few minutes at the painted bunting collage he'd bought that first day at Paradise Found, which made him think of Lois, which made him miss Jane. Then he wrote to the circle group about what he'd seen that day in the woods on the property—but he wrote, *the woods close by*, implying the location was in Delaware. He'd seen a northern flicker, with a flash of yellow in its wings, fly up from the ground as he walked to the back of the property. It was a woodpecker but it mostly dug for ants and beetles in the ground.

The leaves on the maples were already yellowing. Soon the sparrows' nests would be visible. He'd also seen a white-crowned sparrow sitting on the branch of a pepperbush. He wrote about it too. It watched him until the builders' circular saw started up and, startled, the bird flew away.

Had birds left the woods because of the construction? Would they stay away once the market started? A dog on the neighboring farm had barked and a wood thrush darted past him.

Moses wrote about all of those birds, leaving out any mentions of construction, and then addressed the envelope, put the letter inside, and sealed it.

He was tempted to write to Jane again but was sure she—*Lois*—wouldn't write back.

A fence would protect the woods on the market side, just as it did on the neighboring farm side. It would keep both people and dogs out. Although perhaps some people would want to go into the woods. Lois had already incorporated a bird theme into the shop—perhaps they . . . Perhaps *he* could add trails through the woods for customers who came to the market. Maybe even a couple of picnic tables. Perhaps he could add a bird theme to the market too.

He'd have to come up with a way to bring up the topic

with Lois. In the last Flight of Doves report, Teresa had encouraged everyone to emulate birds and be a good parent and/or leader. She'd written about how birds will risk their lives to distract a predator from their young, and how some corvids—crows, ravens, jays—raise their young up to two years, which makes those birds more adaptable and flexible to life's challenges. Teresa had encouraged everyone, in whatever position and stage of life they were in, to emulate birds and be the very best leaders they could be. *Nurture others*, she'd written. *But depend on their strengths too.*

Moses definitely relied on Lois's strengths at the shop. And now she was helping his Mamm too. Who did Lois truly have, besides Amy, to care for her?

The next morning, he tried. He asked Lois how she was doing. She answered, "Fine." After he commented on how many birdhouses had sold that week—nine—he said, "I've been thinking about the woods and how we could incorporate the bird theme of the shop into the market and somehow tie the woods in too."

She gave him a blank stare.

"We could order more birding books, specifically on birding in Pennsylvania."

"You wanted me to get rid of the bird products, remember?"

"Right. But I changed my mind after seeing how well everything is selling." He didn't add, *Remember?*

"So now you like birds?"

He wanted to say he'd always liked birds, but that was something he used to tease her about in school—how much she liked birds. He'd pretended he thought it babyish, all while he was going birding with his Mamm every chance he got. "It's not about liking birds—it's about what's selling in the shop."

She crossed her arms.

He took a step backward. And then another. "Think about it."

She scowled.

A few more retreating steps, and he was in his office. How could he have been so horrible to Lois, fifteen years ago and five years ago and four months ago too? Jane was all sweetness and light, while Lois was a pain.

But she was only a pain to him. And he'd made her that way.

~

Three weeks later, the building was completed and the concrete pads were finished for the outside stalls and food trucks. That Friday, the Paradise Amish Market opened with thirty vendors, including Casey and Amy. It was a warm, sunny day, so Moses put all the vendors outside, hoping the sight would attract more business. He placed picnic tables inside the shelter building and raised the garage doors so people would have a shady place to sit after they bought sausages, doughnuts, slices of pie, lemonade, and coffee.

The lot was full of cars, and several buggies were parked at the hitching posts. The buggies of the vendors were parked near the newly fenced-off section of the remaining grassy area, where their horses grazed.

Moses stopped by Amy's stall and waited until she finished with a customer. "How's it going?" he asked.

Amy smiled. "Better than I expected the first day to be. I've sold fifteen items or so. I'm hopeful."

"Who's watching the kids?"

"My Mamm." She leaned forward a little. "I haven't seen Lois yet."

"The shop has been busy. Evelyn is working too, so Lois should be able to take a break soon."

A few minutes later, Sara arrived at the market. When he excused himself to go to his office, she followed. Without closing the door, she said, "I'm beginning to think I've had enough of you."

Moses sat down in his chair. "All right . . ."

"In fact, I'm done."

"Done?" he asked in a lower tone.

"Jah. Done with the café and done with you."

Moses hesitated for a moment and then said, "I see."

"I'll work for a few more weeks until you find someone to replace me. But then I'm going back to my uncle's restaurant."

Moses stood. "Thank you for the time you've worked for me. I appreciate it."

Sara uncrossed her arms and pointed her right index finger at him. "Is that all you're going to say to me? After all of these years?" More like months. They'd really only dated from February until the end of June. It had taken him that long to—what? Grow desperate about being alone? Get over Lois? And yet he hadn't tried to contact Lois once during that time.

Moses spoke quietly. "I'm sorry. I know I haven't handled this well."

"Sorry?" Her voice was louder. "You're nothing but a jerk, do you know that? A wealthy jerk—"

He winced.

"—but a jerk nonetheless."

"I think you should go," Moses said. "And if you'd rather not work at the café any longer, I understand."

Sara glared at him and then left the office. She slammed the back door. At least she hadn't gone out the front and somehow involved Lois in her antics.

Although he couldn't help but wonder how much Lois had heard of the conversation. No doubt she agreed with Sara. He was a jerk.

24

After Sara slammed out the back door of the building, Lois retreated to the counter, a little mortified that she'd been eavesdropping. But just a little. The office door was open and Sara had been really loud.

A few minutes later, Moses stepped into the shop and asked, "Where's Evelyn?"

"I told her to go spend some time in the market."

Moses said, "I'll watch the shop so you can go look too. Amy's hoping you'll stop by her booth."

"Oh." Lois reached under the counter for her bag. Moses didn't seem upset by Sara's words or exit. "I'll take my lunch with me."

"Does it happen to be a peanut butter and grape jelly sandwich and an apple?" He gave her a smile. A normal, kind smile.

"Jah." She hated when he referred to something from their school days. Sure, she liked peanut butter and that's what she had in her lunch every single day, but it was also an economical choice—both when she was a scholar and now. His knowing what was in her lunch bag felt weirdly intimate. She gave him a wave as she stepped around him. "See you soon." Once she was outside, she made her way toward the booths to the east of the building, stopping at Casey's first. He was counting a wad of money.

"Looks like sales are going well," she said.

He glanced up at her and smiled. "Lois. Did Moses allow you to escape your cage?"

"Something like that." She grinned. "Your Amish birdhouses are selling well in the shop. We'll be ready for more soon."

An Amish man whom Lois didn't know approached Casey and said, "I'm working at the food cart. Moses is letting me store extra propane in the shed, and we need it already."

"All right." Casey held up a key ring. "I can unlock it for you." He put up a sign that read Be Back in Five Minutes.

"I can watch your booth." Lois held up her bag. "I'll eat my lunch while I wait. If anyone's interested in a purchase, I'll chat with them until you return."

A couple of Englischers stopped and looked through Casey's toy trains. "Will you be back tomorrow?" the man asked.

"Jah," Lois said. "I actually work in the shop." She motioned to it. "My friend is the craftsman. He'll be back in a few minutes and will definitely be here tomorrow too."

When Casey returned, Lois walked to the other side of the market to see Amy.

"Finally!" Amy stood at the edge of her booth. "I've been waiting for you."

"I'm here for a few minutes."

"Who's watching the shop?"

"Moses."

Amy's eyebrows shot up. "That's nice of him."

Lois concentrated on the display of candles to her left. "Mind if I do some rearranging?"

Amy laughed. "Did you just change the subject?"

Lois smiled. "Maybe." Then she started moving the candles around. "How do you like working at the market so far?"

Amy stepped closer to Lois. "I feel a little guilty. It's so much easier than my work at home. I'm going to have to think of something really nice to do for my Mamm."

Lois put three pink candles in a row in front. "You deserve a little break. And a chance to have your own business. It's only two days a week. And Bennie will have them tomorrow, right?"

"I'll bring Maggie with me and put her in the front pack. Do you think that will work?"

"Absolutely," Lois said. "She'll be your secret marketing tool. Sales will probably soar." Lois could just imagine the Englischers sneaking photos of the Amish baby strapped to her mother.

The next morning, Lois stood at her window over the market. Moses and Casey had been working together to check in the vendors, but then Moses headed to the parking lot. Lois opened her door. He drove away just before nine, right before the market opened.

And he didn't return all morning. Because Evelyn was also working, Lois went out to the market around noon to see if Casey needed anything.

"A bathroom break."

"You've got it," she said.

When he returned, she headed over to Amy's. Several women had gathered around the stall. One asked Amy if the baby was her first.

"Oh, no," Amy said. "She's my fourth."

"Oh, goodness. You have your hands full."

"Jah," Amy said. "And so is my heart."

Lois smiled. Amy always knew what to say. After the women left, Lois stepped inside the booth. "Do you need a break?"

"Jah." Amy swayed as she spoke. "Maggie is going to wake up any minute, starving."

"Take her up to my place and feed her," Lois said. "I'll watch your booth."

Amy showed her the change box and the notebook where she recorded the sales. "I'll be fast."

"Take your time." Lois handed Amy the key to her apartment. "Get something to eat while you're up there."

Amy grabbed the diaper bag. "See you soon."

When people stopped at Amy's booth, Lois said that her best friend made the candles and soap. "She's a young Amish woman with four little ones." She'd learned in the shop that people were more likely to buy an item if they had information—a story—about the person who created it. "She makes the candles and soaps during naptime and after the kids are in bed." Lois motioned toward the shop. "She has her baby with her today. She'll be right back."

One of the tourists bought five bars of soap—for her friends back home—and another bought a candle. Another said she'd swing back by the booth before she left the market.

"Make sure and stop in at Paradise Found too," Lois said.

"We carry items you won't find here in the market. Greeting cards. Hand towels. Tablecloths. That sort of thing."

"I will," the woman said.

Perhaps Moses would be willing to carry Amy's candles in the shop.

"Lois!"

She turned her head toward the familiar voice. "Scotty!" She stepped outside and gave him a hug. She seldom hugged anyone, but Scotty was an exception. "Are you getting ready to move?"

"Not yet. The farm still hasn't sold."

"That's a shame." But she was relieved. That meant Moses hadn't bought it.

"I've stayed away from the shop on purpose. I didn't want to interfere. But I heard Moses fired you and then rehired you."

"From Isabelle?"

Scotty nodded. "I would have talked with Moses if he hadn't hired you back. He assured me he'd keep you on."

"Jah, well, we seem to have come to an understanding."

"So everything's all right now?" Scotty's serious expression showed how much he cared.

Tears pricked at the backs of her eyes, and her throat thickened. Things weren't all right.

"Lois?"

She tried to smile.

"What's wrong?"

She couldn't pour her heart out to Scotty, even if he was the closest thing she had to a parent. "Oh, I'm just trying to figure out what to do with my life is all." She forced a smile, trying to hide the sadness she'd felt since Menno stood her up. Behind Scotty, Amy approached. "You remember my friend Amy," Lois said to Scotty, as she reached for the baby. "This is her youngest, Maggie."

"Good to see you again," Scotty said to Amy. He reached for Maggie's chubby little hand and shook it. "And nice to meet you." Then he turned his attention back to Lois. "Let me know if you need anything. Or someone to brainstorm with. Barb and I are always available for you."

"Thank you." She hoisted Maggie higher in her arms. She was getting heavy. "I'll let you know."

⁓

Monday, Lois stopped by to see Anna. As they had on Lois's three previous visits, they sat and watched the birds together. A male pine warbler, with its bright yellow throat, pecked away at the seeds.

"He's a pretty boy," Anna said. "What's he called?"

Lois told her.

"Denki. I used to know all their names."

The warbler left and a song sparrow landed in the acrylic feeder. A little brown bird. Anna reached for Lois's hand and said, "Yea, the sparrow hath found an house, and the swallow a nest for herself, where she may lay her young, even thine altars, O LORD of hosts, my King, and my God."

Lois whispered, "Psalm 84:3."

"Jah." Anna squeezed her hand. "Gott takes care of us." Anna exhaled slowly and then whispered, "But I still want to go home."

Lois patted Anna's hand.

After a few minutes of silence, Anna said, "Moses and I used to go birding together."

"Really? Moses did?"

"Jah. He's my boy."

"He is," Lois said. Before, she hadn't been sure whether Anna knew that. She hadn't mentioned Moses yet.

"I had a brother," Anna said.

"What was his name?"

"Paul."

Lois thought of the article on Moses's computer screen. Paul was the name of the man who'd died. "Where did you grow up, Anna?"

"Near Gap."

That was less than ten miles east of Paradise, and according to the article, near where the accident happened.

They sat in silence for a while, but then Anna asked, "How are you doing?"

"Me?" Lois asked.

Anna nodded. "Are you sad?"

Lois exhaled and then took Anna's hand. "I have been sad."

"Why?"

"I thought I'd met someone . . ." She wouldn't go into too many details. "Someone who cared about me, but then it turned out he didn't."

"I'm sorry. Did you learn anything from this person?"

Lois hesitated. "Maybe." She'd shared more with Menno than she had with anyone besides Amy. She'd been vulnerable with him, far more than she'd been with John. Maybe even more than she'd been with Moses.

If she could trust someone she'd never met, could she learn to be more trusting of people she actually knew? Not everyone was like her brother, with her worst interests in mind.

Tears stung her eyes. She missed her own parents, even

more so when she spent time with Anna. But being with Anna reminded her to turn toward God. To trust Him for her future. And for that she was thankful.

On Tuesday during her lunch break, while Moses watched the shop, Lois scootered to the post office. She had a letter from Teresa and the birding circle and another letter from her brother.

> *Why haven't you answered any of my letters? I have no other choice than to write to Bishop Stephen and insist he send you back home.*

Lois eyed the garbage can. But throwing the letter away wouldn't make Randy—or her problems—go away.

She opened the letter from Teresa and first skimmed down to Menno's entry.

> *I saw an American avocet at Delaware Shore State Park last week.*

He went on to describe the bird's stilt-like legs, its up-turned beak, and its white and black body.

> *It was scrabbling around in the sand for crustaceans but occasionally would grab an insect out of the air.*

Lois was tempted to write Teresa and tell her that Menno didn't actually exist, but obviously he existed in some way. Just not in an honest one. But then again, Jane didn't really exist either. And Lois didn't want to have to confess that, not yet anyway.

Next Lois read Teresa's missive.

Like birds, we Plain people tend to flock together. We offer mutual aid when someone is sick, we bring meals when a baby is born, we do chores when there's a death in the family. But do we reach out to make new friends, among fellow Plain people and among Englischers?

She wrote that Menno—Lois sighed—had already mentioned a starling murmuration, which Teresa said was truly enchanting to watch.

Many think the starlings come together to evade predators and meet prospective mates. But a more popular belief is that they do it to strengthen friendships and make new ones. A sort of shared experience. We certainly share many experiences, but do we look for experiences to share with others we may not know well? Ones who don't belong to our district? Follow the example of our feathered friends and keep the bonds you have strong—and look for new ones too.

Lois thought of the Paradise Amish Market. Moses had brought a group of vendors—Amish, Mennonite, and Englisch—together in a community. She'd been so worried about the birds, but they hadn't left the woods, unless it was to start their migrations. And Moses was thinking about opening up that area for people to see more birds. Or maybe just *be.*

She would look for new bonds to form within the vendor group. Honestly, besides Amy and Bennie—and Anna—Lois felt pretty short on friends. For a moment she thought of Moses. Could they be friends again?

She wrinkled her nose. Nee, she didn't think so.

25

The third week of September, Moses and Casey moved most of the Paradise market into the building, leaving a few booths to draw attention from the road plus the food carts outside. Friday was overcast and chilly but dry. Business had been good again. The big sign on the highway helped, but there were lots of local people he recognized—both Englisch and Amish—who came for a cup of coffee and a pastry and sat at the picnic tables and then picked up a few items, such as a loaf of bread and a basket of produce.

When Moses left the market Friday in the late afternoon before the shop closed, he drove straight to the café. It was Sara's last night of work. The new manager, Jennifer, would take over in the morning.

Sara met him with a smile. Relieved, Moses asked if she had time to sit for a minute.

"Sure," she said. "I'll give you an update on Jennifer."

They sat at the back table with cups of coffee. After Sara

ran through a list of concerns, most of which didn't sound too serious, she asked, "Have you heard my news?"

"News?"

She smiled a little. "You never were very good at gossip."

That was true. "What's going on?"

"I've been courting Mark Miller for a couple of weeks. Things are getting serious already."

"Mark Miller? Are you going to join the Amish?"

"No. He's going to become Mennonite."

"What about the family mill?"

"We'll see what his Dat says. He may end up working in Holland with me. Perhaps we can take over my uncle's restaurant in a few years."

"Well," Moses said. "Congratulations. I've always liked Mark." If only Mark had taken Sara home from the river five years ago instead of taking Lois. It would have saved all of them a lot of heartache. "Wait."

"What?"

"Never mind."

"No. Ask."

"What about Evelyn?"

Sara rubbed her earlobe. "They broke up a couple of months ago. You didn't know that?"

"I wasn't sure."

"She's going out with—"

"John."

Sara nodded.

So it was official. Poor Lois. Or lucky Lois. "Well, I'm happy for you and Mark. He's a good guy."

Sara smiled a little.

Moses smiled back. "Thank you for your work here at the

café. You've done a good job. Thank you, too, for your—" he tilted his head— "friendship. I want only the best for you."

"Denki." Sara placed a hand on the table. "I want the best for you too. I hope you'll find your person."

He suppressed a sigh and didn't respond.

As he waited to turn onto the highway, intending to go left and head to the warehouse, he hesitated even though there was a break in the traffic. He flipped his turn signal to the right.

When he arrived at the shop, Lois was vacuuming the carpet. She turned it off.

"How was business today?" he asked.

"*Gut.*" She gave him a questioning look. "Did you forget something?"

"For sure and for certain. I've been forgetting it for the last five years."

She wrinkled her nose.

A lot had happened five years ago. Moses spoke softly. "I should have gone after you to Big Valley."

Her face grew pale as she gripped the vacuum cleaner.

"I'm sorry—"

"Nee," she said. "It all worked out. For the best. I'd prefer not to talk about it." Then she turned away from him and unplugged the vacuum.

"Lois?"

She heard him because she waved her hand, as if shooing him away, carrying the vacuum down the hall with her other hand. He heard her put it in the closet. And then the back door opened and closed and her key turned in the lock.

Moses leaned against the counter and took a deep breath. Once again Lois had pushed him away. But there was something there. Pain, maybe. Perhaps she truly wanted nothing to do with him, but she had cared for him five years ago. Dare he hope she might again?

Because he couldn't deny it any longer. He cared for her. He'd never stopped. If only she'd let him apologize.

~

The next day was cool, but the market drew in the most visitors yet. Moses didn't go to Delaware for the first Saturday in years. He'd asked Joey to call him if needed, but he hadn't heard a word.

When the sausage cart nearly ran out of propane, Moses said he'd go buy some. Casey asked if he could ride along and grab a few more birdhouses to sell while Evelyn watched his booth.

On their way, Moses told Casey about his conversation with Sara.

"That's a relief," Casey said.

"What's a relief?"

"That Sara has a new plan."

"Jah," Moses said. "I felt so bad about the accident all these years that I think . . ." His voice trailed off. He'd escaped the accident without any physical injuries but it had paralyzed him in other ways.

"You've taken too much responsibility for that wreck."

Sara had needed a ride home that night, but Moses hadn't wanted to take her alone in his car. He'd volunteered to drive Casey's and leave his at the river. The two planned to pick it up the next day. "I almost killed both of you."

"Sara could have killed all three of us."

"What do you mean?"

"She reached over the back seat and tried to grab the steering wheel."

Moses didn't remember that. He did remember Sara, unconscious, and Casey, writhing in pain with his leg twisted beneath him, both on the ground as he stumbled from the car.

"As you were going around that curve."

"I was going too fast."

"Maybe a little, but you wouldn't have wrecked if she hadn't grabbed the wheel."

Moses's heart raced. "Why didn't you tell me that before?"

"I tried to. That night, right before they put me in the ambulance. I told the police too."

Perhaps that was why the police hadn't charged him. He'd taken a breathalyzer test at the scene of the accident and passed it with 0.0 percent. He hadn't been drinking. But he still feared he'd be charged with reckless driving. Perhaps Casey's testimony had saved him.

Maybe he wasn't entirely at fault for the accident after all. Maybe Sara hadn't become harsher after the accident. Maybe she'd been that way all along.

Casey asked, "Do you remember how your Dat reacted at the hospital?"

"I'll never forget." Moses tightened his grip on the steering wheel to keep his hands from shaking. His Dat had yelled, *"You could have killed yourself. What were you thinking? Never would I have expected this from you."* Moses had been devastated. His parents had always been supportive and encouraging. Always trusting. When he'd made a mistake, they'd corrected him and then talked him through what to do next time. One time, he'd been helping a farmhand and had fallen in front of a draft horse. Moses rolled just in time and escaped being crushed. Dat had been shaken but not angry.

But the car accident was different.

"He really loved you," Casey said.

"Not that night." Moses exhaled. "I disappointed him horribly." Dat had hired a driver a week later to take both of them to the river and collect Moses's car. It was as if he didn't trust Moses to drive home alone. And then Dat passed away several months later, and Moses realized how much stress he'd been under with Mamm's memory problems and his businesses. Moses had contributed to his stress. He doubted his Dat would have died so young—at sixty-nine—without all of that.

"No, your Dat really did love you. Especially that night," Casey answered.

Moses didn't see it that way—although now the article about Paul's death came to mind. If Moses had been that baby in the car, his parents had already been impacted by one horrible accident Moses had survived. He eased his hold on the steering wheel. Perhaps the accident five years ago had triggered his father's memory—and his fears.

He'd carried the weight of that night for so long. Perhaps he could finally forgive himself.

They reached the farm supply store and Moses had the six tanks of propane refilled. Then they stopped by Casey's workshop. As they pulled away with the birdhouses in the back, Moses asked, "Are you happy with your woodworking booth and managing the market? Is that what you want to do?"

"Oh, I'm happy enough."

"What would you rather be doing?"

"Honestly?"

"Jah."

"Farming."

That had always been Casey's dream. But after he broke his leg so badly, it seemed as if farming wasn't an option for him anymore. "Do you think you can do it now?" Moses asked.

"Jah. My balance is better. So is my stamina. Sure, I limp, but I help Dat with the seeding and dragging and manure spreading. I do as well as he does, if not a little better."

"Can you take over the farm from him?"

"Nee. My oldest brother is leasing a place—he'll come back and take over the farm when Dat retires."

Moses thought about the farm on Meadow Lane that Scotty was trying to sell. If Moses had a couple million dollars he'd buy it for Casey. Or for Lois. He glanced over at his friend. Moses hoped Lois might take him back, and yet, would Casey be the better husband for her? "You should ask Lois out."

"I couldn't do that to—"

"To her?"

Casey shook his head. "I couldn't do that to you."

Moses's heart lurched. He turned toward the shop and drove between the cherry trees, their golden-green leaves shimmering in the sunlight.

"You have a grocery store, a café, a shop, and two markets. You're set business-wise and financially. What do you want? Where is your heart right now?" Casey asked.

Moses turned toward his friend. "Down this lane. In that shop. My heart is Lois. It's always been Lois. But she won't have me."

"Have you asked her?"

295

"I've tried to talk with her."

Casey pointed to a buggy parked close to the shop. A man climbed out. "You need to tell her how you feel. And soon. Because that looks like Bishop Stephen, with support, going in to talk with her."

26

Lois had three customers in line to check out when the door buzzed again. Evelyn was still at the market, filling in for Casey. Hopefully she'd return soon. Lois stepped to the right a little and said, "Willkumm." She froze.

Somehow she managed to force a smile and chirped, "I'll be with you soon." She quickly rang up the first customer, placed the items in the bag, and then ran the woman's credit card as she asked, "Have you been out to the market?"

"Not yet," the woman said. "We're headed there next."

"Make sure and try one of the sticky buns from the food carts. They're a true Amish experience."

The woman smiled. "Thank you. I'll do that."

"The coffee is really good too."

Lois also chatted with the next two people in line as she checked them out, doing her best to keep her normal pace and give the customers a pleasant experience. Then she took a deep breath and said, "Bishop Stephen, hallo." She exhaled. "Randy. Nathan. How can I help you?"

All three had their hats in their hands. Randy appeared annoyed, but Nathan smiled. Creepily. Closer to a sneer.

"We're here on serious business," Bishop Stephen said.

Randy stepped forward. "*Schvesta*, you haven't answered my letters."

"Jah."

"Why not?"

She shrugged. She figured the less she said the better.

"Lois, you misunderstood me before you left Big Valley," Nathan said. "You overreacted."

She took a step backward.

Bishop Stephen stepped forward. "John said the two of you aren't courting any longer."

Lois nodded.

Bishop Stephen cleared his throat. "We've come because it's time you move home to Big Valley."

Lois couldn't keep quiet any longer. "It's not home."

"Your brother and his family are there. And you've had a perfectly valid marriage proposal."

Lois crossed her arms.

"I've spent the last two hours speaking with your brother and Nathan. Both have spent months in prayer for you and want the best for you. You'll be well cared for in Big Valley."

Lois let her arms drop to her sides and squared her shoulders. Then she mounted her stool behind the counter. It didn't make her as tall as any of the men, but it gave her more confidence. "I appreciate your concern for me, but I have a job here and a home. I have a bank account and support. I have a church. Even though I don't live with a family here, I am accountable to others. I am not on my own." Jah, she could use more friends, but she wasn't without help.

"You need to be under the authority of a man," Randy said. "Either me or a husband. Nathan is your only option."

Lois wanted to put her finger to her open mouth and gag, but she knew that wouldn't do any good. "If you remember," she said slowly, "I courted Nathan. We're not compatible."

"Nonsense," Randy said.

Nathan's eyes grew darker. "You're right that we weren't a good match—you were far too headstrong. But I'm guessing you've grown up some since then. I'd hope so at twenty-five. . . ."

The back door opened and closed.

"Headstrong? Because I protested you beating your sixteen-year-old son for arriving home fifteen minutes late because the car he was riding in had a flat tire?"

Bishop Stephen turned toward Nathan, his eyes wide.

"You challenged and disrespected—" Nathan stopped talking as he stared toward the hallway.

Lois shifted her gaze in that direction.

"What's going on here?" Moses towered over all three of the men.

Lois stayed on the stool and kept quiet.

Randy stepped forward, his hand extended. "I'm Lois's brother, Randy Yoder. I've come to take her home."

Moses shook his hand and then turned toward Nathan, taking his. "And who are you?" Was he squeezing Nathan's hand?

"Nathan."

Moses calmly said, "Pleased to meet you," as he finally let go of Nathan's hand. Then he turned to Lois, his back blocking the view of the other men, and mouthed, *Are you okay?*

She shook her head as subtly as she could. He turned back to the men. "Lois just signed a lease on her apartment and a contract for her job, each for a year. I need to hold her accountable to both."

"Nonsense," Nathan said. "You can't do that."

"Business is business." Moses shrugged. "Besides, I have some information I've been meaning to share with Bishop Stephen." He nodded toward the front door. "Do you mind?"

Bishop Stephen glanced at Randy, who said, "Go ahead."

For the first time since Moses bought the shop, Lois didn't want him to leave, not even to step outside for a few minutes. She needed a friend at the moment, and Moses was the only one available.

But he led the way and Bishop Stephen followed.

Lois quickly filled the silence. "How is Deanna doing? How are the kids?" She called them all kids, even though the boys were just younger than she was.

"*Gut*," Randy said. "The kids, the girls especially, miss you."

"So do my children." Nathan twirled his hat in his hands. "All of them. They need a mother."

Lois was hardly mother material for his older children. The boy who had been sixteen when she fled Randy's home would be eighteen now. She hoped he'd left his father's house.

The front door opened and Moses walked back into the shop. Bishop Stephen held the door and said, "Randy, I'm no longer convinced we need to make a decision about this today. We can talk about it in the buggy. Let's go."

Randy opened his mouth and then closed it. Nathan's eyes

narrowed as he glanced from Bishop Stephen to Lois to Moses and then glared at her. She crossed her arms again, waved her fingers, and stayed on the stool. "Please tell Deanna and the children hello," she called out. She wanted to say she missed them, but it felt insincere. Jah, she missed them, but she didn't miss Big Valley.

Randy grunted something—Lois couldn't tell if it was affirmative or negative. Then the three visitors walked out the door.

When it clicked shut, Moses stepped to the counter. "Are you all right?"

"Jah." She climbed down from her stool but her legs were shaking a little, and she stumbled.

Moses reached over the counter and grasped her arm, steadying her.

"Denki." She leaned against the counter. "What did you say to Bishop Stephen?"

"That I, from the talk among the Youngie, believed you'd be courting someone else soon."

Lois wasn't sure whether to be offended or grateful. She wished she hadn't needed Moses Lantz to rescue her, but she had. What he'd said worked. They had left. At least for now.

But no doubt they'd return when it became obvious no one, in fact, did want to court her.

Regardless, Moses had gone out of his way to help her. "Denki," she said. "And I mean that sincerely."

~

Monday morning, Lois hurried down her steps. Something flew overhead. She shaded her eyes against the morning sun. A hawk flew toward the woods. She squinted. A red-tailed hawk. Had the pair returned after all? The bird flew past the loblolly pine and into the trees and disappeared in the top of a maple. Maybe the hawks had simply built a new nest instead of completely abandoning the property. Maybe the first nest had failed long before the construction started.

She pulled her scooter from up against the building and pushed it to the parking lot. Then she jumped on and kicked off, heading toward Paradise. As she reached the café, she used her hand brake and came to a stop. There was a For Sale sign in front. What in the world was Moses up to?

A wave of panic swept over her. Did he plan to sell the shop too? The phone number on the sign was Moses's. The parking lot was full, as it usually was whenever she passed. It seemed business was good. Why would he sell it now? She took a deep breath and let it out slowly. Then she said a prayer. What if he did sell the shop? What would she do?

She doubted the job in Bird-in-Hand was still open.

She continued on, past the park and post office. And the turnoff to the care center. And Meadow Lane. A half mile later, she turned left. When she reached Amy and Bennie's farm, Amy was in the yard putting wash on the line. Other farm wives had their Monday wash out hours ago. Ernie was playing with Oliver, who was sitting on a blanket. Maggie, who was screaming, was strapped to Amy's chest. And Deborah was toddling toward the flower bed next to the house.

Lois parked her scooter, took off her vest, and started toward Amy. As she neared her friend, she asked, "How are you?"

Amy groaned. "Maggie was up half the night. Then as

302

soon as she finally settled down, Oliver woke up with croup. I'm exhausted."

"I'll take over the laundry." Lois picked up one of Bennie's shirts from the basket. "And keep an eye on the kids. Go inside with Maggie. Maybe she'll go down for a nap."

"Denki," Amy said. "You're a godsend."

Fifteen minutes later, Lois held the basket on one hip and Oliver on the other as she coaxed Ernie to hold Deborah's hand. Then they all waddled into the kitchen to find Amy asleep in the rocking chair with Maggie against her shoulder. Lois put the basket down, strapped Oliver into the high chair, and took Maggie from Amy.

Amy's eyes flew open. "Was I asleep?"

"Jah," Lois patted Maggie's back. "I'm going to put the baby down. You go nap while she naps. I'll get the kids their dinner and then put them all down for a rest. Bennie can feed himself."

Amy stood. "Nee. I'm okay."

"Come on." Lois led the way to the bedroom.

A half hour later, when Bennie came in from the field, Lois had the kinner cleaned up from their meal of cheese, apple slices, and bread with peanut butter. "Are there leftovers for you?" Lois asked.

"Jah. There's soup from yesterday evening. I'll have some bread too."

When Lois came down after reading to the kinner from a stack of library books, Bennie had gone back outside. Lois began the dishwater to clean up the kitchen. A few minutes later, Amy stepped into the kitchen, yawning.

"You saved me," she said.

"Why didn't you sleep longer?" Lois asked.

"It was long enough. I feel like I can make it through the rest of the day."

"Get some soup," Lois said. "Bennie left it on the stove. I'll clean up and then let's get supper started."

"I have a roast in the refrigerator. Mamm dropped it off yesterday from their freezer. And potatoes and carrots."

"We can make rolls too," Lois said.

As Amy ate, she talked about the market. "I love it," she said. "Except when I get home, I have a lot of catching up to do. And now I'll need to find time this week to make more product."

"We'll have some time before the kids wake up." Lois started to brown the roast. "Get out your supplies while I put supper together." By the time Lois finished, Amy had her totes of supplies on the kitchen table.

"I think we can do a round of candles," Lois said. "How about you melt the wax while I wash the molds?"

As they worked, Lois asked if Amy knew Moses was selling the café.

"What?"

"Jah." Lois started the hot water. "There was a sign up when I came through town."

"Why would he do that?"

"I don't know." Lois added soap to the water.

"Is it because Sara broke up with him?" Amy put chunks of wax into a pot.

"Are you sure she broke up with him?"

"That's what Sara said."

That was what it sounded like from what Lois overheard, but Moses hadn't appeared to be upset by what Sara had said. Perhaps it was mutual. Perhaps Lois hadn't heard enough to really know. It wasn't her beeswax anyway.

"What if he plans to sell all of his businesses?" Amy put the pot on the stove. "What if he expects us to pay off the farm soon?"

"I don't think he'd do that." But Lois feared he would sell the shop. Perhaps he planned to leave the area. Why did the thought of that make her heart hurt?

"There's something else I need to tell you," Lois said.

"You sound serious."

"It kind of is. Randy and Nathan showed up at the shop on Saturday."

Amy groaned again. "Nee."

"Jah. With Bishop Stephen."

Amy put her hand over her mouth. "What did they want?"

"For me to move back to Big Valley and marry Nathan."

"What did you do?"

Lois began putting the molds into the water. "I protested, but it wasn't until Moses intervened that they left."

Amy's mouth fell open for a long moment as she pivoted toward the stove and turned on the burner. "Moses intervened?"

"Jah."

"How?"

Lois looked at Amy. "He took Bishop Stephen outside and told him, according to the local Youngie, I'd be courting someone soon."

Amy smiled.

"Why are you smiling?"

She shrugged.

"Don't read anything into this. It doesn't erase what happened before." But she did appreciate Moses's help.

She wouldn't tell Amy that Moses had tried to apologize

to her, at least not yet. Why had Lois cut him off? Especially when she needed to apologize too.

⁓

On the way back to the shop, Lois stopped by the post office. She had a letter from Teresa and the Flight of Doves. Lois sat on the outside steps and skimmed through the reports. Mary wrote that she'd seen a flock of ducks flying south. Menno wrote he'd observed a northern gannet, a large seabird. Perhaps Menno, whoever he was, had been back to the Delaware shore.

Lois reread what Teresa had written to the group.

> *Don't be afraid to spread your wings and travel if you're able. Birding in another state—or country— can be enlightening. Just like with birds, a trip to a warmer climate, such as to Pinecraft in Florida, can be just what one needs in the winter. And imagine all the new people you'll be able to flock with, and the murmuration you'll be able to form. But also make sure and follow the examples of our feathered friends who find their way home each spring. You must do the same. You are needed and valued and Gott has a plan for your future.*

Lois let out a ragged sigh. God had a plan. He provided a home for the sparrow close to his altar. He cared for the birds of the air. He would provide a home for her too.

Lois kept reading. Teresa proposed the group meet Saturday, October 12, at the Blue Rock Boat Launch on the Susquehanna River at eight in the morning.

*There should be a good migration of birds moving
through the area by then. We'll have time to observe
them—and each other.*

Lois wanted to see Mary and meet Teresa and the others.
But what if Menno joined the gathering?

*Please let me know whether you can attend. If
you are able, bring something to share for a morning
snack. We'll plan to meet until eleven and then go
our separate ways.*

Should Lois attend? She'd have to hire a driver. And she'd
most likely blow her Jane cover. Perhaps she should let Mary
know she belonged to the circle letter under her middle name.
And what about Menno? Should she let him know she'd used
her middle name? Did she owe him that?

She took out her notebook and pen, an envelope, and
stamps. Then she wrote to the group that she planned to
go to the October 12 gathering at Blue Rock Boat Launch.
Of course she'd have to get a couple of hours off work, but
Evelyn could handle the shop for the morning. She closed by
writing, *I'm looking forward to meeting everyone in person.*

Then she wrote a note to Mary.

*I've been participating in the Flight of Doves
circle letter, that you are a member of, under the
name Jane Weaver, which is my middle name and
my mother's maiden name. I wanted to remain
anonymous. I'll go by Jane at the gathering on*

October 12 and wanted to let you know.

> *Warmly,*
> *Lois Jane Yoder*

As she addressed the letter to Mary, she pondered whether she should write to Menno. Finally, she decided against it. But then she changed her mind. She wanted a clean conscience.

She wrote a similar letter to Menno. Then she added,

> *I also wanted to let you know I traveled to Delaware to the location of your return address in July. I found a mailbox next to a market. But no one I spoke with had ever heard of you. I have no idea if you're even real, but if you are I wanted to be honest with you. Best wishes, whoever you are.*

She mailed the letters and then scootered to the highway. Already she missed Amy and the chaos of her home. *Home.* Lancaster County was home. Paradise Township was home. If only there really was an Amish man in the area wanting to court her, a man she could love.

Instead of staying on the highway, she turned toward the care center. Watching the birds with Anna would take her mind off her troubles.

On Tuesday, when Moses came into the shop, Lois mentioned she'd seen the For Sale sign at the café.

"Jah," he said. "I put it up yesterday morning."

Lois dusted the candles. "Why?"

"It's not working out the way I hoped it would." Maybe Sara had broken up with him after all.

On Friday, Evelyn called right after Lois opened the shop and said she'd be late. Her grandmother had fallen during the night and Evelyn wasn't sure she should leave her. "Stay as long as you need to," Lois said. "Don't worry about coming in."

"Would you let Casey know?" Evelyn asked. "I told him I'd sit in his booth over my lunch break."

"Sure." Lois smiled. Come to think of it, she hadn't seen Evelyn and John together for a couple of weeks. And Evelyn had been spending time with Casey on the market days.

Moses spent the morning at the market, but when he came in a little before noon, Lois let him know Evelyn's grandmother had fallen.

"I'll give you a break," Moses said.

"All I need is fifteen minutes to run out to the market."

"Feel free to take longer."

She shook her head. "Fifteen minutes is plenty."

Moses retreated to his office but then returned with a packet of envelopes. "Would you take longer and mail these in town? I need them to go out today and don't want to put them in the highway mailbox. I'll watch the shop—I just want to stay close in case Casey needs anything."

"Okay." The envelopes all had computer generated labels and return addresses on them.

Lois hesitated for a moment.

Moses asked, "Is everything all right?"

She shook her head. "I appreciate you apologizing to me even though I cut you off."

Moses opened his mouth.

Lois kept talking. "I need to apologize to you."

He shook his head as she continued, saying, "I said mean things to you when we were in school. About how tall you were. About how short your parents were." Her face reddened. "I was cruel. I called you Goliath. I hope you'll forgive me."

"Of course I forgive you." He smiled a little. "I teased you relentlessly. I'm sorry for that too."

Lois extended her hand. "Friends?" Her chest tightened.

"Jah." He took her hand and shook it gently. "Thank you."

Flustered, Lois clutched the envelopes, let go of his hand, grabbed her backpack from under the counter, and hurried out the back door.

Lois stopped by Casey's booth first. He seemed disappointed and then worried when she told him where Evelyn was. "Is her Mammi all right?"

"I'm not sure," Lois said.

"Is it all right if I use the shop phone to leave a message for her?"

"Of course," Lois said. After she told Amy hallo and then goodbye, she scootered toward town. As she passed the café, she noticed the For Sale sign was down. Had Moses changed his mind?

When she reached the post office, Isabelle was at the mailboxes.

"Lois." Isabelle beamed. "I was going to stop by the shop today."

"I was afraid you'd already left for South Carolina."

Lois took Moses's envelopes from her backpack as Isabelle said, "I'd never leave without telling you goodbye."

"When do you go?"

"Well, the shop in Charleston fell through." Isabelle shrugged. "Barb asked if I wanted to visit them in Florida once they move. I might find a shop there I want to buy."

Lois glanced around. They were alone. "What if Moses decides to sell the shop here?"

Isabelle laughed. "Do you think he will?"

"He had the café up for sale earlier in the week—I'm not sure if he still does."

"He seems so unsettled." Isabelle lowered her voice. "I know Anna and Bert did their best but sometimes nature overrides nurture."

"What are you talking about?"

"His mother—she was so impulsive. Going this way and that, which was why her family liked Paul so much. It seemed she was finally settling down. Then they had the baby, and everyone was thrilled. Faith had done a one-eighty. But then she ran off again, this time for good. She was so different from Barb. Sure, Barb was a decade older, but you wouldn't think the girls would be that different."

"Are you talking about Moses's birth mother?"

Isabelle seemed puzzled. "Yes . . ."

Lois stuttered, "Sh-she was Barb's sis-ster?"

Isabelle nodded. "I thought you knew."

Lois shook her head. "Does Moses know?"

Isabelle's expression froze. Then she sputtered, "I assumed he did. That's why Scotty wanted to sell him the shop. To help him out. He knew Moses needed more long-term income to pay for Anna's care. That's why he didn't change his mind and sell the shop to me after I reminded him I wanted it."

Lois furrowed her brow. There was also the fact that Isabelle couldn't put together the financing.

"I'm sorry," Isabelle said. "Me and my big mouth. Please don't say anything to Moses."

"I don't know if I can promise you I won't," Lois said. "I mean, I won't out of the blue, but if the topic comes up, if he ends up looking or asking for answers and I find out, I'd feel compelled to tell him." Wasn't that what a friend would do? "Do Barb and Scotty not want him to know?"

"I don't know exactly. It was his birth father's dying wish that Moses not know, that Anna and Bert would raise him as their own. I think he was afraid Faith would come after Moses and take him far away. Then later, I think everyone thought not knowing all of it would make Moses's life less complicated. But I thought Bert and Anna intended to tell him by the time he was grown."

But Bert died and Anna had Alzheimer's. Perhaps Barb needed to tell him. As it was, Lois felt as if she now knew way more about Moses's, Anna and Bert's, and Barb's business than she needed to.

But maybe Anna and Bert had told Moses. Maybe he chose not to talk about it.

She thought of the article on Moses's computer again. She definitely wouldn't tell Isabelle about that. But it probably indicated Moses did know—at least something.

Isabelle gripped the strap of her bag with her opposite hand. "I'll ask Barb what Moses knows."

"That sounds like a good idea," Lois said. "It's nice to see you. When will you go to Florida?"

"Perhaps soon. Barb said they finally have a bite on the property."

"That's wonderful to hear." Apparently Lois was letting go of the farm, because she was genuinely happy for Scotty and Barb. And for Isabelle. But she'd miss the three Englischers who'd been good to her.

Isabelle continued to the counter, taking a package out of her bag. Lois put Moses's envelopes in the slot, then started back to the exit. But then she decided to check her mailbox. Perhaps she had a reply from Menno. She inserted her key and opened the box. Two letters. One from Mary. The other from Menno.

27

Saturday, as Moses drove to Byler's Corner, he thought about the letter that he, as Menno, had written to Lois, aka Jane, that he hoped had arrived the day before. He said the words out loud.

> I'd like to see you in person before we meet on the river with the rest of the circle-letter members. Would Monday, September 30, at one at the Meadow Lane marsh work? I'll be there in case it does.
>
> Sincerely,
> Menno Stoltzfus

He'd found himself leaving later and later on Saturday mornings for Delaware. At first it had been exciting to have his first business, to figure out how to improve the Byler's Corner Market and collaborate with Joey to work out the best way to run it. But now he'd rather be at the Paradise Amish Market with Casey and Amy. And Lois.

When he arrived, he checked the mail first. Surprisingly, there was a letter from Jane. He hadn't expected that.

He'd felt manipulative yesterday sending Lois off to mail his bills, but he couldn't figure out how else Jane would get Menno's letter before Monday. But when Lois returned she hadn't given any clues to whether she'd checked her own mail.

He tore open the envelope. *Menno . . .* She wanted to let him know that her real name was Lois Jane Yoder, not Jane Weaver. Of course there was no response to Menno's request to meet because she'd written her letter before she'd received his, er, Menno's. He was shocked to read she'd come to Delaware looking for him. That must have been when he thought she was going to Big Valley. He leaned against the mailbox, trying to imagine Lois going from vendor to vendor, asking for Menno Stoltzfus. Obviously she hadn't gotten as far as Casey and Walter's booth.

She closed it with

> *I have no idea if you're even real, but if you are I wanted to be honest with you. Best wishes, whoever you are.*

That stung a little, but he didn't blame her considering what she'd gone through. Menno had stood Jane up. And then he didn't even exist at the address he'd given. Poor Lois. Moses put the letter back in the envelope and put it in his satchel.

He went through the market first, spending several minutes with Walter. "Do you miss having Casey here with you?"

Walter shrugged. "It's nice for Casey to be at the Paradise market. He's getting to know Evelyn. That's a good thing."

Moses had noticed that too. He was happy for his friend.

Next he went to check in with Joey. Moses asked, "Could I ask you a few questions? In private?"

They each got a cup of coffee and a doughnut and then found a picnic table to sit at.

"I'm wondering if I should sell this market," Moses said. "Do you know anyone who might be interested?"

Joey took a sip of coffee. "There's actually someone who might be. He lives in Dover now, but he grew up around here in a Mennonite family."

"What's his name?"

"Eli Byler."

Moses's heart skipped a beat. "Does he have a sister named Faith?"

"That's right."

"Do you have his number?"

"I do." Joey took another drink of coffee. "Would you like to speak with him in person? I could ask if he'd be willing to come out this afternoon."

"Thank you. The earlier the better."

Eli was tall, maybe an inch taller than Moses, and broad shouldered. It looked as if he could pull a plow as easily as a workhorse. He had dark brown eyes and blond hair that was turning white at the temples.

And he knew exactly who Moses was. As Eli shook his hand, he said, "I'm pleased to see you again. You were a tot the last time."

They sat at the picnic table with Joey. Eli wanted to talk about purchasing the market but not about anything from the past.

"How did I end up with the market?" Moses asked.

Eli clasped his hands. "My father deeded it to you when you were a baby."

And yet Moses hadn't even known about the market until after Dat died. Perhaps his parents were afraid of what he'd learn if they spent time in Delaware. "Why do you want to buy it?"

"I helped my father get it started, and then ran it with your father. Then Bert Lantz took it over once you owned it, and he hired Joey to manage it. I got a job in a warehouse in Dover. But I always loved this market. I always wanted to come back."

Moses asked, "When would you want to buy it?"

"As soon as possible."

"All right," Moses said. "I'll go through the books and then we can talk financing. I'll give you a fair deal."

Eli extended his hand and the two shook.

Moses tried one more time. "Are you sure you won't tell me what happened twenty-four years ago?"

"I'm not the one to tell you."

"Who is? My Dat is dead. My Mamm's memory is mostly gone. One birth parent is dead for sure."

"I'm sorry," Eli said. "It was a hard time. I'm not much of a talker—and especially not about all of that."

After Eli left, Moses told Joey thank you and goodbye, and then headed to his SUV to drive back to Paradise.

Frustration filled him as he climbed into the driver's seat. Why hadn't his parents told him he was adopted? He gripped the steering wheel. Why hadn't they told him he had family in the area?

He pulled out onto the highway. On the other hand, he had a sense of satisfaction in meeting Eli Byler, even though he refused to give Moses any information about his origins. He felt selling the market to Eli brought it full circle.

However, Moses had no such sense when it came to his past. He hoped he would in time. The sooner the better.

His phone rang. It was Scotty. Moses let out a sigh and squared his shoulders. It was time to shift gears.

He accepted the call. "Hello, Scotty. I was going to phone you about the farm."

"Have you had a chance to think it all through?"

"I have. Is it still for sale?"

"Yes, but I wasn't calling about the farm."

"Oh?"

"Eli phoned. He said you're planning to sell the market to him. There are some things Barb and I want to tell you."

"You and Barb?" Moses took a deep breath.

"Mostly Barb."

Moses shook his head in confusion. "How do the two of you know Eli?"

"We were with you at the hospital the night of the accident. Anna and Bert were there too. So was Eli. Paul asked us to protect you, but you're grown now. Barb believes it's best to tell you what we know. And if when we're done you still want to talk about the farm, we'll do that too."

Lois was waiting on an older Englisch man in the shop when Casey came in at four thirty, a half hour after the market closed. After she handed the customer his bag, Casey stepped to the counter. "Is Moses back yet?"

"Nee," she answered. "Were you expecting him to be?"

"He said he'd be back by four."

"Are you worried about him?" Lois asked.

Casey shrugged. "He probably got distracted."

Lois nodded toward the phone. "You should call him."

"Nah. I don't need to do that."

Lois wanted Casey to—she was worried about Moses too but didn't want to admit it, not to Casey and especially not to Moses. What if he'd found out—whatever the story was—about his birth parents?

She turned toward Casey. "I'm going to ask you a question. If you don't feel comfortable answering me, don't."

"All right."

"So there was a For Sale sign up at Moses's café on Monday, but then it was down on Friday. Did he decide not to sell it?"

"No. It sold."

"Already?"

"Jah."

"Who to?"

Casey grinned. "Sara Fisher and Mark Miller."

Lois leaned against the counter, as if she might fall down without the support. "What?"

"Jah. Mark is joining the Mennonites. He and Sara plan to get married. Sara has some money from her grandfather, and Mark has been saving for quite a while. They're getting a loan to buy the place."

Was that why Moses was so quiet lately? Was he mourning the loss of Sara? Lois's eyes watered a little. "Is Moses okay? Did Sara break his heart?"

Casey leaned against his cane. "Nee. He and Sara were never meant to be."

"I heard she broke up with him."

Casey shook his head. "Moses broke up with her, but it took a while for Sara to relinquish him." Casey hesitated a minute and then said, "Aside from Sara, he's going through some other stuff. But aren't we all?" Casey sighed. "Say a prayer for him. More than one." A car honked. He turned toward the parking lot. "My ride is here."

"Where are you headed?"

"Evelyn's. Well, her grandmother's. I'm going to do the chores this evening."

Evelyn had stayed home with her grandmother a second day. When Lois closed the shop at six, Moses still hadn't stopped by. She left a message to check in with Evelyn about her grandmother and to see if Evelyn could work on Monday. Lois hadn't decided whether she would meet Menno, but if Evelyn couldn't work the decision would be made for her. Unless Moses covered for her.

She could ask him—and he'd probably say yes.

The image of Moses at the Harris farm the last time she'd gone to the marsh to meet Menno fluttered through her mind. What if Moses was Menno? She smiled. Did she want Moses to be Menno?

No. The idea that he could be was impossible.

Moses might be softening some, but he was no Menno.

Menno wasn't even Menno.

Lois retrieved her backpack and scooter from her apartment and then started toward town. She'd never trust Moses with her heart again, but she'd come to care for him as a friend. And she feared she'd used bad judgment speaking to Isabelle about him. She wouldn't want Moses speaking to anyone about her private life.

Perhaps he was at the care center visiting Anna. She decided to scooter down to see. When she arrived, his SUV wasn't in the parking lot. Lois decided to go in and see her anyway. Anna had her nightgown and robe on but her hair was still in a bun.

"I was just going to brush her hair," the caregiver said.

Lois reached for the brush on the dresser. "I'll do it."

Anna smiled at Lois. "Good to see you."

"It's good to see you too," Lois said. "How are you?"

"Fine. Just fine."

"Has Moses been to see you today?"

"Not yet. He'll be here soon. He's such a good son."

"He is," Lois said.

"I think he'll take me home today."

Lois patted Anna's shoulder. If only.

"Gott was good to give him to us. What happened wasn't good. It was all so horrid."

"Jah." Lois began brushing Anna's hair. "Both can be true."

Anna was quiet after that. When Lois finished the brushing, she braided Anna's gray hair into a single braid. Then she helped her to the bathroom and then to the bed, pulling the blanket and top sheet back. "Here you go," she said.

Anna, with Lois's help, climbed into bed. Then Lois tucked her in, kissed her forehead, and said a silent prayer for the woman. And then she said a prayer for Moses too.

Once she was on her scooter and stopped at the highway, she glanced to the west. The sun was setting in a big orange ball with pink and yellow streaks spreading across the horizon. She didn't like to be out on the highway after dusk, but the café wasn't far. She headed east to see if Moses's SUV was there.

It wasn't. The Strasburg train whistle blew as it rolled into the Paradise station, which meant it was seven.

She could think of one more place close by where Moses might be. She turned west again and then onto Meadow Lane. The earthy smell of the marsh comforted her as twilight fell. It was nearly dusk by the time Lois reached the Harris farm. She squinted up the driveway. Scotty's pickup was parked in its usual place. Barb's Buick was parked closest to the kitchen door. And Moses's SUV was pulled over to the side.

The windows of the house on the first floor were lit and someone was standing at the kitchen sink window. She could tell from the figures in the next window that two people were sitting at the dining room table. One towered over the other. Moses and Scotty.

Lois slipped her backpack off her shoulders, took out her safety light, and turned it on. Then she pinned it to the back of her vest and scootered down the lane to the covered bridge to loop back to the highway. She prayed for Moses for the second time that evening. She didn't know what he was going through—but she doubted it was easy. His life hadn't been as simple nor as golden as she'd always thought.

⌇

Monday morning at ten, Moses pulled into the parking lot of Paradise Found, expecting to find Evelyn at the cash register. Instead he found Lois.

He tried not to show his alarm and asked, as casually as possible, "Where's Evelyn?"

"With her Mammi. Her mother is on her way to take her grandmother to the doctor. Evelyn said she'd be here in an hour or so."

"All right," Moses said. "I have about an hour of work to do and then a few errands to run."

Lois tilted her head a little and stared at him. Did she suspect him of being Menno? If so, he wished she'd come out and say it. Instead, she asked, "How are you doing? How was your weekend?"

Not once since he'd bought the shop had she asked him how he was doing.

"Fine." He started toward his office, stopped, and then turned. "Thank you for visiting my Mamm. She's mentioned it a few times. She doesn't seem to remember other visitors, but she always remembers you. I appreciate you taking the time."

"I really like your Mamm. I always have." Lois's voice choked a little. "You're fortunate to still have her."

"I am." As he turned to go his eyes burned a little. He felt even more fortunate to have her after talking with Barb and Scotty—his aunt and uncle. That was a shock. And a relief. He had family besides Mamm. And now Eli too.

Paul had left a will, which specified Anna and Bert Lantz as Moses Schwartz's legal guardians should anything happen to him. Barb and Eli had both agreed to it. Of course they'd looked for Faith after the accident, even though it went against Paul's wishes, but they couldn't find her. Within a couple of years of Paul's death, Moses's parents legally adopted him after it was determined that Faith had abandoned her son.

Moses would have had a completely different life if she had been found or had returned. He was grateful for the life he had, and yet he mourned for the parents he couldn't remember. Was his mother still alive? Did she think of him?

He'd been abandoned—yet he'd always felt secure with his parents. And he was. Still, as a little one he'd lost both of his parents, and surely that had impacted him in some way.

At eleven fifteen, when Moses left Paradise Found, Evelyn hadn't arrived. He had papers to send to Eli in Dover for the preliminary negotiations on the Byler's Corner Market. And he had an appointment with his lawyer to go over the contract from Scotty and Barb. Once he'd seen to all of that, he'd stop by and see Mamm.

An hour and a half later, before he told Mamm goodbye, he said, "Barb told me everything. About Faith leaving Paul and moving away. About her filing for divorce and giving Paul full custody. About her boyfriend being abusive. She said Paul wanted you and Dat to raise me as your own."

Mamm reached up and touched his face.

"Barb said she heard through a cousin about a decade ago that Faith was in Mexico, but no one's heard from her since." He mourned for her, whatever her sad story was, and for his father. After Faith left, Paul had moved back to Lancaster County and planned to rejoin the Amish, but he still managed the market with Eli's help.

After Mamm and Dat adopted Moses they moved to Paradise Township, looking for a fresh start for their little family. People had heard about the tragedies of the Schwartz and Byler families, but they didn't talk about them. It seemed no one told their children because none of Moses's schoolmates brought it up, except for pointing out how little he looked like his parents. He took after Faith's side of the family, mostly Eli.

"I'm grateful to you and Dat," Moses said. "You gave me a good life." Dat's death and Mamm's diagnosis had cut that carefree life short, but they'd given him the foundation he needed.

Mamm nodded. "You gave more to us. Truly."

His heart swelled.

A tear slid down her cheek. "Can you take me home now?"

He gave her a hug. With the sale of the café and the Delaware market, along with the profits from the grocery, the shop, and the Paradise market, hopefully he could afford around the clock in-home care. Maybe he could make it work. But first he needed a home to take her to.

As he left the care center at 12:55, he crossed the parking lot to the trail and then hurried across the railroad tracks and through the back of the marsh to the willow tree. The whistle of the one o'clock train blew.

He began to run. He'd made Lois wait once. He hoped he hadn't done it again.

＿＿＿＿＿

When Lois arrived at the willow tree, Moses was standing with his back against it, looking down the lane toward the farm. This couldn't be a coincidence, could it? She called out, "Menno!"

He turned.

Lois's heart skipped a beat. Moses *was* Menno.

He waved and stepped forward as she rushed toward him. When they met, he took the handle of her scooter and leaned it against the tree.

"It's you," she said.

"It's been me all along."

"I was hoping it was." She stepped toward him, and he drew her close. She leaned her head against his chest, and he dropped his chin atop her Kapp. He felt as familiar as he had five years ago.

"I'm sorry," he whispered, "for how I treated you. For not contacting you after your mother died. For not going after you when your brother moved you to Big Valley. I have no excuse."

"I didn't know what you were dealing with then."

"I thought Amy would have told you."

"I was grieving my Mamm. I asked Amy not to talk about you. All of it hurt too badly." Lois looked up into his face. "What now?"

"Do you want to start over?"

"Jah, but who are we? Are you Moses or Menno? Am I Jane or Lois?" She reached up and touched his face. "Which one of me did you fall for?"

"Lois. And then Jane. And now Lois Jane. I love your honesty. I love that you're a fighter and stood up to me. I love that you went to Delaware in search of Menno. I love that you love birds. I love what a good businesswoman you are. I love that you care for people and the people of Paradise in particular, including my Mamm. I love that you, even though I've been so awful, still care for me. You give me hope."

Lois turned her face up toward his, and he leaned down toward her, his lips brushing against her face. She tightened her arms around him, and his mouth met hers. This was what she would always remember instead of the pain from five years ago. When their lips finally came apart, Moses lifted her and spun her around, his arms around her middle.

A car horn honked. Lois and Moses both turned toward the lane. Scotty waved. Lois's face grew warm. She waved back and so did Moses.

With one arm still around her, Moses said, "I made an offer on the farm."

"*The* farm?"

He smiled. "Jah, *the* Harris farm."

She clasped Moses's free arm with hers to steady herself. What was he saying?

"I put down earnest money."

On *the* farm.

"I'll let you know when I know."

She finally found her voice. "Will you farm it?"

"No," he said. "Casey will. I'll keep up with the grocery store and the shop and the market. But—" he paused—"I can't say any more now."

Lois cocked her head, hoping he *would* say more. He smiled down at her. She had one more question. "Will you stay Mennonite?"

"Nee. I'll speak with Bishop Stephen about taking the membership class. I'll join the Amish. It's what Dat and Mamm would want for me. It's what I want."

"What about your phone? And your SUV? And electricity?"

"Jah, I'll miss all of that, but I know I belong here . . . with you." He pulled her closer. "But before I give up my SUV, I think a trip to Big Valley is in order. I'd like to put an end to the trouble that visited you as soon as possible."

Lois leaned against him, grateful.

He motioned to the scooter, leaning against the tree. "Want to ride double? I parked at the care center, but we can take the long way."

She climbed on behind Moses and held on to his waist. As they headed down Meadow Lane toward the covered bridge, Lois let go with her right hand and spread her arm wide.

Moses did the same with his left. As he kicked the scooter around the curve just before the bridge, they both leaned into the turn, flying together.

~

By Saturday, October 12, Evelyn's grandmother was on the mend. Evelyn would work in the morning and then, after the gathering of the Flight of Doves, Lois would work through the afternoon.

Mary had responded to Lois's letter about Jane, saying she understood and then that she wouldn't be able to make it to the gathering because of work.

> *But I hope I'll see you soon. I'll stop by Paradise*
> *Found in the next few weeks.*

Moses picked up Lois, who wore her lavender dress, at seven fifteen for the drive across the county to the Susquehanna River. A drizzly rain fell as Moses drove, and a gaggle of geese flew up from a pasture into formation and then swung south. As they drove through Mountville, the rain stopped and the sun poked through the clouds behind them.

Moses slowed for a wagon pulled by a couple of work horses. The Amish man on the bench tipped his hat and Lois gave him a wave.

By the time they reached the Blue Rock Boat Launch, the cloud cover had burned off, leaving a clear sky.

A woman wearing a Kapp and a brown dress with a black apron under her open coat waved from the edge of the parking lot. Lois waved back. As she and Moses approached, the woman said, "I'm Teresa. I'm guessing you two are Menno and Jane."

"That's right." Moses extended his hand. "We are." He gave Lois a wink and whispered, "We can explain later."

Teresa smiled. "Did you two know each other before the circle letter?"

"Jah," Moses said as Lois said, "Nee." They both laughed.

Teresa joined them and said, "You can explain that later too." Teresa was as much a leader in person as she'd been on the page. Several people in the group hadn't been able to make it, including Mary. But a total of seven people did.

Lois took her binoculars from her backpack and put them around her neck. Moses took a pair from his coat pocket.

After thanking everyone for being part of the Flight of Doves and commending them on a successful circle letter, Teresa pointed toward the trail. "Let's go see what we can find." The leaves of the sugar maples and scarlet oaks were changing, and splashes of red, yellow, and orange dotted the east side of the trail. As they walked Teresa said, "Birds are a prime example of the importance of all of Gott's creatures. I believe acknowledging Gott's design and purpose is a form of worship we can share with others."

Birding did deepen Lois's connection to God, and her connection to others too. It brought her peace and harmony. Would Lois have realized her love for Moses if it hadn't been for Teresa? If Amy hadn't brought the circle letter to her attention and encouraged her to join?

As they walked, the group spotted a bald eagle soaring down the river and a black-crowned night heron fishing in the shallows of a tiny island.

A couple of times Moses reached for Lois's hand. One time Teresa noticed and smiled.

When they returned to the parking lot, after sharing a snack, Moses's phone buzzed and he stepped away from the group.

As Lois gathered her container with only a couple of no-bake cookies left, Teresa gave her a smile. "So which is it? Did you know Menno before the circle letter or not?"

Lois wrinkled her nose. "Jah, I did, but we definitely got to know each better because of it. Denki."

Once they were in his SUV, Moses said, "That was Eli who called." Moses had told Lois the details of his family's tragedy and his adoption. "He said the down payment for the Delaware market has gone through. I double checked and it's in my account. I called Scotty and let him know I have the money for the down payment on the farm and my bank has approved the loan. We can pay it off once the money for the café goes through." He glanced at her and then back at the road. "Casey won't live in the farmhouse, which leaves me with a question to ask you." He tightened his grip. "Would you want to live in the apartment or the farmhouse?"

She stared straight ahead. "When?"

"You know—after I join the Amish. After we—"

They hadn't talked things through that far. She leaned toward him.

"I'm ahead of myself," he said. "I'll ask formally, properly, I—" Moses paused.

Lois reached for his hand as hope spread through her. She didn't want him to say more than he wanted to, not yet.

Moses stuttered, "I, I—"

Lois interrupted him. "I want to live in the farmhouse, for sure. With you."

His hand warmed hers.

Lois, fighting back tears as she thought of her own parents, added, "And your mother."

Moses glanced at her and then back at the road. "Denki." His voice was raw with emotion. "We'll need to hire caregivers—we can't do it alone. But we can try to make it work."

A red-tailed hawk flew up from a fence post and toward a grove of trees at the edge of a pasture. Several starlings followed.

Hope filled Lois as she spoke. "We'll be the family we all need."

"Jah." Moses squeezed her hand. "And we'll all be home."

Author's Note

I thoroughly enjoyed writing *The Shop Down the Lane,* the first in my LETTERS FROM LANCASTER COUNTY series, and researching circle letters and birding in particular. Both are common in Amish communities. Life on farms and in rural areas encourages bird-watching, and many people in Amish communities are passionate birders. It's not uncommon for entire families to bird together.

Americans as a whole also embrace bird-watching. Thirty-seven percent reported closely observing, feeding, or photographing birds in a 2023 national survey. Recent research led by the American Museum of Natural History (2016) determined there are 18,000 bird species in the world. Some are colorful, some are plain. Some sing a beautiful song, others caw. But all are fascinating to observe. Sadly the overall bird population is declining. North America has lost more than one in four birds since 1970. Habitat loss is the number one contributor. Window collisions and cats are also significant factors. From my research, I learned that planting native plants, containing cats, and putting decals on windows can all help save birds.

As I wrote *The Shop Down the Lane*, I referred to *Birds of Pennsylvania Field Guide* and *Birds of Maryland & Delaware Field Guide* by Stan Tekiela. If you don't have one already, I highly recommend purchasing a bird-watching field guide specific to your area as a great first step to identifying birds.

Acknowledgments

I have several people to thank for contributing to the creation of this story:

My husband, Peter, for being my biggest supporter throughout my writing career and always giving me hope. This book was no exception. Along with brainstorming the story and talking through plot issues, he also hung a new bird feeder in our yard in honor of this novel. ☺ We have shared many bird-watching memories, from witnessing eagles soar over the Columbia River to delighting in a hummingbird hovering around our grandson's head. I look forward to many more!

My dear friend Marietta Couch for sharing her knowledge about Amish communities with me over the years, explaining her experience as a member of a circle letter, and reading this story for accuracy. Any mistakes are my own.

My agent, Danielle Egan-Miller, of Browne & Miller Literary Associates, for supporting and guiding me in general and in this project in particular.

And the team at Bethany House for turning my manuscript

into a book, and specifically, my editors Hannah Ahlfield and Rochelle Gloege for making the story better in so many ways.

As I wrote *The Shop Down the Lane*, I thought of my parents: Bruce and Leora Egger. My father was a US Forest Service ranger who loved the woods and all they contained from the time he was a young child, and my mother was an elementary school teacher with a deep enthusiasm for life. Their love for each other, for God, the natural world, books, and their children has been the foundation of my life.

I also thought of two other people, specifically, as I wrote the story: my cousin Teresa Walker and my sister-in-law Vel'Dene Jane Gould. I ended up borrowing their names for two of my favorite characters in the story. Both Teresa and Vel'Dene are incredibly strong women who have taught me what it means to be both resilient and vulnerable. Both are incredible mothers and grandmothers. I'm grateful to both of them for inspiring me.

As I wrote the character of Amy, I thought of many dear friends I've had through the years, from childhood to adulthood, who fed and still feed my soul! Thank you to all of you. I can't imagine this life without the friendships God has provided.

I must, before I close, acknowledge two movies that influenced this project, *The Shop Around the Corner* (1940) and *You've Got Mail* (1998), along with perhaps the most well-known romance novel of all time, *Pride and Prejudice* (1813) by Jane Austen. I'm grateful for these classic stories—it was a delight to revisit them as I wrote *The Shop Down the Lane*.

In closing, I'm also tremendously thankful for you, readers, for buying, reading, and sharing my books. This story is for you!

Discussion Questions

1. Lois Yoder believes that working at Paradise Found and living above the shop is a good situation for her. Do you agree or disagree? Why? What is your overall impression of her?

2. When Scotty Harris introduces Lois and Moses to each other, they pretend they don't know each other. What message did that send? What unresolved issues do they have? Have you ever pretended not to know someone? Or avoided someone you had some conflict with in the past? Why?

3. Lois has a cast of supporting characters in her life—Amy, Casey, Scotty, Isabelle, and even the driver, Dave. How do they support her? Which one is your favorite supporting character? Why?

4. Moses Lantz has Casey and Sara for support and he finds comfort spending time with his mother, but he doesn't have an older mentor in his life. How would that be different if he'd joined the Amish church he

grew up in? How did the secret his aunts and uncles (and adoptive parents) keep from him affect his life? Do you think they were wrong to keep the secret?

5. Anna Lantz resides in a care center. Why are people in the Amish community critical of Moses keeping his mother there? Why are they critical of him selling his parents' farms? What would you have done in Moses's situation?

6. Why does Moses fire Lois? Why does he hire her back? Were you sympathetic to Moses throughout the story? Did your opinion of him change? Why or why not?

7. Lois's parents were deeply in love with each other, loved their children, and also modeled an appreciation for nature, including birds. That love and appreciation provided Lois with a standard of what she wanted in marriage and in life. Do you (or did you) have someone in your life who modeled a love of others and of nature? How did that affect your life?

8. Lois's brother, Randy, tries to force her into a marriage with his best friend, Nathan, a harsh and abusive man. Why do you think Randy wants Lois to marry? Do you know anyone who has been pressured to marry someone they didn't love or trust? What saves Lois from the situation the first time? What saves her the second time when Randy and Nathan come to Paradise and ensnare Bishop Stephen into their plan?

9. Lois and Amy have been friends since they were eight years old. What does each contribute to their friend-

ship? Have you had a friendship similar to theirs? What did the friendship mean to you?

10. Why does Lois find it hard to be vulnerable and to trust other people? What allows her to be able to trust Moses by the end of the story?

11. Teresa doesn't appear in the story, besides her letters, until the very end, but her letters about what we can learn from birds inspire both Lois and Moses. What have you learned from birds or other wildlife or domesticated animals? How have they enhanced your life?

Coming soon!

More gently humorous romance in book two of

Letters from Lancaster County.

The first time Joanna Grebel and Adam Slaybaugh meet, he's sure he's found his soulmate—while she insists they be "just friends." Instead of sticking around to work on a friendship, though, Adam flees Lancaster County for Florida. They see each other a couple of times over the years with the same results. Joanna wants friendship. Adam wants something more. When he finally returns to Pennsylvania for good, he finds out Joanna's heart has just been broken by a long-time boyfriend.

Joanna and Adam both work for his grandparents' renovation business, and the two are assigned to the same project, much to Joanna's exasperation. The last thing she wants to deal with is Adam Beyer, so she puts up her guard, determined to keep things professional—and to keep Adam at a safe distance. Then Joanna begins to receive mysterious letters of encouragement she believes to be from her ex. Could it be he's ready to reconcile?

Despite being more attracted to Joanna than ever, Adam finally chooses to befriend her and to try to figure out what makes her so standoffish. But can he be content to be "just friends," or will his love and care for Joanna finally win her over?

Available everywhere books are sold,

Spring 2026

Leslie Gould is the #1 bestselling and award-winning author of forty-nine novels, including the Courtships of Lancaster County series and the Amish Memories series. She holds an MFA in creative writing and enjoys research trips, church history, and hiking, especially in the beautiful state of Oregon where she lives. She and her husband, Peter, are the parents of four adult children and two grandchildren.

Sign Up for Leslie's Newsletter

Keep up to date with Leslie's latest news on book releases and events by signing up for her email list at the link below.

LeslieGould.com

FOLLOW LESLIE ON SOCIAL MEDIA

Leslie Gould Author   @lesliegouldwrites

Be the first to hear about new books from Bethany House!

Stay up to date with our authors and books by signing up for our newsletters at

BethanyHouse.com/SignUp

FOLLOW US ON SOCIAL MEDIA

   @BethanyHouseFiction